In Love and Dead

R.L. Murphy

ISBN:-10:0989288706
ISBN-13: 978-0-9892887-0-5

Also available by this author:
Russian Poker

To those who inspire me,
and don't know it

"You said you needed a break, but now I'm the one that's broken."

Chapter 1

Violet Waits never notices me. She doesn't even know I'm alive. Even if she did know who I am, she would want nothing to do with me. The closest I've ever been to her is walking past her in the hallway and intentionally bumping my arm into hers. Her skin was soft and smooth, I'll never forget it. One time last year in History I got put into a group project with her and found out she was good at math. Judging from the patches on her backpack she has great taste in music. Patches for Nirvana, Pearl Jam, MxPx, and Sublime are scattered on her backpack, no discernible pattern to them as if they were tossed on a magnet board with a blindfold on. I don't know what it is, but I love her smell. I can't tell if it's a body lotion, a perfume, or just the natural sweetness of her skin. It smells like a warm cinnamon roll with vanilla frosting and lilac.

I love her pitch black glossy shoulder length hair. It reminds me of the girl from the Pearl Jam "Do the Evolution" music video. It slightly bounces when she walks down the hallway, and it causes me physical pain whenever she takes her long delicate fingers and moves her bangs out of her eyes. I love how her pale blue eyes contrast with her complexion like a sapphire amid beach sand. I seem to be the only one that has any admiration for her. Everyone thinks she's a loner, but she'll never be alone as long as I'm around.

The only thing she likes as much as I like her is her art. She mostly draws using ink pens of different colors, but mostly sticks to deep dark blacks. Last year I snuck into the art room to take one of her masterpieces. I made a frame for it in shop class and hung it in my bedroom. It's a picture of her in what I assume is her bedroom with a sketchbook in her bed from a birds eye perspective. Plastered on the walls are posters of Nirvana, Lincoln Park, and Sublime. I bet these aren't the posters she actually has over her bed, but the one's she wants over her bed. She's the type to clip pictures from newspapers and magazines in a collage on a wall. The entire picture was done in pencil instead of her traditional pens. She looks as beautiful in black and white as she does in person.

I wish I had the artistic talent that she has. I envy anyone that can take a piece of paper and turn it into art. Hell, I just wish I had a talent. Unless you count stashing porn that my brother gets me from my parents as a talent. Mom locks down our internet pretty tight so we have to get our porn the old school way. Duncan told me he found it in the woods, but I have a feeling he stole it from his friend Toby. His dad is cool enough to just buy it for him. It only slightly grosses me out that three people probably used it for the same reason I do. I think I'm weird for thinking how these adults came to such a low point that porn is their best career choice. Maybe they like it? Maybe this is what they wanted to do their whole lives, who knows.

The rapid clanging of the school bell alarms me. Who knows how long I was daydreaming about her, and she's not even in this class. It was just algebra anyways. I'm always the first one done with the work. I never understood why people have such a hard time with math.

I shove my book into my forest green backpack and sling it over my right shoulder. My mom says I have so much stuff in my backpack that the seams are going to burst, or my back is going to break. I don't use my locker, I just carry all my books. I don't even think I have my combination to my locker. Not having to worry about my locker helps me evade bullies and gives me extra minutes every day to read in the commons area between classes. The time adds up. The bad news is that never happens. I'm lucky to get a book done a year between breaks, and here comes the reason why.

"Hey what's up spaz?" Steven Fargo said. Steven is my best friend, for better or worse. Last year he was one of the popular kids until he stood up to Seth Thompson for me while I was getting pummeled. Seth and his goons extradited Steven. Steven's options were either having no friends...or me. At least I know I'm better than nothing.

"Hey Seth, what did you do last night?" I ask.

"Just the usual stuff, owning some noobs in Call of Duty. Got my kill/death ratio up to two point three to one. Oh and I think I finally nailed the guitar solo in Smells like Teen Spirit," Steven said. Steven loves four things in life, video games, playing guitar, mixed martial arts, and himself.

"Sweet man, I know you've been working on that solo for a bit," I said. He's not very good, but he tries. I'll say he's good enough to impress girls with it. I solely attribute his guitar skills being the reason that he made it to second base with Kelly Dotty.

"I'm going to work on some Metallica stuff next. Probably Enter Sandman. I can hear Kelly Dotty's panties getting wet already!" he said.

"Gross dude," I said as I playfully shove him in the shoulder.

"Oh like you haven't thought about getting some from her," he said sticking his tongue out suggestively. I'll admit, Kelly is cute, but Violet is beautiful.

"I'm not like that and you know it."

"Oh trust me I know you're not like that. You're not like anything because you won't even talk to her. Seriously dude it's a tad creepy how you stare at her," Steven said raising a single eyebrow at me. I always wished I could raise one eyebrow, but to no avail, despite attempts in front of a mirror.

"I can't help it Steven, I love her," I said.

"Dude can you keep that down, someone might hear you? " Steven said. "You can't love someone that you've never talked to man."

"I can too, but it's not about that. We have a deeper connection that I can't explain."

"It's called a boner dude, and you got a raging one for this chick," Steven said.

"Shut up dude. C'mon, it's not like that,"

"You trying to tell me you haven't jerked it at least several hundred times to that picture you swiped of her from art class?"

I blush. I have to admit for the last year I've done nothing but go over every fantasy I could imagine with her. Mostly not even sexual stuff, just being with her, talking with her, holding each other. But Steven wasn't wrong about the drawing. "Dude I'm just trying to help. Look I know talking to her is 100% out of the question for you because you don't want to be happy or whatever. How about I talk to her for you?" Steven said. He really is a good friend. I think he really only wants us together so I can talk about something else.

"No dude, I can't have you do that. Do you have any idea how that would make me look? I'll tell her, it just needs to be the right time," I said.

"What are you waiting for, prom?" Steven said. I wouldn't tell him, but prom would be a near perfect scenario where it would make sense. I can't wait until prom. I can't stand this feeling.

"No, I just...don't want to creep her out. And I don't want to get rejected," I said.

"All she needs to be creeped out by you is to just know how much time you spend thinking about her," Steven said. "And dude, everyone gets rejected it's normal."

"Well, what other options do I have if I can't talk to her, and I'm not going to let you do it?" I ask.

"Whatever you do, just don't do what you did for Homecoming this year, that was pretty wahjah bro," Steven said. I just nod in acknowledgement at how that was one of the worst days of my life. I want to forget that ever happened. Steven often used words like "wahjah" that he made up, or heard from some obscure movie, but expects everyone else to know what it means. I'm guessing by the context it's something super embarrassing.

"You can always be a loser and write her a big long love letter, and have a check box saying 'do you love me, yes or no?' if you think that will work."

"You know what Steven, I know you're joking but I don't think it's a half bad idea."

"Dude, there's no way she can take that seriously. You're not in the fifth grade, a letter isn't going to win her over bro," Steven said giving me a look of doubt.

"No I think it will, girls gush over words man. Think about all the romance novels the girls read. I mean look around, how many vampire books do you see girls carry every day? Girls obsess over words, I just have to make the words speak to her," I said.

"If that's what it's going to take to get your willy wet then so be it captain," Steven said as he messes up my hair with his hand.

"I don't want to have sex with her, I just want to be with her."

"You can get it wet without putting it inside her man," Steven said as he starts pantomiming oral sex. "I bet she'd be amazing at it too yo, with those lips and all." She does have really amazing lips. I dream about holding her in my arms and being able to press my lips against hers.

"Okay man that's enough. Plus it's about time to get to my next class," I said.

"Okay. But seriously man, if you want I can ask Dez to find out what locker number is so you won't even have to look at her to make the note handoff," Steven said.

"You know, if you don't mind that would actually be great," I said as Steven rolls his eyes at the dopey grin I'm sure I have on my face. Am I really going to do it? I mean, I'm an okay writer, but how can I win her with words? I can't just tell her how I feel, that will just creep her out. I also can't pretend like I have no interest in her either. I pick up my backpack, sling it over my right shoulder again and head to my English class.

I like writing and reading, but I never understood the purpose of English class. We either read a book that no one has any interest in and that no one can relate to, or we practice grammar that no one uses. Why can't we read books that someone is actually going to enjoy, and not the ones we're supposed to like? If the point is to make us want to read more, let us read things we're actually going to like. I've read two books by Ayn Rand in this class and zero by Kurt Vonnegut.

I sit in my seat in the front row. Teachers suspect you less of slacking off when you're in the front because they are always looking towards the back, Mrs. Beaker was no exception. She was nice as long as you read your assignment on time. Most of the other boys have a thing for her, I don't understand it, but then again I've never been into blondes. She's a unique mix of being the cheerleader type, but also the librarian type. I think she coaches the girls basketball team. All week we've been having discussions about To Kill a Mockingbird. I read it years ago. No one had to force me to read it, unlike others in the class. While the class is having a discussion about a book that most of them didn't bother to read, all I can think about is the letter I'm about to write when I get home.

I open my notebook and start making an outline of all the things I need to make sure to include. I need to tell her how beautiful how she is, but how do I even start? I guess I'll worry about that part tonight. I need to tell her how much I love her art, but I have to remind myself not to mention I stole some of it, I don't think she'd think too highly of that. I need to tell that I want to be with her, that I don't want a date with her I want a chance to spend my life with her. I don't want to make it seem like it's a crush, I want her to know it's more than that.

I know she's the one for me, I can just feel it. I know one day I'm going to meet her parents. I know one day I'll fall asleep with her in my arms. I know one day I'm going to get on one knee and propose to her. I know one day I'm going to walk down the aisle with her. One day we'll grow old together. One day we will die together. I want to start these days tomorrow.

The next hour crawls by as the rest of the class sat and read what they should have been reading the previous nights. I notice Adam Gaston next to me has been pretending to read the entire time. I really think it takes more effort to pretend you're reading book than it is to *actually* read it. The bell rings, it's lunch time. I don't think I could take it another excruciating minute.

I go to my usual table in the corner and flop my

backpack on it. Steven usually doesn't join me for lunch, it would interfere with his trying to impress chicks time. I move the zipper from the left side to the right and take out two items, my IPod with the ear bud cord wrapped around it tightly, and a plastic grocery bag containing my lunch. I packed my lunch myself so there's no mystery to what's inside. Duncan has cleaned up his eating and packs his own lunch for the most part. My turkey sandwich got smushed under my books again, good thing I didn't put mustard on it. I put my ear buds in and drift away from the lunchroom and go someplace else.

Steven always gives me a hard time for having the first generation IPod. I wouldn't even have an IPod if Duncan hadn't gotten a new one. I don't have a usual playlist I use for lunch like I do everything else. I have a playlist for my walking in the woods, playing video games, and the songs that remind of me her, that's what I'm listening to today.

My favorite song on the playlist is this song "Years Ago" by some Seattle band from the 90's that I've never heard of called Super Deluxe. It sums up how I feel about her in every single way. There's something about 90's rock music that had a bit more emotion to it than current stuff. If it wasn't for her I would regret being born when I was. I eat my sandwich and a couple cookies that were hiding in the bottom of the bag.

"Hey fag, what are you doing at my table?" a voice said directly after ripping my ear buds out with a violent tug.

"What's wrong with you Seth?" Seth isn't so much the school bully as he is my personal bully. For whatever reason he gets special enjoyment in my humiliation and torture. I throw my IPod into my backpack and zipping it up, ear buds still dangling out of it.

"I told you what's wrong with me, you're sitting at my table," Seth said.

"We both know you never sit here and you're just being an asshole for no reason," I said.

"How am I being the asshole? You're the one sitting at *my* table."

"Well then sit down at your table, I'll leave," I said grabbing the strap of my backpack.

"I think I'd rather you join me," he said grinning that asshole smile.

"Piss off Seth," I said as I stand up and start walking away. I'm pulled backwards, Seth grabs the other strap to my backpack and yanks it towards him. The back of my head hits the table. The point of impact feels wet like it might be bleeding. I reach back to check, no blood so far, just a dull throb. I lunge full force at Seth, but I'm pulled back again by the collar of my shirt. It's Steven.

"Seth I swear to God I'll rip your throat out if you don't leave him alone," Steven Fargo said squeezing himself between Seth and I.

"Calm down Steve, I was just playing with him," Seth said.

"I know exactly what you were doing, cut the bullshit," Steven said.

"Sorry Steven, I forgot you were a fag for him," Seth said with a snicker.

"Better than being a fag with you," Steven said turning away. Seth scowled.

"It's no wonder that she cheated on you," Seth said. Steven turned around and charged at Seth. I grabbed him by his collar.

"It's not worth it Steven, he's not worth it," I said.

"He didn't have to go there Matty, that was too far," Steven said.

"I know he didn't, but screw him. You know you would lay his ass out in four seconds flat," I said.

"Yeah, I do know that. I just want to get the chance to prove it," Steven said as we head outside. He doesn't say much. I can tell he's thinking about her, he's obviously not over what happened. Can't say I can relate, but I can imagine what it's like. It's only been a month, I'm sure it takes a while to get over something like that. I'm hoping sometime soon he'll actually want to talk about it, and maybe I'll get to know what actually happened. I heard the rumors that Steven's now ex-girlfriend cheated on him with Seth, then she had the nerve to break-up with him. How much of it is true, who knows?

We sit out on the concrete steps of the main school entrance. The sound of the clanking of the rope against the flagpole is the only thing keeping from us sitting in pure silence. I know he wants to talk about it, but he knows I would think of him differently if he opened up. His image would be shattered if even a tear was sighted exiting his eyes. The warning bell rings. We must have sat there for twenty minutes.

"We better get going. You want to show me that solo after school?" I ask.

"No, that's okay. I got some stuff I gotta take care of," he said. I guess he knew I was trying to cheer him up.

"Okay, I'll be on Call of Duty tonight if you want to play, and Steven, thank you. I know our friendship is mostly forced, but I appreciate you, and I'm glad you're my friend," I said.

"C'mon, lets get going," Steven said as he stands up, puts both of his hands in his jeans pockets and walks off towards the building.

I have to get to Mr. Spalding's class quickly, he doesn't tolerate being late. Randy is constantly made an example of for showing up right after the bell rings. No one really cares because no one likes Randy. It's hard to like anyone who wears nothing but Insane Clown Posse shirts. Mr.

Spalding is as stingy with rules as his wardrobe would lead you to believe. Mr. Spalding was one of those guys that you can really tell cares about the subject he's teaching, too bad no one else cares about creative writing. I mean it's just making stuff up, how hard is that?

His classroom is plastered full of signs that have phrases like "Write what you know" and "Never use clichés" on them. "Adverbs are evil" became his slogan, he insisted on asking at least one of us every day what is the most evil tool a writer can use is. This became almost a catch phrase for him. He ingrained it in our heads so much that when I see an adverb in a book his bald head immediately pops to up, spouting his catch phrase.

Another day, another lesson no one really cares about. We go over an exercise about not mixing up tenses, and how important it is. He gives us the rest of the period to work on our major project for the quarter. We have to write a 10,000 word short story in any genre as long as it's fiction. It's due in two weeks and I haven't even started on it.

I have a couple ideas for my story. I thought about doing a story about an Amish family who goes on a killing spree after finding out their son started doing drugs while on Rumspringa, but I didn't want the teachers think I was some kind of psycho. Maybe I'll do it about a guy who loves a girl so much that he can't handle the rejection if she says she doesn't like him. My life sucks, but at least tomorrow I'll know. I know I'll have no problem finding

10,000 words to describe how I feel about her, it's the Amish I'm worried about. The other idea I had was about people who keep zombies as pets and train them to become fighters like Pokemon.

I decide to use the time to write some characters. You can't have a good story without good characters. I write characteristics of people in the classroom. Jimmy Cello, the guy who always has a runny nose and a wad of tissues in his jacket pockets that have been used so much their turning into cotton particles. Jamie Lucas, the cheerleader who thinks we don't notice the scars on her the inside of her leg from cutting herself. Bobby Porter, the fat kid who everyone had called "Fatty McGee" since they knew him. I realize there's only a few minutes left of the period, so I quickly jot down one last character, Steven. A true rebel, he doesn't let anyone tell him how he should do things, he does it his own way. He's nice to his true friends, and a menace to his enemies.

The bell rings and I make a dash for my last class of the day. Not because I was looking forward to it, but it was the last class of the day, and the sooner I got there, the sooner I could go home. It's also the only class that takes me downstairs into the dungeon. The dungeon is extra hard to get to because it's where all the freshmen lockers are at, and because Seth and his goons hang out at the stairs leading down to it. There are only two classrooms downstairs, pottery and mechanical drawing. There's something about both of the dungeon classrooms that just feel wet, even though there is no actual moisture. The rooms feel dank, like moss should be growing from the corners, and mushrooms should be sprouting from the black and white tiles on the ground.

I took mechanical drawing because I can't graduate without an art credit, and mechanical drawing is the only art class I can take that doesn't take any artistic talent. As long as I can draw a straight line with a ruler for a semester I'm in the clear. I thought about taking an art class just to have another class with Violet, but I wouldn't want her to see me fail at something she's great at.

The teacher Mr. Hamilton, never seemed to care what we do. He knows his class is just a requirement for the artistically inept. As long as we turn something in that's supposed to look like it does in the book, it's a 100% every time. He unbuttons the first button on his shirt sleeve, unveiling his hairy wrists. Mr. Hamilton was shorter than most of the students and built like a linebacker. He sits in his chair with Chuck Taylor's resting on his desk. The bottoms of his shoes are so white he either just bought them, or he spends a lot of time cleaning them.

I pull out all of my materials I need to work on the drawing of a piston. Luckily I don't have to use my backpack or my locker for the supplies, we keep them in the classroom. We have to keep Protractors, five different rulers, a compass, a grip of pencils, a T-square, and art gum erasers. I use the protractor to make one of the curved edges on the piston, then someone bumps my desk, I look up. It's Dez Terrance, Violet's best friend.

"Whoops, sorry Matt," she said placing her finger tips on top of my hand as if she was controlling a marionette.

"It's okay Dez," I say looking back down at my project. She walks out the door with the hall pass. I've talked to her once or twice, I figure being nice to her best friend can't hurt my chances any. I think Steven dated her for a week last year, he would never talk about it no matter how much I probed. Steven never likes to divulge information about himself, so I guess I shouldn't be surprised. It's weird that he's my best friend, and I really don't know that much about him. Some shells weren't meant to be cracked I guess.

I finish my piston and start making a man out of the gum erasers. I scrub the head down into a sphere and use black electrical tape to bind all the pieces together. I put him on the corner of my desk, he's my new mascot. He's going to cheer me on to pass this class. I take a pen from my backpack and draw a smiley face on him. It's a little rude to create a mascot and not give him a face.

Just as I'm putting on the finishing touches on my mascot, Mr. Hamilton gives us the five minute warning, meaning the day was almost over. I haphazardly throw my equipment into my desk, get my backpack ready and place my gum erasure mascot on top of my desk, letting him guard it in my absence. I watch the red hand circle around the clock for the last minute, in what I think may be the most excruciating minute of my life. The bell rings and I rush out the door.

The busses are already waiting for us to get on board. Mr. Ralph greets me with the same expression he does every day, the one that says he just smoked a lot of weed but is trying to act normal. I sit down on the seventh row of seats near the window, which is directly in the middle of the bus. Maybe it's a little OCD to want to sit in the middle, but it just feels right. I drop my backpack on the aisle seat, no one ever sits with me anyways.

The bus always smells like body odor and sweat from the kids who just out of gym and didn't shower in the locker room. Can't say I blame them, I wouldn't either. I get enough harassment from kids, adding vulnerability to the equation isn't doing much for me. The bus is getting more and more full, and no one has been desperate enough to even think about asking me to move my bag.

No one steps on the bus for what must be a minute until Mr. Ralph closes the door. I've seen that little handle close the door for eight years now and I still have no idea how that thing works. The bus starts to pull off and there's a banging noise on the side of the bus. Maybe it's due to Mr. Ralph's drug induced state that made his reaction time become lackluster. He stops the bus and opens the door, and Duncan steps on the bus.

Typical Duncan, he's always late to getting on the bus. If he wasn't my brother it would be hard to love him, although the rest of my family certainly does. He will always be the one my parents brag about. He's already been accepted into police academy after he graduates in a few months. You would think having an older brother in the same school would help get my ass kicked less, but it doesn't. He sits in the front seat on the left next to Jimmy Taff.

I could have done a lot worse in the brother department. Sure when we were younger he used to pick on me a lot, break my toys, and read my journal on the bus, but he's a good guy. He's always known what he wants to do with his life, be a cop. He'll be good at it too, he's got the arrogance and delusions of grandeur that infests most officers of the law.

We are the second to last stop on the bus route. I always liked having a longer route, but Duncan felt differently. The more time we spent on the bus the less time Duncan had to work out, his only hobby. He spends almost all of his gym in the garage either hitting the punching bag, or lifting weights. He's tried to show me how to do it a few times, but I'm not any good at it.

One by one we go through every stop on the route, and every stop another group of kids get off. Only two groups of kids are left, the Adam's twins who get off on Marshall Road, and Robert Slayton who gets off after us so I have no idea where he lives. Robert is the only one who knows where everyone else lives, but no one knows where he lives. It's kind of creepy if you think about it too much, and he doesn't help matters any. He never talks to anyone, and will do anything on a dare. Seth got him to eat a slug last month, and last year I heard he ate Tim Ruff's gym socks.

The bus gets close to our stop and I pick up my backpack and stand up before the bus gets to a complete stop. Duncan waits until we're at a complete stop, and the door opens. It doesn't matter the situation, Duncan will always follow the rules, no matter how stupid they are. Duncan gets up like he's a robot and steps off the bus without saying a word. As I go down the steps I tell Mr. Ralph to have a good day. I look back and see Robert Slayton looking out the window at us. What a creeper.

Duncan has already started walking down our driveway, and by driveway I mean a quarter mile walk down what closely resembles a wooded trail. Tall ominous trees grow overhead like looming monsters. When the wind blows, the tips of the trees from both sides come inwards and touch, forming an organic cave of pine needles and gnarled branches. The road wasn't paved, just a thin layer of gravel that does little more than kick up dust clouds.

I never know what I was going to see walking down the road. Often it's nothing but ferns, and trees but it's not always the case. Recently the blackberry bushes have begun producing blackberries. Duncan gives me a hard time for not washing them before eating them, but they haven't hurt me yet. Sometimes I'll see an animal rustling in the bushes. Usually it's just a bird, but I've seen my fair share of deer and foxes as well. No such luck today.

I stopped to pick a few blackberries before I realized Duncan was already out of sight. I never thought I was a slow walker, but compared to my brother I don't think it's much of a contest. As soon as I see the top of my house through the trees I see my best friend running towards me. Dennis was a birthday present for me four years ago. I still don't know what breed of dog he is, but I think it's a cross between a Scottish terrier and a poodle. I think he might be the only one that really understands me. He runs ahead of me and waits for me at the front door.

I take the key out of the front pocket of my backpack and unlock the door. Duncan locks the door behind him, even though he knows I'm just a few minutes behind him. Dad built this house when I was in the fifth grade, it took him two years to do it, it was crowning achievement. He always built small things, and took on household projects, but he couldn't resist taking on an entire house.

The living room looks like the cabin in Evil Dead. Dad spent every second he wasn't building with hunting. He doesn't discriminate between which animals he kills, or with what weapon he does it with. Once they've been slain he skins it and packs the freezer full of meat, or takes his game to the taxidermist to be posed forever as a victim. Deer, duck, pheasant, and quail have all been frequently caught in the sights of my Dad. His crowning achievement is a brown bear that he caught in Alaska a few years back. No matter what the house always smells like bear fur. Before I had one in my living room I never knew that bears had a smell. I wonder why Dad didn't take any of them with him when he left.

I go up the stairs. This was the only place my mother choose to decorate, which she did with the only hobby that she had, Marilyn Monroe. Small posters, commemorative plates, and a bottle of wine decorated the wall up the stairs. I wonder if it's one of those things that in twenty years mom is going to pop the cork on it. I had to fight Steven last time he spent the night because he wanted to drink it. I don't even really know who Marilyn Monroe was besides the guy who sang Happy Birthday to JFK, I mean she must have done something else right? I never hear her name brought up so I guess she's dead, but who knows. I'll have to Google it later.

I reach the top of the stairs and the bathroom door pops open, followed by Duncan. I guess there was a reason he was in such a hurry to get home. My room is the middle of the three consecutive bedrooms. I'm between Duncan's right to my left, and the guest bedroom to my right. I close my door, and lock it to ensure no one sees what I'm about to do. I pull out my computer chair and sit down. I move my mouse to turn my computer on. I'm about to write the most important paper of my life, the one to confess my love to Violet Waits.

Chapter 2

I stare at the screen with the cursor blinking at me for twenty minutes. I know I made an outline, but how do I actually use words to tell her how I *feel*? I write the first sentence a hundred times over, but nothing sounds right. I need to ease her into it, I can't just expect her to fall for me in the first word. Should I introduce myself? I mean we have a class together so it's not like she doesn't hear my name every day during roll call.

The words aren't coming, and I don't know if they ever will. Maybe I'm looking at this the wrong way. Should I even be doing this? Steven was right, this is dumb, but what's the alternative? Should I keep on going even though I know she's going to say no? I have to, it's the only way that she can say yes. I think I can't do this on the computer, I think I need to write it out on paper.

There's just something about hand written letters that makes it seem more real. The same words typed, mean more on paper and I have no idea why. I get a hand written letter once a year from Grandma, and I save every one, but I delete 30 emails a day. I can't even remember the last time that I actually wrote a hand-written letter. I guess in sixth grade we had pen-pals from Spain that we sent letters to, apparently in Spain they don't have e-mail. I don't think they have the postal service either because I never got a letter back. I take my notebook out of my backpack, unzip the front pocket and grab a pen.

I don't think words are enough, I need a hook, I need something to really show her how I feel. I think I need to write her a poem. If Mrs. Beaker taught me anything, it's how much women love having poems written about them. It's the only way this can work, it's too bad I didn't spend more time practicing in class. I think I need to start it like a story, so it's not so apparent that it's a love letter. If I can sneak the message in, there's no ways she won't fall for me.

The problem I'm having is nothing rhymes with Violet except pilot and quiet. While she is quiet I don't think calling her out on it is going to win me any favors, and as far as I know aviation isn't a hobby of hers. Maybe I don't need to say her name at all; it's not her name I like about her. It's her that I like about her. It's the little things that no one else notices. It's the way she blows her hair out of her face, or the smirk she gets when one of the jocks says something really stupid. I feel like the smirk is just for me, just to let me know we are thinking the same thing.

I put my headphones on and plug them into my IPod, and put it on random. I started writing, and at first the words don't come. No matter how good I think a line is, the second I re-read it I immediately scrap it. I don't have the skill to impress her, the words aren't in me. I need to quit second guessing myself, close my eyes and write. I start writing, eyes fully clenched shut and just let my emotions flow through my pen and onto the paper. When I open my eyes the paper is full, and when I read back what I wrote, it's perfect. It's exactly what I wanted to say to her, and I start to cry. This is my golden ticket to the life that I want. I tear the paper out of the notebook carefully as if I was handling some sort of explosives and put it in a folder in my backpack.

It's done, maybe I can do something to take my mind off things the rest of the night. Mom got me a TV and an Xbox for Christmas last year, Duncan got a handgun. I turn my Xbox on and grab my controller with a headset already connected to it, and roll my chair over to the TV. I see Steven is online playing Call of Duty. I shoot him a message to see if he wants to play. I'm not very good and I know I usually just slow him down, but it's the only thing that we can do together without him getting embarrassed. I know Steven really does like me, I just know he needs to keep his cool status in check with women.

While I wait for Steven to reply I straighten my room. I keep my room as spotless as possible, because I know Mom is going to target one of our two rooms and I've kept an impressive winning streak. As clean cut as Duncan is, he always keeps a messy room; it's so uncharacteristic of him. Mom has been nice enough to give me nice things, the least I can do is take care of them and show I appreciate it. I mean I have a nice bed, computer, a TV, an

Xbox, a bookshelf full of books and graphic novels, and a framed movie poster from my favorite movie The Sixth Sense.

A message finally pops up from Steven and said he's ready and for me to join his game. I put my headset on, and I can tell Steven is already in one of his moods. Winning isn't enough for Steven, he has to rub it in, and I caught him in the middle of his trash talking of a recently demolished team.

"Good game scrubs, learn to play next time," Steven said mocking the other players. I can hear them spouting obscenities back at Steven, which only makes it more enthralling for him.

"Hey Steven, having a good night?" I ask.

"New noobs, new day Matty. Some days I wish some of these kids online would get good."

"Well that's better for you right? Racking up the kills tonight?"

"Yeah, but I like at least a little bit of challenge to keep it fun you know?"

"Yeah I guess, do you care what load out I use?" I ask. Steven sticks to the same weapons and equipment every game, but I always like to try different things out. I hope there's some combination out there that will not make me a liability around Steven. I tend to like single player games. I like my games like I like my books, I want to escape into a world, not to taunt teenagers.

"Naw man, just use whatever you want," Steven replied. I pick a sniper rifle and remote mines.

"Hey Steven, I hate to ask, but did you get it?" I ask.

"Get what?"

"The locker number, I mean her locker number," I said.

"Shh man, the match is about to start, but yeah I got good news for you tomorrow," Steven said.

"Okay, let's go," I said as the game loaded up. My mind wasn't in the game at all and Steven could tell. I was missing my shots, getting knifed in the back because I didn't put a land-mine down, and lost Steven a few times along the way. My mind was in a different place. My mind was with her, my mind was racing. This is really going to happen, one way or another at least I'll know. I was distracted. After three straight matches lost Steven tells me he's hanging it up for the night. I turn the Xbox off and read until dinner.

I hear Mom calling me from downstairs. Neither of my parents can cook, but Mom tries. Dad loves to grill, but I've never seen him inside the kitchen unless it was a late night cereal trip. Mom tries her hardest but she doesn't understand how to follow a recipe. It was always an epic fight between my parents when it comes to food, my Dad always wanted steaks, and Mom always tried to be more health conscious. Since he left, Mom has given up on healthy cooking. I smell grilled onions and mushrooms, then baked potatoes, then as I reach the final step down the stairs I smell the glorious steaks.

Duncan has already set the table and is sitting down. We have to wait until my Mom gets her plate before we get ours, I guess that's one of the perks of being an adult. The table is a huge breakfast nook that takes up half of the kitchen. It was moms dream to have a diner for a kitchen, black and white checkered linoleum, 50's style décor, and teal bar stools. I wonder if that's really the type of chairs they have in a bar? That's one of those questions if I asked Duncan he'd probably laugh at me.

Duncan and I get our plates. I guess I have basic tastes compared to the rest of my family. I don't like the taste of steak sauce and the only thing I like on my baked potatoes is salt. The rest of my family slathers their potatoes in every kind of sauce and cheese imaginable. I eat quickly, but not as quickly as Duncan. I guess for how much he works out he needs it. By the time I got to my potato Duncan asked if he could be excused. I could tell it always weirded my Mom out; she never demanded anyone be excused from the table, but he always asked.

I finish my food quietly, thank Mom for dinner and put my plate in the sink, the juices from the steak swirl down the drain. I head back upstairs to watch some TV in my room. I spend more time watching TV than I like to admit, but it passes the time, and tonight is all about passing the time. I probably should be doing my homework, but even if I wanted to I don't think I can force myself through it tonight. I lie down in my bed and think about tomorrow.

My head jerks up and I feel disoriented, my thoughts are cloudy. My body feels different, no, the room feels different. It's night, I must have fallen asleep laying down on the bed. I roll off my bed and into my computer chair. I move the mouse on my computer to wake my PC out of sleep mode and see what time it is. The monitor illuminates the room. It's almost midnight. I hope it's not one of those nights where I take a nap and can't sleep through the night. Of all the nights to not be able to sleep, this would be the most excruciating.

I get up quietly knowing that if Mom, or hell, even Duncan, catch me up I'll be in trouble. I turn on my lamp, the clicking of the knob breaks the silence of my house. I just need enough light to read. I think diving into a good book is about the only thing that will get my mind off of tomorrow. I pick up the *Art of War* by *Sun Tzu.* It's one of those books I've always heard about but have no idea what it's about.   I'm five pages in and realize this isn't a story but some sort of collections of insightful messages. Every page is more engaging than the previous. As I turn the last page over I feel an odd feeling, like I actually got something out of it. I've always enjoyed reading stories, but I rarely feel different after I put it back on the shelf.

I look at the clock and it's almost one in the morning. I turn my lamp back off and let the darkness in my room overtake the light. It's like the darkness is just waiting for an opportunity to overtake the light, and it always capitalizes. I close my eyes just to see more darkness, hoping soon the light of dreams will flood my brain until morning.

I wake up vaguely remembering my dreams. There was something about a cat with a dislocated jaw, a weeping willow tree, and a woman who wanted to be an Olympic gymnast. The further I get away from my subconscious the cloudier the dream becomes. Within minutes I start doubting if I even dreamed it or not.

I take a shower and I realize for the first time in my life that it actually matters what I wear today. I put on the jeans I wore the previous day and my one nice Ralph Lauren polo shirt. Grandma got it for me for my birthday a few years back, she died a few months later. Wearing it always reminded me her which always made me a little sad. My best memory of her was a summer I spent with her where we just talked, and we could talk about absolutely anything. She treated me like an actual adult for the first time in my life. I miss you Grandma.

Throw on my socks and shoes, pickup my backpack and head downstairs. Duncan was putting his cereal bowl in the sink as I enter the kitchen. Duncan never sleeps in. Duncan never skipped breakfast either. I'd much rather sleep for an extra 15 minutes than eat.

"C'mon bro, the bus is going to be at the end of the road in five," Duncan said.

"Alright, let's go," I said. Duncan always waits for me no matter what. He would rather be late than leave me behind. I don't want to put the idea in his head, but he'd be a great soldier. There's no other man I'd rather have by my side than Duncan if I was under fire, except maybe Vin Diesel. However, when we're walking home it's every man for himself.

"What were you doing last night?" Duncan asked.

"Couldn't sleep, I was trying to read to fall asleep, it didn't work," I said.

"What were you reading?"

"The Art of War, I think you'd like it. It's all about war and techniques to defeat your enemies," I said as Duncan smiles.

"It's my favorite book, I bought it for you on your last birthday, don't you remember?"

"Oh crap that's right I guess you did. Well I'm really enjoying it. It's rare that I dig something non-fiction," I said.

"That's the difference between us. I don't want to read about things that never happened," Duncan said reaching the bus stop before me.

"I just read for an escape, to experience things I'll never get to experience in life, you know what I mean?"

"Opportunities multiply as they are seized."

"Huh?"

"It's from The Art of War. Guess you didn't get that far yet. You can do whatever you want, you just have to work at it," Duncan said. I never thought of him as the insightful type, but I guess I underestimate him. "But I wasn't talking about what kept you up, I was wondering what was bothering you yesterday?"

"Just girl stuff, you know how it is," I said. Duncan didn't know what I meant. He never wanted to date seriously, he didn't want girls getting in the way of his goals, but he never had a shortage of girls to go to formal dances with. Every time I go to the refrigerator I'm reminded of all the dances he's been to. Mom makes it her purpose in life to post the pictures of them in chronological order. I change the order from time to time, and it never fails before I wake up the next morning to find my mischief has been corrected.

"Yeah I know," Duncan said. "More than you probably know."

"I seriously, seriously doubt that."

"Well, whatever it is, don't let the opportunity pass you up. Live life with no regrets if nothing else you know?"

"Yeah, that's the part that's messing with me. I'll only regret it if she says no," I said as the bus comes over the hill in the distance.

"Trust me, it's the only way you'll know. And if she rejects you, then that's her loss because you're a great guy," Duncan said putting his hand on my shoulder. Why is he touching me? Duncan never touches me.

The bus pulls up and Duncan lets me on first. I sit next to the emergency door as always out of pure paranoia. Duncan takes his usual place in the first seat behind Mr. Ralph. I close my eyes and play the scene of her reaction a million times through my head. There's the one where I come up to her just as she finishes reading the last sentence, she looks up at me with her gorgeous eyes and gives me a hug, and whispers yes in my ear. Then there's the scenario where she tears my soul apart. I have no idea what's going to do to me. I can't even imagine how I'm going to react to that if that happens. Luckily those are the only two options.

By the time I've run through the scenarios fifty times, I open my eyes and we're almost at school. A girl had sat next to me and I didn't even realize it. I've seen her at school but I never bothered to ask her name. The closer I get to school, the closer I realize I can't back out even if I wanted to. The ball is already rolling, I have other people involved and I've already written the letter. The bus pulls to the school and I know I'm ready. I'm ready for my new life to begin. I'm ready for my life with Violet. I step off the bus and head to head to my first class, Gym.

I have a love/hate relationship with gym. I don't mind the exercise, the running, or physical tests, but I can't stand any game that's based around points. Even something as seemingly fun as dodge ball always turns ugly for me. I have all the physical traits of an athlete but none of the dexterity or talent. I can't catch a ball, turn quickly, or throw a ball worth a damn. When Duncan used to wrestle with me it was just a matter of when I was going to be on my back screaming in pain.

I go to the locker room to change. Any day besides today this is when I usually get my anxiety build up. Not because I'm afraid to change around other people, but because Seth was also in the locker room at this time. He wasn't in my gym class but all the jocks are in the weight lifting class first period. I can't help but notice the amount of bacne on the lifters. If that's the consequence of being able to break state records in rushing yards I think I'm good. Apparently they are too preoccupied with a game that happened last night to worry about tearing away at my self-esteem.

It's funny that the gym is the only place I use a locker. I put on my green shorts and white shirt and head into the gym, not knowing what we're going to be forced to do before throwing open the locker door. Four basketballs were placed in the center of the court, well it could be worse. I'm a terrible shot and not that tall, but as long as I just pass the ball when it happens to come my way I'll be fine. The teacher Mr. Zang who is also the wrestling couch blows his whistle and we do our usual stretches and laps around the court to warm up then get broken up into teams of five.

My team consisted of Travis, Daniel, Angela, myself, and Danny. Luckily Danny actually plays on the varsity team, so we might actually have a shot at not being embarrassed. Danny was one of those guys who could be popular but choose to have better friends rather than popular ones. He couldn't stand bullies, the preps, or the hipsters, he was the champion of the weird guys with good hearts. Danny would also stick up for kids who routinely got made fun of, I guess kind of like Steven did for me except he's not worried about being excommunicated.

Danny led the way with our opening four points. After he rebounded a missed shot from Travis he passes it back to me. He gives me the nod to take the shot so I do, air ball. It falls into the hands of a kid from the other team and he immediately runs it back to half court. Danny taps me on the shoulder and tells me good try, and I think it's the first time anyone has said that to me un-sarcastically. We squeaked out a 21-18 victory over to the other team. Danny scored all of our points but four., none of which were mine.

I would never shower in the locker room at school if didn't have a class with Violet. Showering at school just became a necessary risk I have to take every day. The last thing I want to do is offend her with my smell, so I endure the risk. I get in and out as fast as I possibly can and get dressed and ready for History, my second period class.

History was a weird subject for me. It was either one of my best subjects, or my worst depending on what part of history we were studying that year. Anything involving guys in armor swinging swords I can get into, but most American history just bores me. I mean, look at all the pictures of the founding fathers; they all have the most boring expressions on their faces. I don't think the founding fathers knew how to smile or swing a sword.

Mr. Kemp is my history teacher, and he's the only one that could make this subject bearable. We're going over Ancient Egypt. Why should I care about a desert with triangles in it? Even their art sucked, all they could come up with is stick figures of men with birds for heads. But Mr. Kemp has a way to making it interesting by throwing in topics he knows would intrigue us. Like for instance yesterday he told us how even today no one knows how they built the pyramids.

Today Mr. Kemp is back on pyramid theories. I am especially intrigued by the idea that the Egyptians didn't build the pyramids, but there was another civilization with technology that lived there before the Egyptians, but were wiped out. What could wipe out a civilization that could move 100 ton slabs of stone? What could wipe us out? I would hope asteroids couldn't take us out, but if it could take out a planet full of T-rex's what chance do we have?

The rest of the period we were given to study for our test on Friday. History tests were always a breeze for me. It's just memorization of the people and the dates that they did some sort of act. Memorization always came easy to me so it was always an easy grade for me as long as I put the time in. I just can't stand to study boring people who I can't relate to in any sort of way. Mr. Kemp realized this and tried to humanize historical figures as much as he could, he would try to tell us their favorite food, or other hobbies that they had. Last year I learned that George Washington was a big gambler and loved cockfighting.

It always bothered me how they taught Christopher Columbus, and the founding of America. If you read anything outside of a text book he was really one of the most horrible people ever, but we glorify him as a hero. If you put him in a movie he would be one of the greatest villains ever! You know, between killing babies and forcing Native Americans to change religions or be murdered. If you made this guy up in a movie it would be too over the top, you would think it's unrealistic. His favorite hobby was fishing.

Fortunately, lunch comes quickly. I take my usual seat at the table off to the corner. Steven plops down several minutes later. He lurches over the table as if to tell me some of secret information he doesn't want anyone else to hear.

"Hey man I got it, you owe me big time," Steven said.

"You found her locker?" I ask with must seem like a cartoonish smile on my face.

"Yeah dude, its 068, took some work but yeah, don't back out," he said.

"Why would I back out, this is what I want, remember?"

"Keep telling yourself man, if you do it she's yours."

"Why do you say that?"

"I can't say my exact reason behind it, but there's a rumor that Violet likes someone, and from the description given, it could match you."

"What's the description?" My heart drops.

"Dude, it doesn't matter just know you got a good shot at this, okay?"

"Alright, Steven I trust you, I'm doing to do it between 5th and 6th period, she goes straight to her next class then," I said.

"How do you...never mind," Steven said as rubbed his hand against his face in disbelief.

Is it that weird that I know her schedule? The only thing standing between me and happiness is to slip a piece of paper through a small slit in a locker.

I eat the lunch my mom packed me without saying a word to Steven. Steven was talking about his usual heroics of online gaming, and nailing guitar solos for 20 year old songs. I politely nod when I know he expects a response. He knows I'm not really paying attention, he just has no one else to talk about guy stuff with. The warning bell rings amid Steven talking about his current sniper layout in Call of Duty.

No sign of Seth today, maybe he's found someone else to be an asshole to today. I guess he could be sick, but I didn't know pure evil could get the flu. I put the remains of my lunch back and get ready for creative writing.

Mr. Spalding was sipping a cup of coffee as I stepped into class. It was no surprise to him that I was the first one in class even though the warning bell had already rang. He looked like he was intently focused on his computer, but why?

"You okay Mr. Spalding?"

"Shh, one minute Matthew, I'm writing," he replied with one finger in the air to silence me while typing with the other.

"Yes sir." Minutes pass and most of the class has already piled in the room. Even Randy the juggalo came through the door a split second before the bell rang. Mr. Spalding was too discouraged to even give him a hard time about it. Whatever he was doing on his computer was really bugging him out. He slams his fist on his desk, it's super unlike him to show any emotion that's not sarcasm.

He steps away from his computer and tells us today we're pitching ideas for stories. He wants to hear three ideas from each of us for premises of short stories. Mr. Spalding looks for the student who doesn't make eye contact, a dead giveaway of who doesn't want to be picked. Misty Murphy is the first selected. Her first idea is about a vampire in high school who falls in love with a girl who happens to be a fairy. Snore-fest. Her second idea is about a fairy in high school that falls in love with a guy who happens to be a vampire, Mr. Spalding cringes and I smirk. It's one thing to have a really bad idea, it's another to use it twice hoping to fool a teacher. Her third concept is about a girl who gets her heart broken by a guy who plays guitar so she learns to play to be better than him. That's actually not too bad of a character motivation. Good ideas can come from the least likely places.

Ellen Blackwell, the quiet girl who everyone has assumed is a lesbian is Mr. Spalding's next victim. Her first idea is about a girl who tries to solve a murder involving a homeless man. Her second is something about a dystopian future where the internet is banned but there's a secret anarchist type group of people keeping it up. Her third idea is about a man who goes crazy and beer starts talking to him, and tells him to do crazy things. She sits down as if she had just schooled us all and raised the bar.

She didn't.

Mr. Spalding makes direct eye contact with me and gives me a nod. Oh shit, I'm next, and the nod means he thinks I have something good. I'm right, Mr. Spalding calls my name and I grab my notebook and head to the front of the class. I only had two written down and I didn't like either of them. I start off with the Amish Rumspringa idea, but it mostly gets laughs. My next on I had written down is about a man who used to be a rock star but quit the band because his girlfriend got pregnant and couldn't tour anymore. The girl ends up spending all the money he saved and has to get a job in a factory. I didn't have a third idea, but I had to think of something, Mr. Spalding is expecting something phenomenal out of me. I blank for what feels like an eternity.

"What if uh, God came to earth, but not like God, but just like his body? Like he had died or something, and when he did his body crashed to earth. What would happen to society? Would people argue over whose God it actually was, and what would they do with the body? I guess that's it," I said and walked to my desk as fast as I could. There as a dead silence in the room as Mr. Spalding called the next student up. I laid my head down on my desk hoping I wasn't going to cry. How could I have said something so dumb? I clench my eyes and feel tears forming around them.

I hear Becky Pike's name called next. I try to block out her voice and concentrate on not breaking into full fledged tears in the middle of class before I deliver the important letter of my life. Classmate after classmate goes up and I can't bring myself to lift my head up. The heat of my breath bounces back to my face with every breath, but the humidity is better than crying in public. The bell rings and I lift my head up. I take a deep breath, and take the letter out of my binder.

Mr. Spalding is staring at me.

"Matthew, can I see you for a second?"

"I...I really got to get to my next class."

"I'll write you a pass to your next class."

"But..."

"But nothing, it will only take a minute or two of your time I promise," Mr. Spalding said. He's not going to let me go, I better just get it over with.

"Look, I'm really sorry Mr. Spalding I'm really sorry if I offended you about the whole God thing," I said.

"Well that's actually what I wanted to talk to you about. I like your idea. Actually I need your idea. With your permission I'd like to use that premise and incorporate it into something I'm currently writing," he said.

"Okay, but I was going to use it for my short story, what do I do instead?" I ask, knowing full well I had no intention of using the idea.

"If you let me have it, you can submit ten-thousand words of the phrase 'I hate this class' and I'll still give you an "A"," Mr. Spalding said. I think he's serious.

"Okay, go ahead it's yours," I said. "But I'm still going to write you 10,000 words that actually mean something."

"That's entirely up to you, but thank you Matthew, you got me through a rough patch of writing," Mr. Spalding said.

"You're welcome...I guess," I said.

"You better get to class, here," Mr. Spalding said as he handed me a late pass to my next class. I guess I better hurry up and drop the letter off. I take the pass in my left hand, and the letter in my right. I head down to the dungeon and look for the magic number, sixty eight. I walk down the hall hearing nothing but my footsteps. Her locker is at the very end of the hall. It has a slight dent below the number, there's no way she did that. I take the letter and fold it over again to make sure it will fit through the slit. I close my eyes, my hand is shaking. I take a deep breath and slide the letter into the locker.

Chapter 3

I barely even remember Mechanical Drawing. The last thing I clearly remember was putting the letter in the locker and now I'm on the bus on my way home. Did I double check the punctuation? Should I have put my phone number on the note, or at least my e-mail? Maybe if I had I would hear back from her tonight, and wouldn't have to wait until tomorrows English class when I see Violet. It's doubtful but I might run into her in the halls between classes. Or maybe I'll go to her first period class before it starts and surprise her. No, that really seems too stalkerish, even for me.

I get off the bus and run to catch up to Duncan who's already 20 feet ahead of me.

"Hey man, can we talk for a minute?" I ask between gasping for breaths.

"Yeah of course, you alright? " Duncan asked not even short of air and slows down to what must be a crawl for him I would really like to be his sort of shape someday.

"Yeah, just not used to running."

"I'm not running, this is just a jog."

"Well whatever it is, it's going to murder to me. So I

was hoping we could continue our conversation from earlier.

"Sure, you never did exactly say what was bothering you."

"Well…you were right, it's about a girl," I gasp out, still trying to catch my breath.

"And?"

"Well…I wrote her a note, well a poem telling her how I felt."

"And you can't work up the nerve to give it to her?"

"Well, that was the issue, but I slipped the note in her locker," I said looking down at the ground making sure not to make eye contact. I hope my lungs don't explode.

"And I take it didn't go well?" Duncan said as he starts to breathe a little harder.

"No, well I don't know yet. I dropped it off at the end of the day and she only checks her locker once a day," I said stumbling forward struggling to keep pace with Duncan.

"How do you know how many time she…never mind. So what's the issue?"

"It's out of my hands now, and I just don't know what I'll do if she says no," I said. My lungs are burning so bad that feel like they might explode.

"Look for someone else. There are plenty of other girls in school, just focus your attention to one of them."

"But they aren't Violet."

"Is that who this is about, Violet Waits? C'mon man, you can do better than that," Duncan said slowing down for a moment, giving me a light shove on the shoulder.

"There is no better than that. She's perfect Duncan, and no one else seems to realize it."

"Could be, or it could be that you are the one person who doesn't see her for who she really is," Duncan said as we reach the front door of the house. I double over with my hands on my knees. "C'mon, get some water it helps. Just remember when you're running that the first day is always the hardest."

"What do you mean first day?" I said still not able to stand up straight without my hands on my hips.

"You're running with me every day after school. I'm getting you in shape bro," Duncan said.

I say to Duncan "Why would I want to feel like this every day?"

"Well that's the thing Matty, you always felt like you do now, you just weren't forced to prove it."

"Yeah well I wouldn't hold your breath for your chance to torture me again," I said after gulping down a glass of water. I don't think I've ever drank anything that quick in my life.

"I guess we'll see. Just don't let it ruin your life if she rejects you," Duncan said.

"I don't think I can help it, it's probably going to ruin me," I said.

"That's what girls do to boys, they ruin them, and then it turns them into men."

"I don't get it."

"Give it a couple of years, you will," Duncan said finishing his water then placing it in the dish washer.

"I think you're crazy."

"And I think you're too young to understand."

"You're not that much older than me you know."

"I agree but those two 'n a half years make a huge difference." I don't think Duncan knows what he's talking about. I mean he hasn't even had a girlfriend, at least none that I know of.

I sit on the couch in the living with a mounted deer head looming over me. I turned on the television and stare blankly at whatever bad reality show was on. It was something about women who are married to drug dealers and they talk about how they openly spend their money. I don't understand how they are okay with just telling the world that they are involved in the drug world, or that no one has just simply arrested then yet.

I think the anxiety of waiting might be killing me. I know I need to take my mind off of it, but I've never had to wait on something so important before. I flip the channel to a show about people who run pawn shop in Portland Oregon. I think we've completely given up as a society on creativity. Why do I want to watch people do their jobs? Shouldn't I want to watch people do things I'll never get to do or see?

I can hear Duncan in the garage beating the heavy bag into oblivion over some woman on the show haggling to over the price of some old coin. I turn off the television and go to my room. I turn on my Xbox and see if Steven is online. He's not. I guess I'll just play Call of Duty until he logs on, God knows I need the practice. After two rounds of getting an even kill to death ratio I finally hit my stride. I get my third knife kill in a row when Mom calls me down for dinner. I quit the game despite my streak turning around and head downstairs to the kitchen.

Mom cooked. I can tell that she burnt the chicken just based on the smell permeating in the room, and the fire alarm that had went off as I came down the stairs. The charred remains of what was once a chicken sit on a plate surrounded by vegetables that came out of a bag from the freezer. I'm starting to think that Mom is a vegetarian and this is how she's trying to win us over to her side. I sit down and realize Mom and Duncan have already started eating. I figure I better eat the chicken before it gets cold. Nothing is worse than cold burnt food. I shovel it into my mouth while she talks about her day at work. I try to listen and answer any questions that come my way. I clean my plate and excuse myself from the table. I know if Mom questions me about what's going on with me that I'll break down and tell her. I can't let them know, they can't possibly understand.

I grab a random book off the bookshelf, it doesn't even matter what it is. I just need something to take my mind off tomorrow. I wish I could just hit a button and have it be over. I know there's no way I can go to sleep right now, the knots in my stomach are almost painful. Duncan is right, the worst thing she could say is no, and I can't handle that. I wish I wouldn't have written the stupid poem. I could just be enjoying my night and not having to worry about anything. I could just not have to worry about who likes me or who doesn't. I could just stare at her from afar as I've always done.

There's a knock at my door that breaks my train of thought like obese men on thin ice. My Mom opens the door before I verbalize that it's okay to come in, which doesn't surprise me in the least.

"Hey honey, can we talk?" She said still with one arm braced against the ridge of the bedroom door.

"Yeah, just let me finish this paragraph," I said. I wasn't actually reading at this point, I just needed a minute to fight back the tears. After 20 seconds of her starring at me I put the book down. "What's up?"

"I'm worried about you, are you sick?" She asked. "I haven't seen you this bad in a while. I'll call the doctor in the morning to make an appointment. Hopefully we can get you in tomorrow. I'll take your temperature here in a few minutes, and then I'll get the Theraflu going."

"Mom stop, I'm not sick," I said to keep her from freaking out. "I just ate something bad at lunch today, no biggie...seriously."

"Did Steven make you eat something? He did didn't he? What was it? Dog food? Boogers? Was it boogers Matthew?" She said with her arms nearly flailing.

"Mom no, he didn't make me eat anything. Why don't you like Steven?" I know why she doesn't like him. She thinks he's only friends with me to make fun of me because he's "the cool kid", even Mom knows I'm a dork.

"I just don't think he's good for you Matthew, that's all," She said with her hands on her hips.

"It was sloppy Joe day okay? It's doing wonders to my stomach as you can imagine," I said.

"Okay well, if you need any Pepto let me know okay babe?"

"Yeah I will Mom, thanks."

"And if you need to talk about anything I'm here for you okay hun?"

"Yeah I know Mom. I'm just going to lay down for a while okay?"

"Of course that's fine, but I still think we should take your temperature."

"Mom I'm fine, really."

"Then just let me feel your forehead."

"Mom!"

"Okay, okay I get it. Just rest up okay? If you need to stay home from school tomorrow tell me okay?"

"I wouldn't miss it for anything as much as I'm dreading it."

"Dreading what dear?"

"I...got a presentation tomorrow for Creative Writing class, that's all," I said as she nods and walks out of the room. I don't think she suspects anything but who knows. Mom is smart when you least expect it. It's only eight I have no idea what I'm going to do for the next few hours. Duncan used to have problems sleeping, I think he used to take some sort of sleeping pill.

I knock on Duncan's door, his is right next to mine but without the Nirvana poster over it. I can hear his music through the door, I think it's Lynyrd Skynyrd, but everything he listens to sounds the same to me. I knock again a little louder, seconds later I hear his music turn off. He opens the door and I notice he's incredibly sweaty. His tank top was soaked in his own perspiration.

"Hey bro, what's up?" He asked panting only half as hard as I was running down the road earlier.

"I was hoping you could help me out with something," I said rubbing my hands nervously.

"Of course, come in." I step in his room, something I rarely do. It's strange to me that we have the same amount of space, but he uses it completely differently. He has no bookshelves, no TV, no Xbox, no computer, no desk. He has a small table with an iPod he got for Christmas a few years ago hooked into a pair of portable speakers, he must absolute awful sound out of that setup. He has a dresser for his clothes and a safe where he keeps his gun. He has a gigantic hammock in the dead center of his room. I never saw him beg for anything in his life like when he wanted a hammock in his room. I don't see how sleeping on ropes can be comfortable in any sort of way. "So what's up?" He asked.

"I'm having a hard time sleeping, is there any way I can, you know, take one of your sleeping pills?" I asked thinking he might punch me just for asking.

"Did you ask Mom?" Duncan asked. Shit, do I lie or do I just hope he will help me out because he's my brother?

"No, she already thinks I'm sick, asking for medicine will make her call the CDC," I said as Duncan gives me a blank stare. "Center for Disease Control."

"Yeah that sounds like Mom."

"So?"

"I'm not going to give you a full one, but I don't think a half will kill you," Duncan said. I don't know if he's being serious or not. "If you tell Mom I gave it to you I'll break your femur."

"Sounds like a solid plan to me. Trust me, I don't want to tell anyone. I just want this night to be over."

"Okay. Also know you're not getting any more," Duncan said as he turned his back to me and went over to his solid wood dresser. He opens the top drawer and I see him shove socks out of the way. He must really not like the fact he has to take these pills. I see something shiny and metal gleam out of his sock drawer like a beacon. I wonder what that's about? I better not ask, he's already helping me out enough today. I hear the sound of a top popping off a bottle. He takes one out, puts the cap back on and hides it. He snaps it in half like a pencil and extends his hand with the half pill sitting in the palm.

"Don't take it on an empty stomach, and drink it with a glass of water, trust me," Duncan said as I grab it from his hand.

"Sure thing Duncan," I said. "Thank you, I really do appreciate it."

"You're my brother, it's what I'm supposed to do," Duncan said giving me a half smile that he rarely blesses the world with. "Oh and lay down as soon as you take it, there's a window which you'll fall asleep with it, if you miss it, you'll be awake all night for sure."

I don't waste any time. I go to the kitchen downstairs, get a glass of water and toss the pill in my mouth, drinking the water as fast as I could. I dash upstairs, and without even taking my clothes off, I get under my covers, close my eyes and go to sleep.

I wake up with memories of my dreams bombarding my stream of thoughts. None of it makes any sense. I was trapped in prison a cell in a mansion with a few friends, there was an old man in a wheelchair carrying a shotgun. He rolled up to each of my friends and killed them. He pointed the gun at me, pulled the trigger and paper bullets came out. I crushed it with my hand before it even hit me. I throw it back at him and it turns into a real bullet. It kills him but I'm just trapped in the cell forever. The more time that goes between the dreams and me being awake, the less clear they become. Five minutes later I remember almost nothing about it.

I thought I would be excited or anxious, but I feel normal. It feels like just another day. I better go downstairs and eat breakfast. I'm going to need something to throw up if she says no. There are two packages of Pop tarts in the cabinet. I take one and put it in the toaster. Duncan reaches over me and grabs the last package and starts eating it right away.

"Hey Duncan, Mom is gonna be pissed you took the last one," I said.

"Wrong again, Mom hates strawberry. She keeps the blueberry ones she likes in the cabinet above the oven," Duncan said with pastry chunks falling out of his mouth. There are two long standing rules when it comes to food, the first is never drink the last Pepsi or Mom will do unspeakable things to you. The second unwritten law is any cereal that contains chocolate shall not be eaten by anyone but Mom or face the horrible consequences. The only times I've seen Duncan in trouble is when it's involving food. I don't think Duncan has a weakness, but if he does it probably has something to do with baked goods.

The toaster pops, I roll off a paper towel off the kitchen counter and pull the pastries out of the toaster. I take a bite and a rush of fruit filling ignites my mouth in agony. I open my mouth fan my hand into it, knowing it must look ridiculous and I'm sure isn't actually helping.

"And that's why I never toast them," Duncan said taking a bite of his, grinning with satisfaction. His mockery is not appreciated as I can feel my taste buds melting away. What seems like an eternity passes before it stops hurting. Duncan has already finished his first, and has started on his second. "Well look at the bright side, this will probably be the most painful thing you experience all day. You got it out of the way before you even got out the door."

"Let's hope it's the most painful thing I go through today," I said. I finish my breakfast and leave while Duncan is still getting ready. I open the door and brisk autumn air slices at my cheeks. I make it halfway up the road before Duncan catches up with me. He gives me a nod and runs past me. I guess he doesn't realize the bus is going to be there at the same time regardless of when he gets there. Nothing is going through my mind, nothing is affecting me except the wind. I walk forward knowing every step is going to determine the rest of my life.

Once I reach the end of the road Duncan was already half way through his stretches. He does the same stretch routine at the bus stop. I wonder what benefits he's really getting from it? He finished as the bus pulls up. He doesn't even say anything to me. No words of encouragement, no extra positivity, nothing. I get on the bus and sit by myself near the front, Duncan has decided to sit next to Becky Pike, I have no idea what he sees in her. Even though he never really has a girlfriend Duncan is always talking to girls. I wonder what he gets out of just talking to them? They all want to date him but he never gives in. Why doesn't he want to score?

Jimmy Tucker just wiped the gunk in the windowsill onto Roger Pain in front of me. I want to feel bad for him but Roger is going to murder someone when he's older. Hell, it might not even be that long before he starts. I can't put my finger on it, but something tells me that he's a psychopath. His eyes look like they are from a zombie movie. Everyone teases him but it doesn't seem to bother him, like he's hiding his emotions. I don't know what it is about him, but I know he's got cats hung up in his basement. The thing that terrifies me is that Roger doesn't fight the torture, he just endures it. He didn't even flinch when Jimmy wiped the wet black filth from the windowsill on his jacket.

The bus pulls to the school as Mr. Ralph was finished singing along to the song Enter Sandman that he had playing on a small portal radio. Maybe someday he will realize that IPods exist. I mean bus drivers can't be that poor right? I mean why would you want to do that as a career if it didn't pay well? On the other hand, if it makes him happy, isn't that what he should be doing?

I feel the cold air rushing through the bus as soon as Mr. Ralph opens the door, it sends chills down the aisle. I grab my backpack take a deep breath and sling it over my shoulder. I overhear Bobby Thomas talking about a fight that broke out yesterday that I didn't hear about. I didn't catch the names of who was fighting but apparently someone's nose was broken. I guess I could always look around for someone with a broken nose if I really want to know who it was. The warning bell rings, the sooner I get to gym and get changed, the less likely I am to get made fun of.

John Parsons is the only person in the locker room. Gym is always the class the slackers sign up for first period. We get 15 minutes to dress down so most people just come 15 minutes late already in their clothes. It's mostly the kids who smoke prior to coming, which I always thought disturbing that you would want to ruin your lungs before using them. The basketballs were already placed on center court when I went in. I didn't have the luck today to be put on Danny's team again. I manage to actually put up six points, by far the most I've done in any game of basketball.

"Good job out there Matt," Danny said patting me on the back of the shoulder. "You really have a decent jumper, keep at it."

"Thanks Danny, I don't think I have much of a future in the NBA, but I appreciate it," I said as I head to the locker room. I undress and take the quickest shower that a human can possibly take with it still being considered a shower and get dressed. I latch my lock on my locker, grab my backpack and head towards History early, not in the mood to read today.

Mr. Kemp was really excited for class today. I don't know if that's different than any other day but he seemed especially jazzed for today's lesson. Mr. Kemp had to be right out of college, late 20's tops. He has a real passion for teaching which is pretty refreshing, but he wants to act like he's the guy from Stand and Deliver, a movie we've watched no less than a dozen times in school. We have our final next week on Ancient Egypt, and knowing the kind of tests he gives it'll probably be open ended questions.

The lesson is about mummification. Mr. Kemp goes into every single gory detail of how they extract all the vital organs, drain the blood, and fill it with fluid without disrupting the body. They stitched it with a symbol of an eye, then put all sort of jewelry on it. They then wrapped in 20 layers of cloth before finally being laid to rest. I think cremation sounds a hell of a lot less work. I think Mr. Kemp is doing less of a history lesson and more of a research of his demise.

The second half of the class he gives us to study for the final. I open my notes and stare at them as if I were reading them. As long as I don't bother anyone, no one is going to say anything. I just can't focus on Ra and pharaohs when in two periods I'll know the truth. Dez is in my next period class but I don't think she'd tell me, hell Violet might not have even told her yet. What if she didn't check her locker today? Should I just let her talk to me until I know she got it? If she says no, would she even let me know? She's too nice to do something to intentionally hurt me, right? Isn't the point of this to seize the day and not wait around for the things I want in my life? Just waiting around is what I have been doing the last five years and it got me nowhere.

The warning bell went off and I recklessly shove everything in my backpack as if I'm in a hurry. Mr. Kelp is talking to Seth about his test scores. He's bullied me into doing his homework before so it's no surprise Kelp sees a difference between assignments and test scores. I don't think I can read today, I'd need a bottle of Aderol to focus.

I head directly Algebra class. I'm the first student in class, not even Dez is in her seat, writing. I've always wondered what she writes, but with the amount of time she spends with her face in a notebook it's got to be something pretty important to her. I can see her working on the next big teen romance book, or a movie script for an action movie starring a female lead.

Mr. Sim stumbles through the door, obviously flustered from his smoke break that the class can always smell on him. I don't see how it's fair that teachers can leave school grounds to smoke but students can't. He logs on his computer presumably to check his e-mail while the rest of the students come in at random intervals. The bell rings and Mr. Sim starts going over yesterday's homework fielding questions which as usual the room is silent. For some reason no one wants to ask questions in a math class. It's like if you don't get it, you must be dumb for needing him to go over it again. We pass our homework forward and Randy, who obviously doesn't have anything to turn in for once looks guilty about it.

Mr. Sim calls Randy out for having ear buds in while

he was talking about scientific notation, Randy called him a hater and was promptly sent out of class. He complies with two middle fingers extended while he backs out of the door. It's almost expected that Randy gets kicked out of class for something every day. He always claims it's because he's a juggalo, and not because he's a fat annoying asshole. I know I'm not the most popular kid and it's really not my fault, but Randy has brings it upon himself. Before he identified himself as a juggalo he was a fairly normal kid. I think he desperately wants to identify himself as being something that everyone will hate just so he stands out. Some people would rather be hated than to go unnoticed.

I feel like someone is staring at me, I look to my left and see Dez, Violet's best friend. I know the look wasn't a good one but I can't tell exactly what it is. Maybe Dez thinks if Violet has a boyfriend she will lose her as a friend? I think I should talk to her before class is over, I can't let Dez sabotage things between me and Violet. I need to let her know that I have no intention in getting in the way of what they have. Hell maybe the three of us could be friends, or four of us including Steven. I guess I'm missing the main point, if she's mad at me, it's because Violet read the letter. That fear has left me.

As each minute passes of class, my heart beats faster. I'm sure I look like a wreck, hopefully no one calls me out for it. The more I try to act normal like my heart isn't about to pop out of my throat, the more nervous I get, and the more I start to sweat. I wipe my brow and my palm comes away drenched. I scrape my soggy hand against my jeans even though I'm slightly worried it will soak through. It didn't. I rush through the math work, only half absorbing the lesson. There would be time tonight to either drown my sorrows in learning scientific notion, or I use it thinking about my life with Violet.

There's only three minutes until class is over, I put my book away and get ready for lunch, then my only class with Violet. I better plan on getting to class early just in case I don't see her during lunch. The bell rings and I make a mad dash for the door. I know the teacher she has always lets them out a few minutes late, I might be able to meet her as she gets out. It might spare me the next thirty minutes of torture.

I turn the handle of the door, and immediately turn left down the hallway. I see Violet's classroom at the end of the hall, they still haven't left. I speed up. I get flung back, and the clang sound of my head hitting the locker dazes me more than the pain. Dez has her left hand around my throat with death stare that only occur when acts of violence are imminent.

"How dare you do that to her?" said Dez in a low voice, tightening the grip around my windpipe making me gag for air.

"What?" I squeak out.

"You got some fucking nerve to do that to her. I always thought you were a nice guy, I guess Steven turned you into an asshole."

"What?" I said struggling to breath, thinking that every word I utter gets me closer to suffocation. I feel her nails digging into my skin, making indentations in my neck.

"I hope you die Matthew, you know she doesn't deserve that, no one does. If you only knew what kind of shit storm you've just caused in her life. Here keep it." Dez says as pulls out a folded piece of paper in her right pocket and shoves it in my face. The outer edges of my vision start to go black as she releases her death grip. Oxygen flow starts back into my brain and I feel dizzy. I see her walking away towards the commons. After a moment of gathering myself I unfold the note that Dez gave me. I read it even though I already know what it says because I wrote it.

I bet you don't know me but I know you Violet
You make me feel like my hearts on auto pilot
I've adored you since you moved here years ago
I've kept this from you and you've never known
You're silky hair, milky skin, and perfect smile
Makes my life worth living even though it's vile
You give me something to aspire to, motivation
To change my life for the better, no hesitation

My name is Matthew Masters, nice to meet you
I sat behind you last year in history, period two
We were on a group project once I think in math

You're as smart and as beautiful as Sylvia Plath
I'm writing this poem because I want to know you
 I want to be David Carradine, and you to be Kung-Fu

I love you Violet Waits and it's been ever so long
That I've hid this fact from you, it was so wrong
It's been so ever long that you've tickled my fancy
I'm a lonely Sid Vicious, looking for my dearest Nancy

Something seems off about it, the ink I wrote it in looks faded, looks different. It's a different color. It's a copy. She made a copy of it? Why would she make a copy of it? If it was just for Dez why wouldn't she just show it to her?

"Good job fag," I hear near me from a familiar voice...Seth. I look up in time for Seth's palm to meet my forehead, forcing my head into the locker. My ears are ringing and my vision is out of focus. Once my eyes adjust a throbbing pain streaks from the back to my head to the front. I look around to see if Seth is still around to brace for a second attack. He isn't.

I turn around to see if there were any dents or blood on the locker. There wasn't. There was a note taped to the locker, I rip it off. It isn't an advertisement for the play or cheerleader fundraiser. It's my poem to Violet. This locker wasn't alone. It's everywhere. She made copies and posted them around school. I'm sure it's not just this hallway, but all the hallways. Why would she do this to me? Was my confession to her so disgusting to her to she felt the need to embarrass me? I need to find out.

The first people start piling out of Violet's class. I don't see her in the crowd, I get closer and the people leaving the room get fewer and fewer. She comes out last, head to the ground, she must already feel bad for what she's done. I approach her for the first time in my life but not in the way that I had hoped I would.

"Why did you do this to me?" I said to her holding the paper to her face. She looks up, glances at the paper and claws at it with her nails, slicing it into strips.

"Why did you do this to me? How could you think that was a good idea? Why did you think that was an okay thing to do?" She said to me. She's speaking to me, but my stomach is turning over like a dryer. I don't understand why she's acting like this is my fault. I can't help it.

"This isn't my fault," I said.

"How is this not your fault? Are you trying to tell me you didn't write it?"

"No I did, but," she interrupted me.

"Okay then, how the fuck isn't this your fault? How did you not just ruin my life?" Violet said an inch away from my face. I can feel her warm breath against my face. A small crowd around us started gathering. Lewis Kelley started making kissy faces towards us and Cody hands copies of the poem to people standing around.

"I'm sorry," I said hanging my head towards the ground.

"Fuck you Matthew," she said as she slaps me in the face. It stings. For as long as I've wanted her hand to touch my face, I never thought it would be from contempt. There's an uproar of "oooohhhhh's" from the crowd that had gathered as Violet stomps away more furious than I had ever seen anyone.

I don't know the emotion I'm feeling but it must be what heartbroken is. I feel the empty loneliness crawl up from the pit of my stomach into my throat. My eyes start to well up and feel the warm tears of depression stream down my face. I get shoved into a locker for the third time today, this time by Steven.

"Hey, we need to talk," Steven said.

"What Steven? What do we have to talk about right now? Did you just see what happened? Do you know how I feel right now? Violet just fucking ruined my life. I never thought she'd do that to me."

"She didn't Matt, she didn't."

"What the fuck are you talking about? it's pretty obvious that she got the letter, laughed her ass off and decided to humiliate me in front of the whole fucking school," I said shoving Steven out of pure frustration.

"Matthew listen to me, it wasn't her." Steven said grabbing me by the shoulders.

"Then who did this to me? Who would do this to me Steven?" I said trembling. My knees feel weak and I can feel my skin going pale. Steven's frowns. "Who?"

"It's my fault Matt."

Chapter 4

"You did this? Why would you do this to me? Was this your plan all along Steven? Were you pretending to be my friend just to humiliate me? "

"Matty, of course not. It's not like that."

"Oh yeah, then tell me Steven what is it like?" I shove him into a locker, the clanking echoed down the hall.

"I didn't make the copies Matt, someone else did."

"So it was Violet then?"

"No it wasn't Violet."

"That fucking bitch, it was Dez right? That's why she gave me that look in class."

"Matt, it doesn't matter who it was, I'm here to say I'm sorry it happened because it's my fault," Steven said as he let out a deep sigh.

"What did you do?" I said to Steven as I feel my heart pounding like a sledgehammer.

"I wrote it down wrong Matt. I gave you the wrong locker number. I wrote it down as 068, but 086 is her actual locker number. I'm sorry Matt," Steven said with actual remorse coming from his voice. I don't know what to say. I was set up to fail. No matter how she felt about me, no matter how much she may like me my chances with her were doomed before I even wrote the letter. My heart sank to my stomach and my head hung several inches lower. I could tell he felt bad about it, but it didn't unscrew the dagger I felt twisting inside me.

"Who did it?"

"I don't know whose locker it was, but I'm sure it's not too hard to find out. That's not what I'm concerned about Matt, are you okay?"

"Of course I'm not, but I'm going to fuck up whoever did this," I said clenching my fists so tightly that anything they hit will explode on contact.

"Dude, you know it's not worth it."

"Didn't you fight Seth when he came between you and your girl?"

"That was different, and she's not my girl. Not anymore. Plus you don't even know who did this to you."

"I don't want to smash his face because of what he did to me, I want to murder his face because of what he did to her."

"Matt seriously, just let it go," Steven said putting his hand on my shoulder. Why is he picking this moment to be all touchy feely?

"I know you're right. I know beating whoever it is up won't help, and it's likely I'd get my ass kicked, but right now Steven, I don't care," I said as I brush his hand off my shoulder a and walk off to English class. It's going to be super awkward with Violet in the class. I'm sure it's all anyone will talk about until someone else does something stupid. Maybe I'll get lucky and Cody Mills will shit himself in gym class again. Maybe for once I will be that guy who handles it the wrong way and punch the first person who looks at me funny. Who am I kidding? I'm not that person. Just thinking about it makes me worried about breaking my hand. The thought of broken bones and shredded skin makes my skin crawl.

Mrs. Beaker is already writing on the whiteboard when I come in the room. Ritchie and Lewis used this as an opportunity to stare at her ass, and I could see why. I overheard Ritchie telling Lewis that if you stare hard enough you can see an outline of her thong. I never understood how people could wear those things. However, they were right, you could see the outline of her thong from the outside of her tight business skirt.

I lay my head on my desk. Several minutes pass when I notice the room has gone quiet. I get the sneaking suspicion that the class was staring at me, I was wrong. I look up and see several students who had entered while my head was firmly planted on my desk to that had their necks cranked towards the door. It's Violet. She looked stunned by the glances she was getting as if she'd never had that many people looking at her. Now that I think about it, she probably hadn't as she wasn't quite the attention seeking type. After several moments walked to her desk with her eyes pointed to the ground making sure she didn't accidently make eye contact with anyone.

Ritchie made a kissy face to Violet, it made my blood boil. I wanted to lop his lips off with a cleaver and throw them in a garbage disposal. I start breathing heavily and stare at Ritchie hoping that I gained the ability to make people explode with a glare. I didn't. I did however gain the ability of creeping someone out by staring at them for too long. He didn't have to say anything, the look he gave me said it all as we quickly avoided eye contacted and averted his eyes back towards Mrs. Beaker whose thong was no longer visible as she was facing the class.

It wasn't any surprise that all the boys in this class paid extra attention to Mrs. Beaker. Duncan told me when she got divorced a few years back all the students took bets on who would "nail" her first. Several had lied about it, or at least I think they were lying. She got married last year much to the chagrin of horny teenagers all over the school, and was to someone her own age. It was also no surprise that the girls hated the attention that she got. Even though it's not my favorite subject, and I wasn't attracted to her, she was rather good at teaching English. She was much better than my middle school teacher Mr. George who put us to sleep with stories of how he loved the classics.

I couldn't help but slyly glance back at Violet who sat two rows behind me, and three seats to the right. She was doing everything she could to not look this way, which is in all honesty just like every other day. The difference today was that everyone wanted *her* attention, it was just a shame I'm the only person that wants her attention because I like her. She looks up slightly to brush her hair out of her eyes, but part of her hair had stuck to her cheek. The adhesive keeping her hair attached to her face made my stomach drop when I realized it was tears. I couldn't tell how much she had been crying but an even gleam across her left cheek matched with an extreme puffiness of her eyes. She raised her hand up again to get the remaining hair out of the way, when she looked up at me. My body froze, and I couldn't look away. It wasn't a look like she hated me, it was a look like she wanted my help. She wanted someone to get her to escape. She was looking for a hero.

I can't stand having Violet needing someone and I am the sole person who can't be the one to help her. Noticing her face is moist she smears her hand against it and wipes it on her jeans. The rest of the class saw this as a sign of weakness, a bleeding fish in shark infested waters. Jayden Douglas puts his fists to his eyes and rotates them slightly calling her a cry baby. I want to jab a pen through his eye. Jayden had his gym shorts pulled down by Billy Wyler only to discover that he didn't wear underwear, and he cried before pulling his shorts back up. He has no right to make fun of anyone else. I clench the pen that's in my hand so hard I think it might break. Without thinking I throw it at the back of his head, secretly hoping it gets lodged in his skull.

"Who did that?" Jayden said after the pen had bounced off his head. The girl in back of Jayden, Becky Pike pointed a finger my way. "Oh, that figures. You trying to stick up for your girlfriend?"

"She's not my girlfriend," I said.

"Can you blame her for saying no? Who would say yes to *you*?" I'm suddenly regretting the fact that I don't have a pen to jam into his eye socket.

"Hey guys anything that you want to share with the class?" Mrs. Beaker said.

"Yes Mrs. Beaker, did you know that Matthew is in loooooove with Violet?" Jayden said. I want to kill him, I literally wish he would keel over from an aneurysm. Violet stands up and the entire class looks at her, including Mrs. Beaker. Violet walks towards the door and slams it shut.

"Jayden go to the principal's office, and Matthew I want to talk to you after class," Mrs. Beaker said. How the fuck am I getting in trouble for this? I mean yeah I threw a pen at him but I mean c'mon, he's clearly the asshole here.

"Yes ma'am," I said to her with my head lowered. Even though I still wish him a thousand deaths I don't want to get in trouble over him. The rest of class didn't acknowledge what had happened since Mrs. Beaker was on a detention giving mood, but I can feel that Johnny Byerly had to hold back from making a remark. Class couldn't end soon enough but once I did I knew I had to endure an embarrassing conversation with the teacher most students would love some one-on-one time with.

Students began piling out of the class, but slower than they do most classes as Mrs. Beaker was wiping off the dry erase board from the lesson again. It was no surprise to me that that Ritchie and Lewis were the last two to leave trying to catch one more peep of her panties. Once they reluctantly left class Mrs. Beaker finally addresses me, sitting on the desk in front of me.

"So, what's going on with you Matthew? You're always so quiet, what's with the rumors going around?"

"They aren't rumors Mrs. Beaker, I just did something stupid," I said doing whatever I could to keep from making eye contact.

"Oh, so you asked her out and she said no?"

"That wouldn't be a mistake that would be being rejected, this is far worse."

"Did she slap you then tell you no?" Mrs. Beaker said with a half smirk that made me realize that she also has a beautiful smile.

"Actually she did, but I deserved it. I wrote her a dumb poem that told her how I feel about her and put it in her locker," I said but Mrs. Beaker cut me off before I could finish.

"That is so sweet Matthew, if someone had done that for me there's no way I would have said no."

"Well, that's the thing, it didn't go in her locker, it went in someone else's by mistake. Whoever did get it made copies and posted them all over school. I was mad at Violet because I initially thought it was her, and then she was mad at me because she thought that was my idea of getting her attention."

"Oh, I see. Have you gone to the principal yet? I mean, you want to get whoever did it in trouble, it's a pretty terrible thing to do," Mrs. Beaker said.

"No not yet, but I probably will, it just happened so I haven't had much time to think about it." This was a lie and she knew it. She could tell I was fighting back tears, but she didn't know is that I didn't want to go to the principal, I wanted to physically hurt the person responsible.

"Okay Matthew, but if you need to talk about it just let me know okay?"

"Okay. Is that why you asked me to stay after class?"

"Partially yes, but I have Violet's friend Dez in another class, and I overheard Dez talking about you," Mrs. Beaker said.

"What did she say?" I said completely perplexed.

"She was talking to another student about how Violet had a crush on someone. While she didn't say the name of the person, the description sounded an awful lot like you. I don't want to get your hopes up, but she's acting like a girl who is smitten with a boy. Trust me, I've been there before, it's not hard to see in other people," Mrs. Beaker said. I don't know how to take this, it's kind of weird and I can tell the longer the silence is the more awkward this whole thing is becoming.

"Well I really appreciate it, but I'm pretty sure even she did have those feelings that my mistake annihilated my chances. I guess the single life isn't such a bad thing though right?"

"Matthew, don't be so hard on yourself, you'll be fine. You better get on to your next class. Do you need a pass?"

"I'm actually on lunch so it's no big deal. I bring my lunch so I don't need to worry about being last in line," I said. Being last in line for lunch meant you were given the bottom scraps of what was left in the giant metal bins of food. A lot of times they don't account for the number of people correctly and the people at the end of the line don't even get a full meal. I was near the back when Kimberly Harris got the last serving of pizza last month. I brought my lunch since then but I wasn't hungry after all that's gone on.

I wasn't in the mood to read either. I thought it was take my mind off things at least for 30 minutes, but the stares I got from other students was unbearable. Most of the copies had been taken down around school but everyone already knew, and everyone was talking about it. One student that I've seen around school but didn't know his name was brave enough to ask me why I was eating lunch and not making out with Violet? Instead of responding with a witty retort that I had yet to think of, I ignore him.

Hoping to avoid anymore embarrassment I go to Mr. Spalding's classroom. I know he never locks it, and he has lunch the same time I do. As expected its empty and I sit down at my desk enjoying the silence in the room with my forehead firmly planted on my desk. I haven't really been alone with my own thoughts since it happened. I hear footsteps approaching the room. I don't acknowledge whoever just came in the room, but I assume it's Mr. Spalding.

"Good afternoon Mr. Masters, are you feeling alright?"

"Yeah I guess," I said without removing my head from the desk.

"If you need to go see the nurse you're more than welcome. The lesson today is just writing a main character for the ideas we pitched yesterday. Something tells me you already have that covered."

"You're right I do but I feel fine. Just...personal stuff going on."

"I know Matthew, we were talking about what happened in the teachers' lounge earlier," he said and immediately regretted afterwards.

"Great, so the entire faculty knows how pathetic I am. You're a wealth of encouragement Mr. Spalding."

"It's not like that Matthew, but I can see how you would take it that way. Every teacher in the lounge sympathized with you, and not because we feel pity for you, but because we've been there before. Matthew, putting yourself out there and getting rejected is a part of life, we've all done it and it's all destroyed us."

"Not like this, this is a bit of a uniquely terrible situation."`

"I agree that it's different, but even though it feels like the way you're feeling is unique, it isn't."

"Okay then how do people get through this?"

"Everyone deals with these things differently, but I'll tell you what I did. When I was 20 and in college I asked a girl out in my psychology class. I did the traditional passing her a note in class. I stared at her the entire time she was reading it, when she got to the end she made a disgusted look and tore it up in front of me. She didn't even look at me to tell me no. The look on her face haunted me for a long time. You know what I did? I wrote about it in excruciating detail. Every little aspect of not only what happened and her reaction, but also how it made me feel went into a character I made. Once I wrote about it, it went away, because it didn't belong to me anymore, those emotions belonged to the character."

"So you're saying I should write it out?" I was slightly confused about how transferring my misery to a character worked, or if there was some other dimension where that characters I write come to life and I create some miserable guy whom nothing goes right for.

"No, not exactly, I'm saying that you need to find an outlet. Two things are for sure though, first is that brooding about it isn't the outlet. Secondly, you will look back at this moment as a valuable lesson in life that a lot of people go through."

"Thanks I guess," I said. I hadn't removed my head from the desk during the entire conversation but I felt the urgent need to come up for fresh air.

I decide to take Mr. Spalding up on his offer and I tell him I'm going to the nurse's office. He doesn't object. I had no intention of going to the nurse however. I've never liked the nurse, and I wasn't alone in this feeling. There was just something very cold and artificial about her. I always wondered if all nurses were that way or if there were some that were warm and comforting.

I walk out the front door of the school to get some fresh air. As soon as I step through the doors I know I wouldn't be coming back to school for the rest of the day. I wasn't much of a walker, but walking home sounded a lot better than staying in school for the rest of the day. I think it's an eight mile walk, I'm not sure if I've ever walked that far before. Maybe I'll get lucky and get run over somewhere around the first mile to put me out of my misery.

It's weird how your mind just works different when outside even in a small town, rather than in school. I wasn't worried about getting beat up, made fun of, or trying not to fall asleep. Instead my mind was thinking about how intricate the world is, how empty houses look during the day, and how lost I feel. I don't think I have a place in the world. If there is a God, I don't know if he gave me a purpose, and if there isn't, I don't think there's a place I fit in. I'm not cut out for physical labor and not smart enough to get an engineering degree. I'm a grasshopper trapped in an ant farm with no queen to lead me.

I walk by the Johnson's house on the outskirts of town. I've driven by it since I was a kid but it looks so different when you walk by it. You start to notice the little things, like the assortment of lawn gnomes the Johnson's have on their porch. Their house had burned down a few years ago, the town came together and helped out to help pay for and build their new house. I think this may be the first time in my life I've ever sweated in jeans, not a pleasant experience. The denim starting chaffing and sticking to my legs with beads of sweat like dabs of glue.

The more I walk the more I feel farther away from what happened at school today. I don't know if I feel any better about it, but it feels good to not be surrounded 500 people who would love nothing more than to remind me of the most embarrassing thing that's ever happened to me. The bad news is that no matter how far I walk away from it today, I'll have to come back to it tomorrow. At least tomorrow is Friday and hopefully things can blow over after the weekend. The only good thing about school is that drama has a short shelf life. Around the corner is the railroad tracks which is about the half-way point. I hear unmistakable sound of a train horn in the distance. It's interesting to me how fast trains turn into a thing of fascination to kids to a thing of pure inconvenience. As I approach the tracks I realize it's already passed and won't delay me getting home.

So what do I do from here? Do I just give up on Violet? I mean pursuing her even further is just going to push her further away, and there are no other women I want to be with. She's the one I'm supposed to be with, so not pursuing her means being alone forever. I know Duncan is going to tell me that in five years I won't even remember her name...but that's not true. She's the one, I feel it in every single cell in my body. If she's not the one for me then I can't trust my body, and if that's the case I have bigger issues.

If I would have thought about it I would have stopped by the gas station and got a bottle of water. My mouth is so dry that I think my tongue might be permanently stuck to the top of my roof. I try to pry it off with sticky and painful resistance. Step by step I get closer to home. I wonder if anyone's noticed I ditched school, and if anyone tried calling Mom yet. I only had two classes left; they may not even notice. Mom might give me a hard time for ditching school; but once she knows the reason I have no doubt she will understand albeit with concern about my mental well-being.

As soon as I reach the beginning of my driveway I notice that my legs hurt worse than I think they ever have. I don't think I've ever walked this far in my life. The contender is when we took a family vacation to Disney Land, but even then we took breaks between rides. I wonder if Duncan feels this bad after exercising, or does getting in shape prevent this pain?

I made it; I'm at the front door. I'm fairly certain this is how the soldier whom the marathon was named after felt after run his run right before he died. I don't know the last time I've beat Duncan home, but I'm sure he's not far behind me. I stopped carrying my key because Duncan always has his and he always beats me here. I'll have to start bringing it from now on. Mom is probably taking a nap, and waking her up is about the most unwise thing I could do. She never really gets mad, but I know better than to poke the bear. I lay my backpack down in front of the door and use it as an impromptu stool until Duncan arrives. I had forgotten during that entire long walk that I had an extra 20 pounds strapped to my back. I wedge my head in the corner of the door frame and close my eyes.

"You charging admission now?" A voice said as I open my eyes. As I start to realize I had fallen asleep I stand up. It was Duncan, of course it was who else would it have been?

"I left my key on my desk. I never beat you home so I never bring it anymore," I said while picking up my backpack which had my butt-print on it.

"Well I hope you learned your lesson," Duncan said gently pushing me aside to get to the keyhole. "I was worried about you when I didn't see you on the bus. Glad you're okay." He unlocks the door and steps inside. Before I can get through the door I can hear him already heading upstairs towards his room. I was in no rush to get to my room. I shut the door behind me and lay my backpack by the stack of umbrellas. I had no intention of doing homework tonight so there's no point in bringing it into my room. In fact I have zero intention of doing anything remotely responsible tonight. I plan on dicking around on Facebook, reading, and spending some time on Call of Duty.

I decide to go on my computer and check my e-mail. There's nothing besides an offer for boner pills and a notice that Faith No More would be playing near me soon. I refresh my inbox, my own little form of OCD and a new message pops up. I set-up Facebook notifications to send me an e-mail whenever someone messages me, mentions me, or tags me on a photo. Usually this happens when Steven sends me message to get answers to math questions, or other homework assignments. This was different, this wasn't from Steven. It was from Xavier, a friend of Seth's. The message said that Xavier Michaels tagged me in a photo and provided a link for me to view the photo he tagged me in. I clicked the link.

My heart was beating so loudly that I thought Duncan would tell me to quiet down as the page loads. It's the poem. Xavier uploaded the fucking poem to Facebook and tagged me in it. As I hover over the photo I realize I wasn't the only one tagged in the photo, Violet was too. I didn't know she had a Facebook account. This is partially because I tried to find her account to no avail, and partially because she's more of the Twitter type. I already see the post getting several "Likes" from other people friends with Xavier. As I stare at the screen I see the "Likes" and "Shares" increasing steadily. The more these numbers go up the more visible they are. Comments start to pop up as well from familiar names saying things like "haha" and "What a fag." While I was used to name calling and peers laughing at me, something just popped on the screen that grabbed my attention, a comment from Violet. "Matthew

Master is the biggest piece of shit I've ever known. Why would he think I would ever want anything to do with him? Even if I did the lame-ass poetry wasn't going to win me over, so pathetic. Matthew, please do the world a favor and go kill yourself."

Chapter 5

I read the words over and over hoping I just read it wrong. I hadn't. The life that I wanted was vanishing in front of me like a ghost. I won't have my first kiss with her, I won't take her to prom, and I won't ever put a ring on her finger. I won't grow old with her. I won't get to raise our kids together. My entire life lost all of its meaning in a single Facebook post. Devastated isn't the right word for what I feel, despair may be the closest. My worst fear has just come true, the woman I love hates me. I hold down the power button to turn off my PC, I just want it to go away.

If I can't live the life that I want to, then what's the point? When adults ask me what I want to be when I grow-up the only thing that comes to mind is being Violet's husband. That's not going to happen, so what's the point in living if I can't get the one stupid thing I want? I start sobbing over the keyboard not caring that the tears are dropping into the cracks between the keys. I place my hands over my face as if I was playing peek-a-boo, tears squeezed through the cracks between my fingers. I take a deep breath and exhale, trying to get the tears to stop. I didn't stop crying but I stopped sobbing.

With tears drying to my face I get out of my chair and open my bedroom door. I can hear Duncan hitting the punching bag in the garage from here. I close it as silently as I possibly can and do the same to open Duncan's. If I was going to do this I wanted to do it right. I never went into Duncan's room with permission or not. I see his small lockbox where he keeps his gun...locked. I'm not surprised, I was just hoping for a miracle. Where would Duncan keep the key for something that important? He wouldn't hide it somewhere in the room, he would keep it on him more than likely. His keys!

I know he doesn't keep them on him when he works out, he always talks about making sure there's nothing in your pockets that would hurt you, and keys would most certainly do that. I look around and see no place that he would put his keys on. I pick up his pants and I hear a slight jingle. I try the left front pocket and...nothing. I reach into the front right pocket and immediately feel something sharp poking the tip of my finger. I grasp it despite the unpleasantness and pull it out like a fish on a hook...bingo. I threw his pants to the ground haphazardly and got to work trying to figure out which key went to the safe. He had around ten keys on the metal ring that kept them in place, I tried the smaller ones first with no luck, but also no confidence that I was even doing it right. I try the sixth key; it turns and the safe clicks open.

Inside the safe has exactly what I was hoping for; Duncan's Smith & Wesson 686 pistol. I only know that much about it because Duncan talked about it a lot. I pick it up. It's a lot heavier than I expected, but I honestly didn't know what to expect. It was somewhat comforting knowing that this is what was going to kill me. Most people go their entire lives fearing what may or may not kill them, at least I know. I fumble around with the weapon like some sort of alien artifact until the chamber opens up. Six brass colored bullets are loaded into the chambers. I spin it like the movies and with a flick of the wrist snap it shut. I close the safe and take it back to my room.

I lay the pistol next to my computer keyboard. This is a pistol right? I don't know the difference between a pistol, revolver, or a gat except from what I learned from Call of Duty. I stare at it, half expecting it to turn towards me and just randomly shoot me. There's something about it just seems dangerous, even without a finger around the trigger. I open it back up and push one of the bullets out of its snug home. I hold it between my fingers like I was investigating a strange bug. I place it back in making sure the sharp end goes in first.

A kid in my school killed himself in the sixth grade and no one knew why. Someone started a rumor that it was because his dog died, and even postmortem kids made fun of him. Thinking about it now it makes sense he did what he did. It wasn't his dog, but the relentless harassment from other children. There has to be a reason kids are so mean, something in nature that *makes* them act like complete assholes.

I need to write a note. I don't want rumors to get out about me. I think in this case, if rumors did start as to why I committed suicide that they would probably be correct. A lot of people aren't going to understand why I'm doing this regardless of the note, but I can't do anything about that. I go to my computer turn it back on. Upon pulling up a word processor I realize that doing something so personal as a farewell letter would be impersonal as text on a screen. An actual hand written letter was the only way this was going to have the impact that I want it to have.

If you're reading this, then for once in my life I finally got what I wanted. Mom if you're reading this first, I'm sorry. No mother should ever have to see the child they gave birth to like this. I wish there was a better way for me to do what I had to do but there wasn't.

Duncan if it's you, don't let mom see. I don't care if you have to hold her down, don't let her see me like this. Duncan I'm sorry to you too, but I know even though you're still young, you can handle it. You're my older brother Duncan, you can handle anything. I don't think I ever told you how much I look up to you. All I ever wanted was your admiration and respect, and I'm sorry that I never did. I know I'm just your dorky little brother, but I love you Duncan, and I've never been able to tell you that. I don't know what it is, but you're going to grow up to do great things.

The reason why I'm doing this is because there was only one thing I wanted in life. I wanted to be with Violet Waits, and after the events of today...it's not possible. Because someone decided to play a practical joke on me, my life is going to end early. I don't want anyone to be sad for me even though I know it will happen. Dozens of people will come out of the woodworks claiming they knew me and how close we were...it's bullshit. The only friend I have is Steven. Steven, even though you were more or less forced to be friends with me, I'm still glad I had you. You got me through some really hard time and I genuinely care for you. Keep pwning the noobs and shredding those solos, and never give up your dreams. Trust me when I say all you have is your dreams.

Mom, this wasn't your fault. Don't be so hard on yourself, there's nothing you could have done. The girl I love doesn't love me back, no mother in the world can do anything about that and I'm really sorry. Don't cry for me Mom, I wouldn't want that, remember the good times we had? Remember when you took us to Disney World and I met Woody and Buzz? Remember when you took me to the zoo and I got to feed a penguin? Remember when you took me out to Chucky-E-Cheese for my birthday and let me play arcade games all day? Remember when you took me out on a random day and just bought me a Game Boy out of the blue? You did a lot for me Mom, you gave me more good memories than I would have dreamed for. You're a good mother, continue being one for Duncan's sake. I know he's your favorite, and he's got his shit together, but he still needs you. Those are the things I want you to remember when you wish I was by your side. And Mom, you need to unwind a little bit, you worry too much and it can't be good for you. Enjoy life, have fun, do the things I would have wanted to do. See Japan, learn a second language, go to the coliseum, and shake hands with Shigero Miyamoto. Mom, I don't know a lot about relationships but I know you shouldn't doubt yourself just because dad left you. You should start dating mom, and if you meet the right person...re-marry. I trust your judgment and I want you to be happy not just with yourself but also with someone else...because I couldn't.

Violet, I owe you the biggest apology of all. I know doing this will cause you some sort of pain for the rest of your life. This isn't your fault, it's mine. It's mine because I knew I didn't deserve anyone as smart, funny, talented, or beautiful as you, but I wouldn't settle for any less than perfection. I don't want you to dwell on what happened to me Violet. I want you to live the perfect life that I know you will live. As sad as it makes me, I want you to find someone special, someone that is worthy of you. Never settle for someone who is any less than who fills your dreams at night.

I wish my life would have been different. I wish I could have the life I want to live. I don't know what I did to deserve the life I got. Wishing your life was different doesn't get you anywhere. I never wanted anything extravagant. All I ever wanted was for someone to love me as much I as love them. This is too much to ask. I see couples all around me that have everything I want and they never give it a second thought. Why can't they understand I'm miserable? Why can't they understand that what they have is all they ever need?

I'm not doing this because you don't like me Violet, I'm doing this because I embarrassed you and there is no greater sin I could commit than hurting the one I love. I don't deserve to live if I'm going to hurt the one I care about the most. I know I said earlier it's because I couldn't be with you, but that's just because it's what I really wanted, but what I want more than that is for you to live the perfect life that I know you deserve. I was just hoping that life would involve me by your side.

Always yours,

Matthew Masters

I place the paper which was completely full front and back on the keyboard. It should be noticeable when whoever enters the room. I grab the gun and go to my bed and lay down on top of my blanket. Think of all the things that I'll miss. I won't get to see the end of How I Met Your Mother, I won't see if they ever make a good Superman movie, or if Half-Life 3 ever comes out. None of that will matter when I'm dead I guess, and it's a little silly to worry about entertainment right now. I guess this is where I'm going to do it, right on my bed. Should I do it under the covers? No, I don't want the last thing I see to be darkness, I have an eternity of darkness ahead of me.

I look at the painting of Violet's that I took from her art class hanging on my wall. I put the back of my head onto my pillow and press the barrel of the gun to my temple. I guess this is how I do it right? I hope I didn't forget anything in the letter, and I really hope mom doesn't find me first, Duncan is still working out and I'm not even sure if Mom is home from work yet. It doesn't matter I guess. I wish things hadn't turned out this way.

I close my eyes and tears begin squeezing out of the corners of my eyes. I open my eyes deciding my last living moment should be seeing something, something I want to see. I tilt my head slightly to the left of the painting that Violet did, the one that I stole, the one of her in her room doing what she loves most. "I wish things were different," I whimper out loud, as my quivering finger wraps around the trigger of the gun. I squeeze the trigger slightly expecting that's all it would take to set it off. Every little bit I squeeze I expect it to go off but it doesn't. The metal of the trigger is close to touching the metal circle surrounding it. "I love you Violet."

-Bang-

Chapter 6

Everything is black. I look around but no matter where I gaze there's just darkness. Am I in a coma and this is what it's like being trapped inside your own body, or is this just death? Maybe the afterlife is just darkness, darkness forever. I guess this could just be some sort of messed up dream. I see a small dot of light somewhere above me, but not a light like I've ever seen. It's like an alive ball made up of neon green, and purple lights like a lava lamp. I am drawn to it, and I seem to float towards it. The closer I get, the bigger it gets, and I don't think it's because I'm getting closer, I think it's actually getting bigger. I notice that it's pulsating like a heart ever so slightly. I try to float to it faster to get to the ball quicker but to no avail.

When I finally reach it, it has grown to the size my head, or least my head before I put a bullet through it. It was just floating there in darkness. I can't see my hands in front of me, even with the light from the ball, but I reach out to touch it. As soon as I make contact with it, it explodes into a kaleidoscope of colors all swirling around me as if forming a giant spinning bubble all around me. It regroups in front of me but in a different shape, instead of ball it's turned into a large bird. I think it may be a crow or a raven. The giant prism crow stares not just at me but through me not making a sound. The gaze of the crow is hypnotizing, I try to look away but I can't.

It speaks to me without words, without thoughts, and without sound. I felt what it wants me to know with light, and what it wants me to know is blatantly clear. The Crow showed me my mistakes in life. My insecurities, my neediness, and my self-doubt is brought to my full attention. It makes me see that those are the weaknesses to led me to where I am now. Wherever I am now. After the crow has decided that I've had enough time to digest what he has shown me and not shown me at the same time, he explodes. Again a Crayola box of colors surround me forming a chain link net around me covering my body. I can feel the warmth of the net of colors and it's oddly soothing. I can feel the net sinking into my skin, and now the warmth inside of me. I can feel the net inside my body crawling to the center of me. I can feel it contracting back into a ball in the pit of my stomach like a bear getting stuffing put into it. As the light disappears inside me everything goes black again.

I'm somewhere familiar but I don't know where. My eyes adjust and I realize I'm in my room, but I'm seeing it for the first time at a different angle. I'm above it, I'm clinging to the ceiling by some invisible glue. I look around and everything looks just like I left it with one glaring different, my body. I never realized how frail the human body looks until I'm looking at my own deceased vessel. My body is laying in an awkward position, all my limbs laying at different jagged angles. One hand still had the gun tightly wrapped around the gun as if they fused together. My head was down on my pillow with a pool of blood being sopped up by the white pillow case. How long had I been in the dark place? I look at the walls and see a smattering of blood sprays, including at the art I stole from Violet.

There's a loud abrupt knock on the door promptly followed by a twisted of the door knob. The door opens very slowly. I don't want Mom to find me, please anyone but Mom. I know that just leaves Duncan but Mom couldn't handle it, and Duncan would be okay. Duncan wouldn't let it get to him, he would understand. I see a hand emerge from the darkness of the other side of the door, the side of the door that believes I'm still alive. Thick, black hairs like spider legs protrude from the wrist of hand attached to the knob.

It's Duncan. He steps in the room cautiously like if makes a wrong move that it'll set off a trap. He scans around the room starting from his right and works his way over to the left to where I am...or was. I guess that's not me anymore. When Duncan sees it, he rushes over to my body. He tilts my head over to see the quarter sized hole in the side of my head. Pieces of skull shake loose like chipped paint onto the bed. Duncan puts his hand over his face then shakes his head in disbelief. I'm sorry Duncan, I really am. I float to the corner nearest him. I see tears running through his fingers and dropping onto my sheets.

Duncan sees the gun. I know he's going to be pissed about it, but I hope he understands. Duncan drops to his knees now with both hands covering his face, blocking his view of my arm dangling off the side of the bed completely slack. I can only imagine what's going through his mind, but I wish I could tell him it wasn't his fault. Maybe I can. I float down next to him, I still find the absence of needing floors disturbing. I whisper in his ear "It's not your fault." It didn't come out in my voice, it came out like a subtle gust of wind. Duncan responded like he felt a cold breeze against his neck. He didn't hear me. He eventually stands up, rubs his eyes with the palm of his hands and smears it into his almost non-existent hair. The only time I've seen Duncan cry is the night when Dad left, and it caught me off guard then. I wonder if he just doesn't understand why, or if he actually misses me?

Duncan leaves the room and shuts the door behind him. Dead silence in the house lasts minutes, until I hear Mom give a high-pitch, blood curdling scream of "noooooooooo!" I shut my eyes only to realize ghosts don't see darkness when they close their eyes. Heavy footsteps rush towards the room, and mom throws open the door. She instantly spots me laying in my bed and wraps her arms around me sobbing. I feel so bad for her. I just want to come back to life and hug her back, but I can't. She just clings to my lifeless corpse.

"Why did you do this? Why? What did I do wrong? God I'm a fucking awful parent. I'm sorry Matthew, I'm sorry I messed you up. All I ever wanted was to make you happy. I'm sorry I wasn't there for you, I'm sorry I couldn't make your father happy either. I'm sorry he was such a lying cheating bastard that he couldn't try to make it work. Matthew why did you leave me? Why does everyone I love leave me? Why am I so fucked up? Why Matthew, why?" Mom continues to go on, but I block it out. I don't really have feelings anymore but I can sense emotions and the intentions behind them, and this wasn't a positive thing happening between my corpse and my mother.

I go to the door and try to twist the door knob, but my hand passes through it. So I guess I pass through everything? I start with my hand, watching it disappear into the door. The section inside the door feels like it has a weight on it, but it doesn't hurt. I don't know if I can feel pain, I mean if I feel bad for Mom over what just happens but it doesn't get an emotional reaction out of me I don't know what would. I step through the door. The head is the weirdest part because it's like you're looking at wood in a magnifying glass. I wait, and I don't exactly know what for.

When I was alive the point was to grow up, get a job, find a wife, settle down and have a family. What is the point in the afterlife? There's no one I can ask about it. For all I know I may be the only ghost roaming around. Do I sleep? Do I eat? What happens if I go into outer space?

 Do I ever die, or do I have to pull a Groundhogs Day and make everything in my life right? Or maybe none of this matters and there is no reason for any of it. I wasn't given a rulebook so I have to assume there isn't one. The door opens as I contemplate my afterlife. Mom steps out holding the letter in her hands with her head hung deep between her shoulders. There's a ring around her collar where her tears have been landing.

 Mom walks past Duncan who was standing next to me in the hallway and goes into her room, shutting the door behind her. I follow her into her room, still slightly hesitant about going through the wall. She was on the phone. Mom didn't believe she needed a cell phone, so she kept the home line active. In fact she hasn't even sprung for a wireless phone; the cord of the phone has uncoiled and intertwined enough to drive someone with OCD insane. I could tell by the way she's talking that she's calling the police. After a few minutes mom hangs up the phone and sits on her bed.

 After several minutes of quiet contemplation, she lets out a deep sigh and reaches into her nightstand. She pulls out a package of cigarettes that have probably been there since Mom quit smoking a few years ago. Well...from my earliest memories she smoked, then she quit when she went on a health kick when I was in 2nd grade or so. She started smoking again when dad left a few years later. It took her seven months to kick the habit, and has been on the straight and narrow as far as I know, until just now.

She stands up, opens the door that leads to her outside deck that my dad built for her as an apology after he cheated the first time and flicks the butt off the side.

Mom goes out to the hallway, by the time I catch up Duncan and Mom are already mid-discussion about something. Duncan looks scared by whatever Mom is saying to him. I've never seen him thrown off like this before. I listen in while the volume of the conversation increases.

"So you're saying he broke into your safe, how could he have done that Dunk? You really expect me to believe you didn't give him the gun *or* were the one that did it?" Mom said.

"Mom, you know I wouldn't do that! You have to believe me, I'm telling you the truth," Duncan said as he flaps his arms at his side in frustration.

"Duncan, you need to tell me the truth, I'm not playing around. You need to tell me everything you know."

"I did, you just won't believe me! Just believe me Mom, I'm telling you the truth."

"Duncan, I'm sorry but I don't. So what you need to do is tell me everything you know about how Matthew got the gun," Mom said sticking a finger in his face. Duncan swats away the finger from his face.

"Fuck you," Duncan said and turned away from her and headed downstairs. Mom didn't know what to say, so she stood there stunned until Duncan was out of sight.

I better check on Duncan. It wasn't right for Mom to doubt Duncan, especially at a time like this, but I somehow understood where she was coming from. She's only doubting him because of how careful he is. It's unlike him to do something as careless as leave his keys mere feet from a firearm. I guess he never assumed that someone in the house would take it from him...he trusted me. I pass through the floor and descend from the ceiling of the first floor. I don't see Duncan, but the front door is a half second away from being slammed shut from the other side.

By the time I pass through the main door and outside Duncan was already booking it down the driveway. I try running after him but to no avail. Since I have no muscle mass to fuel my legs, I move at the same place regardless if I float or walk. I feel more comfortable walking than floating, but I have to make sure I don't accidently start floating into the ground. I see Duncan taking a sharp left into the brush ahead. When I get to where he veered i noticed something I had never noticed before...a path. I walked down this road to get to the bus stop, and to get home and I never noticed this path. The deeper I go into the trail the more thick the stinging needles get. I remember when Duncan and I had gotten into a fight on the way to school and had pushed me into a patch of them. My legs itched for a solid week afterwards.

After 30 feet of following the path it suddenly breaks into a clearing. It looks like one of those scenes in a fantasy movie where someone is spying on an elf in the woods feeding a deer and being one with nature. It's so...serene. I knew what that word meant, but never felt it before, but this was definitely a fitting definition. Surrounded by fading light from the break in the trees above, Duncan is on his knees crying into the palm of his hands. I wish I could help him. I wish I could do something to make him okay.

"Why don't you believe me? Why won't you believe me Mom? Why can't you just fucking believe me? What did I ever do for you not to trust me? You stupid bitch," Duncan said slamming his into a nearby tree. He repeats the act several times, pounding the tree to the point where shards of bark begin splintering off. Duncan stands up and reaches into his pocket and pulls out a small plastic bag. He pulls out what looks like a cigarette and a lighter, and shoves the bag back into his pocket. He lights the cigarette and takes a long drag from it, the end of it burns bright orange. Duncan sits on a stump from a tree that looked like it was cut down ages ago and continued to smoke. I know I haven't been exposed to a lot, but I've seen enough movies to know that it's pot. Never in a million years would I think Duncan would smoke pot. Maybe it's for "in case of emergency" sort of situations, but if that's the case, why was it already in his pocket?

Seeing my brother smoke pot changed my perception of him. I don't think any worse of him, but I just don't look at him the same way. Duncan was always the one who followed the rules, never disobeyed orders, and never did anything illegal. If someone told me he smoked I wouldn't be believe it, but there he is, smoking a joint in the woods by himself. He smokes pot, I wonder what else Duncan does that he doesn't tell me about? I wonder if he's still a virgin or not, I had just assumed that he was because he never had a girlfriend, but now I'm not convinced.

Duncan's head perks up and he listens intently like a hunter hearing a rustling in the bushes. A moment later I hear it too...sirens. I wonder if I just have worse hearing because I'm dead, or if Duncan has some sort of supersonic hearing. Duncan, looking nervous, takes the bag out of his pocket and shoves it in small hole in the stump he was sitting on, hidden by a flap of moss that Duncan laid back over the hidden compartment. He walks back through the trail pushing back branches with his hands and carefully stepping over the stinging nettles while I float through them without a worry. I've gotten the hang of this floating thing quicker than I thought I would. If I don't concentrate on walking on the ground I start slipping into the earth. I wonder how long it would take me to float to the center of the earth? I wonder if I could just float into space, I've always wanted to see space.

Duncan casually strolls up to the house, probably

trying to act like he wasn't just smoking pot, and two police cars were in our driveway. I float through the front door ahead of Duncan as he's hesitant to open it, though I'm unsure if it's because of the cops or Mom. Mom is sitting on our couch talking to the officer as he writes down notes. I can hear other voices upstairs talking about each other. Duncan goes to the kitchen and grabs a souvenir coffee cup we got from Disney World and fills it with water from the sink. He walks to the side of the officer and offers him the cup, he declines and Duncan shrugs and takes a drink. The officer who was tall, white and bald shifts his attention over to Duncan.

"Hey son how are you doing?"Asked The Tall cop.

"I guess considering what happened I'm okay. I guess I'm still in shock officer," Duncan said trying his best to maintain eye contact.

"Understandable son, but I need to ask you a few questions, do you feel up to it?" The Tall Officer asked.

"Yes sir, whatever I can do to help," he responded after he took another swig of water and leaned forward.

"It was your gun that he used right?"

"Right."

"How did he take possession of it?"

"I'm not a hundred percent sure, but I think he stole my keys and unlocked the safe, it's where I always keep it.

I know for sure it was locked when I put it there, I always double check it to make sure."

"Did Matthew know you had the gun?"

"Of course, the gun case is out in the open." Duncan answered as the question gave him a suspicious look on his face.

"Did you show him how to use it?"

"I felt like it was my responsibility to show him how it works, I didn't want him to be scared in his own house because of it," Duncan said as The Tall Officer continues to write in his notebook.

"Did he ever shoot it?"

"No, he refused to even touch it. He had no interest in ever learning how to shoot, just to ease his concerns about it," Duncan said as Mom looked at him a bit concerned, I guess she never knew he taught me about gun safety. The officer also picked up on this.

"Miss Masters, were you aware that he did this?" The Tall Officer asked.

"No, no I didn't, and I don't really know how I feel about it," she said still sobbing.

"How did Duncan get the gun?" The officer asked.

"It was a birthday gift last year. He wanted to start practicing because he wanted to be a cop...sorry I meant police officer," Mom said.

"No offense taken. Duncan, did Matthew know where your keys were?"

"Mom didn't even know where I kept the key, she had a hands off approach to the whole thing,"

"Miss Masters, is that true?"

"Yes, I mean I assume he either had it on his keychain or hid it somewhere secret," Mom said. The clatter of footsteps overhead gets louder, I better go check it out. I float up through the roof to where I estimated my room was on the floor above. I come up right under an officer's foot. Still getting used to this whole being able to move through people thing, I politely move to the side unbeknownst to him. Two officers were in the room taking pictures of everything I own careful to not touch anything. They took pictures of everything from the position of my body, which is still weird to look at, to the books on my shelf. I wonder what they're thinking? This is probably just another casual day at work for them, no big deal. I wonder if this is the job that they always wanted, or if they thought it would lead somewhere they really wanted to be?

The walls start flashing red, I look out the window to see the lights of an ambulance and a trail of dust kicking up behind it. The photographers pack up their equipment into small black bags with shoulder straps and wait. A burly man followed by a petite woman come through the door with a metal fold out stretcher with an empty body bag laying on top. The photographers move to the back corner of the room then exit and head back downstairs presumably to talk to The Tall Officer. The man lifts my body by the shoulders with little effort while the woman struggles to get my feet in the bag. They carry on the conversation they had when they entered the room, something about a body they found in the Prairie Dog River. They hoist my body onto the cart and the woman lets out a small grunt with the effort. As they exit with my body the woman flips the light switch off. I'm gone now, it's officially not my room anymore, Mom is going to be referring to it as "his old room" from here on out.

I float down through the floor and instantly wish I hadn't. My body was half way down the stairs, and mom has her arms wrapped around the metal slab with her head pressed against the bag where my head is. The petite woman tried to pry her off of my body but to no avail. She gave a nod to burly man as if they were communicating telepathically and he squeezed between the banister and the stretcher to get behind my mother. He wrapped his muscle bound arms around my Mom's waist and heaved her backwards while the petite woman held onto the cart for dear life. The man sets her on the floor at the bottom of the stairs, slightly embarrassed of what she had just done. The stretcher makes it down the stairs and into the living room with no further incidents from Mom. Duncan opens the front door for them unable to look at the body bag that I'm now resting in. Duncan closes the door behind them.

Duncan and mom talk to the officers for a few more minute, then they leave as well. They don't talk to each other until Duncan tells Mom he's going to bed. Mom, whose eyes were puffy and swollen in such a way I hadn't seen since Dad left sat downstairs for a long time before heading up to her room. Now knowing exactly where my room is located from the bottom floor I float up above the kitchen table and into the center of my room. Even though I've sort of gotten used to it, I still close my eyes when passing through solid material. There's just something unsettling about having wood and whatever sheetrock is made out of that close to your eyes like a horror movie where a syringe is edging closer to someone's eye. I guess I'll try to sleep to see if I can. I'm not tired but I lie down on my bed and close my eyes. I start sinking into the bed the more relaxed I get, once I open my eyes my body pops back on top of the bed.

Chapter 7

I fall back into the darkness, back to the place with the ball of kaleidoscope light promptly greets me. I get the feeling it's trying to tell me something but I'm not understanding what. It wraps around me like a bodysuit, I can feel its immense love and warmth. I can feel it...cleansing me? It gave me the feeling of love, that everything is connected, that life and death has a purpose, and that purpose is love. Everything turns white and I feel like I'm falling. My head is inside my pillow. There has got to be some sort of trick to staying on top of things without sinking into them.

I hear light but steady noise coming from Duncan's room, a slight but constant thud. I float through to Duncan's wall and see where it was coming from. Duncan is sitting at the edge of his bed, his head down, chin touching his chest. Duncan is slamming a clenched fist into the wood headboard. The skin on his knuckles is peeling away with small drips of blood smear on the wood. I want to tell him to stop but I know that it won't do any good, I can't talk to him. The more times his fist hits the headboard the more skin layers open up on his hand revealing another spurt of blood. The speed and strength of the punches increases with each blow, his skin now shredded wide open. The blood is dripping down the headboard and each punch is making a wet sound like stepping in a shallow puddle. Duncan winds his hand back which now looks like a carcass mangled by farming equipment for one final punch. He's going to break his hand if he follows through with it. He slings the punch forward, I sling my body forward, half jumping and half floating towards him at full force. His hand moves to the side.

I moved it, I moved his hand. Holy shit I moved his hand. Duncan looks puzzled, but he didn't try it again. Maybe he thinks his arm just gave out or something. He stands up and looks at his hand realizing what damage he's done to himself...he doesn't look surprised. My brother stands up and goes to the bathroom. I follow him. He pops open the medicine cabinet and pulls out a clear bottle of rubbing alcohol and a hand wrap. He spreads his hand over the sink and pours the rubbing alcohol over the open wound. He bites his lower lip to fight through the pain. He straightens his fingers out and wraps the bandage around his hand so tight that I think it might cut off the circulation. Duncan pops the cabinet open and puts the rubbing alcohol back where it was on the top shelf and closes it shut. I follow Duncan back to his room and finally feel like I'm able to protect my own brother.

Duncan lies down on top of his blanket and turns

towards the side facing the wall. I sit on the end of his bed all night to make sure he doesn't try to do anything else. He didn't. I had no intention of going back to sleep and meet the weird all knowing space-ball tonight. I could feel something strange in the room, like a whisper but without sound. Duncan's body was making some sort of noise, a noise like hearing a concert from outside a stadium. I climb over his body and the noise gets louder. My press my ear against his head where it seems it be the loudest.

I put my right ear into his head and an explosion of sound attacks me. I quickly pull away and turn my head like an owl and peer inside his forehead. A world opens up in front of me, a vague one. Duncan is sitting in a doctor's office packed full of patients. I recognize some of the people in the waiting room from school, people in Duncan's grade, while others are adults that I don't recognize. A nurse comes in calling out names of people and every time she does someone in the waiting room stands up and follows the nurse. This happens until Duncan is the last person in the room. The round-faced receptionist in her 40's with curly red hair and glasses stayed busy with her paperwork, not paying any attention to the waiting room. Duncan's name is finally called by the nurse who has absolutely no distinguishing features and he follows her...so do I.

I don't quite understand how I'm in Duncan's dream and also looking into his head in his room, but there's a lot about being dead that I don't understand. I guess it's no different than Duncan being both in his bed sleeping as well as being in his own dream. The hallway is deathly quiet, the eggshell white walls have chipped paint sporadically, and the smell of antiseptic fills the air. There are three doors on each side of the claustrophobic hallway each marked with a number. The nurse led Duncan back to the last door on the left, door number three and told him to have a seat and the doctor would be in shortly. I'm reminded that this is a dream by how quickly the doctor actually came. He stood nearly seven feet tall, and was lanky and frail. He looked like an African-American Jack Skellington in the land of doctor town, his gleaming white lab coat hanging off his body as if it was on a coat rack.

"Duncan how are you feeling?" he asked.

"I don't know how I feel," Duncan responded, slightly shaking his head.

"What symptoms are you having?"

"I guess I'm just really depressed sir, and don't know how to handle it," Duncan said. Good to see that even in an alternate reality that Duncan has kept his manners.

"That's normal son. There's also a simple solution. When you're feeling down and don't know what to do," the doctor said reaching into his pocket. He pulls out a gun, the gun that I had used hours ago to end my own life. "Here, take it," The Doctor said extending out his arm from across the room as if they were on stilts. Duncan takes it and looks at it as if he'd never seen it before. "Now put it to your head and pull the trigger. This will make all your troubles go away." Duncan gives the doctor a nod and presses the tip of the barrel against his temple. Duncan closes his eyes and slowly squeezes the trigger.

In Love and Dead

R.L. Murphy

- Click –

Chapter 8

Duncan sits up from his bed not realizing he was dreaming. I fall through his head and into his flannel sheets. I regain my balance and float above the bed. I can feel Duncan's heart racing trying to burst out of his ribcage, a bead of sweat rolls down his forehead. He catches his breath then picks up his watch from his night stand, it's almost morning. I can tell Duncan is debating going back to sleep or just getting up. He throws the blankets to the side, stands up and stretches. Wearing only the boxers he slept in he goes towards the bathroom, grabbing a towel from the closet next to the door. I decide to go check on Mom, she was already up, throwing her long brown hair back into a ponytail. I notice she's only partially clothed and avert my eyes. Mom leaves for work by the time Duncan gets out of the shower. Mom was rarely mad at Duncan, but even if she was she always wished us a good day at school. Today she said nothing. I can't believe she's even going to work. If she thinks she's going to escape what happened she's wrong.

The water stops running in the bathroom. I go to Mom's room to snoop a little bit. Mom's room has always been a forbidden place for us. We never went in unless we needed to ask her something, or to report something that happened, like the time Duncan accidently broke the chandelier while throwing a football around. Luckily that wasn't a conversation I had to have with Mom as Duncan turned himself in after he picked the glass out of the carpet with his hands. Mom was more concerned about Duncan's shredded hands from handling broken glass than the chandelier. I find a small square piece of plastic on her nightstand. I turn it over to see a picture of her with her name under it. It's her work badge. It's not like her to be forgetful; she must have not gone to work. Where the hell could she have gone?

I trust my head into her nightstand and wish I hadn't. A long purple plastic sex toy would have poked me in eye if I still had them. Yeah, I think I'm done poking around Mom's room. I saw some face down Polaroid's that I don't even want to guess what's on the other side. I glance down the hallway and catch a glimpse of Duncan heading down the stairs. I float down to the kitchen. Duncan already had his hand on the door knob. He takes a noticeably deep breath and tilts his head back as if to expose his neck to an executioner and clenches his eyes. He swallows his spit and his Adam's apple travels up and down like the test your strength meter at the fair and opens the door. He steps through the door and slams it shut so hard the whole house seems to shake.

I follow him out the door. I expected to see Duncan halfway up the road by now...but he wasn't, he's mere steps in front of me. Duncan's walking at a slow steady pace up the road. I don't think I've ever seen Duncan walk the road, he's always ran it, and he only jogged it when he was sick. He kept his head hung low and his hands in his jean pockets. The rain starts to lightly drizzle on the trees overhead, then dripping on Duncan, but he doesn't seem affected. The glowing lights of the school bus looms in the distance like red beacons. I float in the middle of the road and let the bus plow right through me. When it stops I'm standing in the middle of the third row. Everyone talking gets deathly quiet as Duncan steps on board. He scans around the bus for a seat and finds his usual one behind the bus driver empty. Duncan faces the window and watches everything pass him by.

It takes several minutes and several more stops before the talking resumes. It takes me all of those minutes to get used to being in a bus, this time with the added difficulty of concentrating on not falling through it. It's sort of like walking on an elevator with a cracked glass floor. I sit in my seat next to Missy Jones who was writing in a notebook, probably doing homework. I hesitate a second before reading over her shoulder. It wasn't a notebook, but her journal. She was writing about me, about how things like this shouldn't happen to nice people. She continued on to write that she always had a crush on me but never could speak a word, hoping that I would make the first move. I don't know what to say. I never knew, I just thought that she felt sorry for me. I guess I was too busy focusing on Violet to notice. She writes a bit more but I don't want to see it, and a few minutes later she puts it back in her backpack and zips it up as we are approaching school.

Duncan stands up and waits near the door before the bus even fully stops. Mr. Ralph flips what looks like an oversized Dr. Frankenstein switch and the door opens. Duncan doesn't wait for the door to open fully before he steps off and walks towards the front doors. I shift through the side of the bus and tail him. Why am I following him? Why did I even come to school? I guess out of habit, it's all I've done for the last decade or so. There has to be a reason I'm here, something I'm supposed to learn to pass through to the real afterlife. What if this *is* the real afterlife? Maybe all I do is wander around for eternity with nothing to do. Maybe that's why ghosts haunt people, out of sheer boredom. If this is the afterlife then it makes real life look pretty damn important by comparison. Maybe if I was a better person I wouldn't be here right now.

While I contemplate the meaning of the afterlife, I'm startled by the warning bell ringing. I guess I should go to my first class and see if they even noticed I'm gone. One of the best parts of being dead is that you never have to change your clothes. I don't even know if I can change my clothes, I'm still wearing the clothes I shot myself in, but it's like they are molded to my skin now. Kids were changing and bantering back and forth about some game last night, I couldn't even make out what sport it was by the slang they were using. No one spoke a word about me, as my locker stayed locked with my gym clothes inside. I go through the cold brick wall into the basketball court where Mr. Zang was already waiting for them to line up.

"Good morning class, go ahead and line-up. We're going to have a special announcement here in a few minutes, so just hang tight and listen up," Mr. Zang said dressed in red short and a grey school t shirt. After a short moment of whispering between classmates the speakers came on in the gym.

"Good morning students. I regret to inform you that today we mourn the loss of one of our students. One of our brightest and inspirational students, Matthew Masters passed last night. We cannot discuss any specifics, and will not tolerate any rumors being spread. If you need someone to talk to, the guidance counselor will be available all week for anything you may need. Thank you." The voice which I'm fairly certain was the vice-principal trailed off and the audible click of the PA system being turned off followed. Tony Stewart whispered to Jonathan Myers if he thought they'd let them out early because of it. Jonathan tried to hold back his laughter...badly.

"Is everything okay Mr. Myers?" Mr. Zang asked giving him the look that I only got when my push-up formation wasn't up to his standards.

"Yes sir everything is fine," Jonathan said still

struggling to regain composure.

"If anyone needs to talk to the counselor talk to me in private and I'll write you a pass, but if I catch you anywhere else you *will* be suspended," he said as sternly as he possibly could, then blows the whistle around his neck. The boys run towards the basketballs in center court and immediately break into teams. I don't think anyone really wanted an organized game today, they just wanted to play around. They're treating my death like a free day at school, knowing no one is going to really force them to do anything because they're "grieving."

I guess there's no point in hanging around watching other people play, but what else is there to do? I pass through the gym, the locker room, and back into the commons. It's weird being in the place where everyone in the school gathers, but no one is here. I guess it's creepy in the same way that being in an abandoned hospital must be creepy. I wonder what the office is talking about. I've only been there when seeing the nurse after getting beat up, or to deliver a message from a teacher. I catch a glimpse of beautiful black hair and perfect skin entering the counselor's office. It was Violet.

Okay I know it should feel wrong to invade in her privacy, but I don't. Maybe it's because I know I can't get caught, so there's no penalty. I close my eyes and step through the counselor's doors. Before I opened my eyes I knew the tone of the conversation. Violet was crying, crying over me. I stand next to the where the counselor is sitting. Violet's eyes were puffy and the tissue in her hand was scrunched up and soaked with her tears. I want to make her feel better, I want to comfort her.

"I almost did it again Cathleen, I came so close," Violet said with her fingers a sliver apart.

"What stopped you?" Cathleen Grey the school counselor said.

"That's the thing I don't even know, I just didn't. I gave up like I do on everything else in life." Violet slammed her fists on the table in frustration, her hair flopped over and fully covered her face like curtains.

"That's not a bad thing Violet. You didn't give up you realized it was a bad idea. There's a part of you that realizes it wants to be happy, but you're letting the rest overpower it. You have such a good future ahead of you Violet. First you'll break yourself, then you'll bend the world."

"Do you understand how infuriating it is to hear you say it's going to get better time and time again? This doesn't just go away you know, this stays with you forever."

"I know, but the problem isn't your condition, you just need time to adapt to it, once you adapt to it you learn to defeat it," Cathleen said leaning back slightly in her brown leather office chair and crossing her left leg over her right. What condition is she talking about? I never knew she had anything wrong with her. Maybe that's why she never talked to anyone but Dez.

"I know, it's just frustrating! I just want to live a normal life. After the whole thing with Matthew, it guarantees I'm going to be screwed up. I mean, he wrote me a love letter and I slapped him! Then he kills himself! how is it *not* my fault?" Violet says with her hands still on the desk like cement blocks.

"You know it wasn't you're fault, Matthew he." Cathleen was interrupted.

"But it *is*! When I slapped him I sealed his fate, I may not have tied the noose for him but I made his life not worth living," Violet retracted her fists from the desk and lowered them on her knees.

"We can't discuss what happened to Matthew because we don't know, nothing official has been announced. The cause of death has remained undisclosed," Cathleen said.

"Right, a 15 year old boy just dropped dead after a girl crushed his fucking heart?"

"Language Miss Waits. I understand you're frustration but we still have to abide by some rules here."

"Sorry, I just," Violet trailed off and couldn't think of the words to express her outburst.

"It's okay Violet, it's perfectly normal to be feeling the

way you do," Cathleen said.

"I mean, it's just, I liked Matthew you know? He was such a good guy, and if could have gotten over my issues, I would have gotten to know him better," Violet said finally pushing the hair from out of her face revealing fresh tears piling over the ones soaked into her pale skin.

I never knew she liked me. Why couldn't she have just told me? Why couldn't have I just talked to her?

Violet continued. "I was just so embarrassed by what happened that I took it out on him. I thought he spread it around the school because Dez told me that's what happened."

"Do you think Dez lied to you?"

"No, she told me later it was just a rumor she heard, but it was the *only* rumor about it going on."

"Do you know who is responsible for what happened yesterday?"

"No one knows anything. Usually when shit, I mean stuff like this happens someone is dumb enough to brag about it later," Violet says wiping the last of her tears away and throwing away the crumpled tissue in the trash next to Mrs. Grey's desk. "I wish I knew who could be so mean to do something like that."

"It's no surprise to you that kids can be cruel. Just remember it's usually because they feel insecure about themselves and don't know how to express it any other way than to lash out at others."

"I know, I know. Look can I go back to class now?" Violet says looking visibly drained from their talk.

"Of course, but anytime you need to talk Violet, just let me know okay?"

"Okay, thank you Cathleen," Violet says as she stands up out of her chair towards the door. Cathleen opens the door for her and shuts it behind Violet. Cathleen Grey sits back down at her desk and starts typing on her computer. I leave.

My routine is off. I'm so used to having most of my day scheduled, now I'm unsure what to do. I never really had the option to live my life the way I wanted to. I sort of want to just follow Violet around, and see what it's like to be around her. I could get to actually know her. The thought of being close to Violet for an extended period of time makes me giddy, and filled me with happiness. It's probably still second period which means she has geometry. I head across the school and into Mr. Sim's class, who also taught my algebra class.

I float into the room and half expect the class to turn and look at me. They don't. Every girl is currently in the trance of Mr. Sim's lesson which means about zero percent of it is getting absorbed. Every student is bored shitless except for Violet. Violet in the direct middle of the room, is furiously and intently writing every word he says. She occasionally looks up to make sure she's getting what he's writing on the board, but it all looks like gibberish to me. I never understood geometry. There's just something about correlating numbers to shapes that just throws me off. I float through Sandy Yates and Jack Preston to Violet's desk. I sink into the floor until I'm level with her. I can hear the jostling of a plastic pen cap in her mouth, anxiously biting it as she continues to jot down information on her paper. I look at her paper, she's not writing down math equations and formulas...she's writing. I read a little of what she has on the paper and it appears to be a poem, but her left hand is covering most of the paper so no one else notices. I smell her perfume as I draw my nose close to the side of her neck. I want to touch her, I want to caress her neck but it would be wrong. I inhale deeply through my nose and think if I'm actually smelling it or if I'm just remembering what she smells like.

I've always wanted to touch her hair, just a strand of it. I reach out my hand and inch it closer and closer towards her jet black straight hair with my phantom fingers. I start at the very top of her head and slide it down towards her shoulders like a ski slope. It's so soft and comforting I could do it for hours, but the bell rings. I reel my hand back and as I do she scratches the back of her head, did she feel it? I guess if I felt it she should have too right? This whole thing of being able to touch things when I want to is confusing but I'm sure I'll get the hang of it. Violet closes her book and walks out of class without saying or looking at anyone.

I follow her to her locker, the one that I *should* have put the letter into. If I would have put the letter in the right locker I'd probably be next to her in person right now, talking to her about her day, instead I'm next to her but she doesn't notice...just like when I was alive. She opens her locker and it's exactly what I imagine her room is like. Magazine clippings of favorite bands like Nirvana, Sublime, and Smashing Pumpkins scattered haphazardly. Miniature movie posters from Fight Club, A Clockwork Orange, and Requiem for a Dream line the inside of the door. It's like looking into her own world, seeing only the things that matter to her. She removed a piece of paper from her notebook and grabs a Pennywise magnet currently holding nothing in place and clamps the paper under it. I glance at the paper for a moment, because it only took me that moment to realize what it was. My poem.

Chapter 9

I stood there a long time thinking about what it meant. Why would she put it in her locker? Is it a reminder of how she thinks she killed me, or is it a sign that she's loved even if she doesn't know it? I phase through her locker and lower my head until I'm eye level with it. I just want to make sure it was my poem and not some other random piece of paper. No, it's the poem all right, and the original copy. I can see where I accidently ripped the paper. I look around her locker but the only light is from the three small slits currently illuminating a piece of the poem.

I think Violet has art class next, but I feel like I better check on Steven. I haven't seen him in the halls at all, and I would have noticed him waiting for the counselor. He should be in shop class on the other side of the building. Shop class was one of two classes that had a separate building not connected to the main school, with agriculture being the other. Even before I enter the stand alone stone building I can smell the unmistakable scent of saw dust. John Matthews is using a plane to shave layers of wood off of what looks like a toy car. Dennis Prince was secretly making a bong while the shop teachers back is turned. I could never remember his name since he only taught shop and I never had to take his class but he seemed nice enough. Steven's not in class.

Where could he be? He could just be getting to class late, or in the bathroom smoking. He could be seeing the counselor, or he could have just skipped class. It certainly wouldn't be the first time that Steven bailed on class, but something just feels off. I leave and go back to wandering the halls aimlessly. There was always a rumor that the school was haunted, but I never believed it. Who would have guessed that the paranormal skeptic would have ended up being the one haunting the halls of my high school?

I heard a familiar laugh from around the corner. If I still had a stomach it would have dropped at the sound of Seth Thompson's cackle echoing from inside the boy's bathroom. Hearing his laughter almost exclusively meant humor was being had at someone else's expense. I see Seth's long narrow fingers wrapped around the neck of a classmate forcibly kneeling in front of the urinal.

"Lick it, lick my piss dipshit," Seth said as the boy outreached his arms to the wall to the sides of the urinal.

"Fuck you, you prick," the boy said. I finally recognized the voice. My feeling was right, it was Steven.

"No, fuck you!" Seth put full force on the back of Steven's head. As much as he resisted, the pressure was starting to be too much as his head inched closer to the porcelain. I move between the two of them and place my hands over Seth's head resting my palms on his temples making sure not to go through him. I focus intently and hover my thumbs over his eyes. I close my eyes and concentrate as I thrust my thumbs through his retinas.

Seth jumps back, immediately loosening his grip from Steven as he leaps to his feet with anger in his eyes I've never seen. Seth still covering his eyes with his palms gets slammed to the floor by Seth who slams his shoulder into his gut. The back of Seth's head bounces twice off the damp ceramic tile with dull thuds. Steven jumps on top of him, firmly planting his backside on Seth's stomach. Still unsure what happened, Seth removes his hands from his face and cracks his eyes open like ancient doors enough to see Steven's fist about to collide with his face. The unmistakable sound of snapping bones and the crunch of cartilage echoes in the bathroom as his fist lands dead on to his nose. Blood immediately oozes out of his nose like sludge out of a leaky barrel.

Steven gets up and looks at his hand, notices that it's already red and swollen. He shakes it from the wrist once. Steven walks out of the bathroom. I wait a few minutes for Seth to get up, his shirt slowly staining from his own blood. I feel like I'm watching a bear about to wake up from hibernation as he lazily stumbles to his feet, wiping the blood off his face with his hand and flicking it on the floor, splattering in long red streaks. He looks down at his shirt and lets out an audible sigh lifting it up so his eyes which are still only half open and bloodshot as hell from my handiwork.

"I'll kill you Steven Fargo," Seth yells out the door unsure if he would be able to hear him. "I'll fucking kill you."

I leave the bathroom when Seth starts draining the blood his nose into the sink, dark crimson swirling down the drain. I check back with the shop class but Steven wasn't there. I better go check to see if he went to the nurse's office for his hand. I'm not as familiar with the blueprints of the school as I am of the house, so I'll avoid going through the walls when I can. At least I've finally stopped flinching when someone walks through me. If I try to touch them when they walk through me I wonder what would happen. It might make them split in half, or maybe that's what spontaneous combustion is about. I work my way through the corridors to the front of the building near where the office is. I take a right through the main hall and into the commons. It was still before lunch so it was quiet except for the cafeteria workers sitting down at a table taking a break before the swarms of hungry assholes line up.

The stage where after school performances are held is against the north wall, the curtains were drawn most of the time. The lip of the stage is where most of the cool kids hung out before and after school. There was almost always one kid with an acoustic guitar performing, trying to impress any girls that happen to cross by. Though

Steven was never the type to jam out on the lip, he was sitting there now holding his right hand. I could see streaks of red on his knuckles but unable to tell if the blood was his or Seth's. It was swollen, and it looks like he either dislocated a few fingers or he broke his hand outright. After several minutes of quiet contemplation Steven hops off the lip of the stage and heads towards the nurses office. I follow him.

The nurse was inspecting his hand when I catch up. She wrapped a blue gel pack in a brown paper towel and placed it on his hand. Those gel packs may be the coldest things ever invented. When I got hit in the face with a baseball in gym last year the nurse made me put one on my face. I thought I was close to frostbite by the time she told me I could take the ice pack off my nose. The nurse tells him she'll be back in a little bit and shuts the door behind her. Steven's eyes wander around the room looking at the random objects. After staring at a glass jar of cotton balls for what seemed like forever, the nurse comes back to look at his hand. I could tell by Steven wincing in pain that it hurt to the touch, but he tried to pretend like it didn't. Steven was bad at pretending.

"Well Steven, I don't think it's broken, but you're going to need to keep it wrapped for a few weeks. The office is already talking to your parents to inform them of the injury," the nurse said. Steven tried to not look angry but I knew he was pissed, and rightfully so. Steven's parents are always super harsh on him, this isn't going to be an exception.

"Oh man, are you serious?" Steven said in a sigh of frustration. "They are going to flip. I'm dead, I'm totally dead."

"It'll be alright Steven, it's not my job to determine how you hurt yourself, just to fix you when you do," The Nurse said re-tightening the hand-wrap, tugging at it securely. "They will be here shortly, you can sit here until they arrive, or you can sit out in the office." The Nurse walked out of the room leaving the door behind her slightly cracked. Steven thanked her for her help as she exits. Steven looks at his hand, wrapped in bandages like a mummy in progress.

I leave before Steven's parents show up. I don't want to be anywhere near the discussion that is going to take place. I sit on the lip of the stage, the one place I always wanted to be but was never allowed. The lunch crowd was starting to pour in, and kids would randomly sit around me, not knowing I was there. If I tried to sit on the lip when I was still alive I would have been shoved off violently. Not that I ever dared try to sit there, I just knew the consequences if I tried, so I stuck to tables far, far away.

Bells ring, students shuffle, trays get dumped, and more bells ring. More bells, more students, and more shuffling of feet. I watch this pattern go on until the end of the day. Once the busses pull up I don't even wait for my bus to come to a complete stop before I phase through the emergency exit door. I stand by Mr. Ralph while he waits for students to load on the bus. No one at this point is even talking about me. They've already moved on with their lives. Not surprising as I didn't mean anything to them, but I figured the gossip would last longer. Duncan gets on the bus and sits down in his seat.

I sit next to Duncan who is not talking to anyone. He stares out the window at the flagpole, watching it wave and hearing the flapping sound of the cloth in the wind. I wonder what he's thinking about? As the bus rolls on he keeps his head planted towards the window. I can the reflection of his face in the window, and notice the sheen of tears streaming down Duncan's face.

When we reach our stop I forgot I didn't have my backpack with me, but I still reached for it. I wait for the door to open not for fear of falling through it, but just out of habit. Duncan steps through me on the last step and hops off. Duncan lowers his head, hands in his jean pockets and shuffles down the road. I stand there watching him walk down the road, getting engulfed by the trees around him until he disappears. The passing of a car behind me jolts me out of my train of thought and I start walking towards Duncan.

I reach the front door without catching up to Duncan, he must have picked up the pace. I go through and immediately notice that the television was on, and loudly. Mom was lying on the couch with bottles of wine lined up on the coffee table like bowling pins on a bad split. Her laugh was almost as loud as the ones coming out of the blaring TV. She was watching stand-up comedy, I didn't recognize who it was but he was doing a bit about Hot Pockets. Mom howls with every punch line and takes a swig straight from the bottle. Duncan probably walked right past her in disgust.

Duncan doesn't deal well with Mom's drinking problem. She started when Dad left, or at least it's when I started noticing. It started off only on the weekends at dinner, Mom would make herself a drink, sometimes even offering us a half a glass. We would usually take her up on the offer. As occasional weekends turned into weekdays and the offers for red-wine increased, we turned it down. If there was one thing that Duncan and I agreed on, it was that we didn't want to be like our Mother in that respect. As timid as she usually is, she's as loud and boisterous as dad was sober, and probably still is. She never became violent towards us, but she didn't exact act like the responsible parent that we needed her to be. However, it was the only time we could get her to talk about Dad, although the things out of her mouth didn't exactly show him in the most positive light. It was better to just leave her alone when she's drinking.

The door opens, and Duncan steps through it. As Duncan steps through me I could smell the stench of pot engulfing him. Guess that explains where he's been.

"Hey, where are you going?" Mom asks Duncan.

"Upstairs, I have homework to do," he replied as he starts to ascend the stairs without a glance towards her.

"Hey, come back here, I need to have a talk with you," Mom said motioning towards him with a nearly empty bottle. Duncan turns around and gives her a blank stare.

"Mom, you're drunk, there's nothing you can tell me right now that can't wait until you've sobered up," Duncan says.

"I just need to be with you Dunk, I'm just lonely," Mom says stretching her arms out to him still lying down on the couch.

"The bottles can keep you company." Duncan races upstairs, and Mom starts sobbing into her hands. I feel bad for her, she just lost her son, but I don't disagree with Duncan either. She stops sobbing long enough to tilt the bottle into her mouth until the red liquid slows to a drip. She slams the bottle back on the coffee table sloppily, and rolls towards the couch covering her face again.

"I just want him back, I just want him back, I just want him back," Mom said pounding a fist against the armrest of the sofa.

I crouch next to her and whisper in her ear "I'm still here." She stops sobbing and wipes away the remaining tears from her damp face. She sits up like she has seen, or heard a ghost. Her head scans the room looking for a source of the noise that she apparently heard, but found none. She carries the empty bottles to the trash and stands with both hands pressed over the sink, looking out the window into the yard. I don't know what she's looking at, but she looks at it long enough for me to want to go check in on Duncan.

I knew no matter how distraught Duncan is, he wouldn't miss his workout. I wasn't wrong. I could hear the rattling of the chain and the dull thwack of the heavy bag before I could phase through the garage. The first thing I notice is the intensity in Duncan's eyes, he's so focused a marching band couldn't distract him. Duncan lands two left jabs then follows it up with an overhand right rocking the bag back, nearly hitting the wall. When it returns Duncan meets it with a spinning back fist sending it flying in retreat. Several more left jabs meet the bag upon its return, slowing its movement. Duncan and I used to watch the MMA fights that came on TV, we could never afford the big pay-per-views so we rarely got to see the big name fighters outside of highlight reels online.

It takes me a minute to realize Duncan is hitting the bag without any gloves on. He's not even wincing with the big hits, but I can see his hand is turning red from the stings. The more punches he throws, the harder he's throwing them. I see the skin on his right knuckles spread open as he lands with a hook. He lands five consecutive straight rights each tearing the skin off his hand a little further. Blood transfers from Duncan's hand to the vinyl of the punching bag with every blow. Elbows start getting incorporated into the barrage and the skin gets shredded like deli meat in a blender. Blood streaks across the ground in a perfect line as a kick from the shin lands and the bag jumps back almost to a horizontal state.

The bag settles and Duncan's essence drips from the bottom of the bag onto the cold cement floor of the garage forming a small pool like a morbid mud puddle. He looks at his limbs to see how much damage he's inflicted upon himself. He doesn't seem to be disturbed by any of the wounds and walks back in the house, leaving the mess to congeal.

Mom moved back to the couch, but this time sitting up staring at the blank television. She didn't even notice Duncan walk past her and he rushes upstairs, presumably to disinfect his open wound. I sit next to Mom on the couch and put my arms around her. Even though she can't feel it, it still feels good to be near her. I know when I whispered to her last time it freaked her out, but I think she needs me in some way. I whisper "I love you Mom, and I'm okay." Her eyes widen, but the rest of the body remains completely still.

"I must be going crazy," she mutters to herself. Great, now I've given my mother a complex. I need to let her know it's me somehow, and not a sign of her mental stability deteriorating. I'll have to think it through before I try to make another move to console her. It is a little weird that it's easier to talk to someone while dead than it is to move objects in the real world. Or maybe the ghost world is the real world and they just can't affect anything in my world? I shouldn't think too much about it, I'm sure I can ask the glowing orb thing and it will tell me the ways of the universe.

I go to my room to prevent further damage to Mom or Duncan, not that I feel responsible for Duncan massacring himself, but I didn't stop it either. I stood there and let him abuse himself like I was helpless, I could have helped. My room was almost untouched, except the sheets were cleaned and the blood stains were washed off, though I'm sure Mom will always see them when she steps foot into my room. Nothing can wash memories away. We used to talk about creating "forever memories" when she took us to do special things, but I didn't intend on creating this one for her. I sit on my bed Indian style and wait for something to happen. It doesn't. Duncan eventually goes downstairs to get something to eat then promptly goes back to his room. Mom eventually goes into her room locks the door behind her. I fall asleep in my bed.

Once again I slip into the darkness, and once again I'm met by the psychedelic ball of light. The color of the light changes from a ever changing rainbow to a solid reddish orange, like an intense glowing fire. The sphere starts expanding into long vertical strands of independent light like some sort of space eels. The eels start curving and twisting into each other forming a figure, a person of sorts. The figure towers above me and isn't solid, but is formed like a three dimensional grid of a human shell. Inside each of the intersecting squares are videos of my memories of different parts of my life. Inside the left hand is me unwrapping my Xbox on my last birthday. The video pans up to Mom who's smiling bigger than I've ever seen, then it loops back to the beginning. The right shoulder shows a video of me at the 8th grade dance sitting alone while I see everyone else dancing having a great time. The one over my heart is me putting the letter into Violet's locker over and over again.

I don't understand what this all means. Why would the ball turn into a figure of flaming eels and video clips of my memories? Maybe the ball is where my memories are stored after I die, or maybe this thing was collecting them my entire life, and I just never knew about it? Maybe this *thing* is my soul? I reach out and touch one of the memories, careful not to get near the fire. My finger pokes through the memory like a knife going through jello, and it creates small circular waves inside of the video like throwing rocks in a pond. The memory monster starts to condense to my size, my exact size, and it walks through me, or into me. Suddenly the fire eel grid is around me like an exoskeleton. I can feel the warmth from the eel grid, but not the heat, it's not fire, it's energy I guess. I look at my hand to see the memory of opening the Xbox, the flames burning around it. I attempt to pinch my skin to between my thumb and forefinger to grasp at the memory. I wake up.

R.L. Murphy

Chapter 10

I sit on top of my bed thinking about the memory videos, the fire eels, and the ball of energy. The longer I think about it, the less of a consensus I come to about it. Is it God, an angel, my soul, or something else entirely? All I do know is that it's trying to tell or show me something that I still don't comprehend. If it can turn from a ball of light to a flaming eel person, why can't it just tell me what it wants me to know? My concentration is broke by a light whimpering noise coming from the other side of the wall.

Duncan is on his side, curled up into the fetal position on the floor with his shirt off sobbing into his chest. I lie down next to him and notice he's clutching something in his hands. I catch enough of a glimpse to realize it's the picture of me from vacation last year. He must have grabbed it from the refrigerator when he went downstairs. Every year we got a new picture on the fridge and we got to pick a new magnet to pin it up with. Every year Mom took a picture of her feet and posted it with some sort of beach related magnet. She loves the beach. We always joked that we would need to get a larger refrigerator once ours was filled up with pictures, I guess now it'll take longer to take up that space. I don't want to scare Duncan into paranoia like I did Mom, but I feel like I should do something to help him. Duncan was always there for me, it's not right for me not to be there for him.

I know I can whisper to him and he will hear it, but what could I say that would help him? He lost his brother with the weapon that was under his surveillance, he blames himself. I don't think anything but time will relieve his guilt, but knowing Duncan, he won't want to let go of this guilt. I know I can interact with the physical world in different ways, but it's limited. It seems like I can move small objects or get in the way of things, but I don't think I possess the same kind of strength I had with a physical body. Maybe that's why in all the ghost movies all they do is slam cupboards and slam doors; it may be the only physical way they have to communicate. Maybe slamming dresser drawers is some sort of afterlife Morse code.

An e-mail, I can send an e-mail. There's no doubt that I can push keys and move a mouse. I'm going to have to make it seem like I sent these e-mails on a time release. If I send messages to him saying that they are from beyond the grave will make him think it's a hoax, but Duncan doesn't know enough about computers to be able to know how it was delivered. I phase through the wall and push my desk chair out of the way. It still bothers me to be halfway phased through things even though it doesn't feel any different.

I push the power button of the PC and the blue LED lights illuminate the dark room. A second later the internal fans kick into gear and the LCD monitor comes to life. As the operating system starts to boot I remembered how late it was and that drawing attention to myself isn't in my game plan. I turn down the speakers so the startup noises don't wake anyone and I lower the brightness of the screen just in case anyone walks by. My desktop background, some picture by Gustave Courbet popped on the screen before my icons and folders did. I find the mouse is still hard to navigate and half the time my hand falls through it, so I try to rely heavily on keyboard shortcuts. I open my e-mail account and draft an e-mail to Duncan, telling him I set these e-mails up to send after my death as a reminder that this isn't his fault and to remember all the good times we had. I finish it off with a quote by Carl Sagan and send it. I better delete anything on the computer that I wouldn't want anyone to see. I delete all of the illegal music and movies I downloaded, all of the half-finished writing projects and a folder full of internet pictures I just found to be funny, but would offend Mom. I clear my browsing history to ensure no one sees all porn and gross stuff that Steven sends me, and shutdown the computer.

I stare at my Xbox for a long time, not because I can't really play it, but because of how much I did play it instead of doing something that mattered. Maybe if I had worked out instead of playing Halo, Violet would have liked me and I wouldn't be where I am right now. I guess I used playing video games as an escape from how miserable my life actually was. I should have used that time to fix the problems instead of being an escape artist from them. I wish I was more like Duncan, he at least has the courage to work towards a goal to better his life. I did everything I could to run away, especially in death. Did I kill myself because of the harm I did to Violet, or did I do it because I didn't know how to preoccupy my time without obsessing over her? I wish I knew why I did it, I wonder if I'm starting to regret it. Obviously I didn't want to hurt Duncan or Mom but that was inevitable. Maybe I can ask the ball of light about it.

Eventually Duncan's alarm goes off. It's Friday, which means that Mom will be home late tonight. She says she has to wrap up some reports but Duncan thinks she goes and drinks with coworkers and just doesn't want to tell us. I think I agree with Duncan. Weekends for me usually meant that I got to play Call of Duty with Steven all night and sleep in till noon. I guess Steven will have to find someone else to play with. I would say maybe Steven can be friends with Seth and his crew, but pretty sure breaking his nose sealed the deal on that. Duncan usually doesn't make plans on the weekends, he sees two days off as two full days of working out. He has a group of friends he goes on hikes with in the mountains while I shoot insurgents with Steven on a video game console. While mine is worn out, Duncan's snooze alarm button is pristine, but he pushes it this morning...twice.

I phase to the kitchen and flip the light on for Duncan before he heads downstairs. I halfway do it to see if he will notice, and even if he doesn't it makes me smile, so why not? He comes down and either doesn't notice or doesn't care as he heads straight to the cupboard for a bowl, and to the refrigerator for the milk. Duncan pulls out Fruity Pebbles from the cabinet and drowns it with milk. He hunches over the kitchen counter eating it savagely and throws the bowl in the sink once he's slurped the milk from it. I hear Mom above us getting ready for work, as Duncan flicks off the light switch that I had turned on. He grabs his backpack by the door where he left it when he got home yesterday and heads out the door.

I dread going down the stupid quarter mile driveway more now that I'm dead than I did when I was alive. I close my eyes and wish I could just magically appear at the end of it. I open my eyes and I'm staring at the cows in the field at the end of the road. Okay so apparently thinking about being in a place will now take me to that place. I was unaware that ghosts had magic powers other than floating through objects. I wonder if I can make a cows head explode? I think it's better not to know that actually. I close my eyes again and wish I was back in my room, I open my eyes and I'm there. I close my eyes and wish I was in the Area 51 hanger...nothing. I guess it has to be someplace that I've already been to before. I think I'll put exploring Area 51 on my checklist of cool places to go to. Maybe that's why all the cool places are haunted, not because people died there but because dead people want to vacation there. I wish myself to the lip of the stage at school and sit down in the near empty commons of my high school.

Randy the Juggalo is one of the kids who gets dropped early. He sits at a table by himself wearing his Insane Clown Posse shirt and listening to his CD player. Even now that I have nothing to fear, not even death, I still find myself doing nothing useful with my time. What could I do? I figure there's still a reason I'm here, but what is it? The only thing that makes sense to me is that I'm supposed to be with Violet, and being dead is the only way it's going to happen.

I catch Violet walking with Dez before the busses arrive. She must have spent the night with Dez and walked to school since she lives a few blocks away. I couldn't tell exactly what they were talking about but it seemed to be some reality show that they watched the night before. As close as Dez and Violet are, they couldn't be more different. Dez is loud, perky, energetic, and has a very bubblegum feel to her, she's nice but always finds herself in a fight with someone. Violet is quiet, calm and collected and solves most of her conflicts with her quick wit or self-deprecating humor. Her ability to talk herself out of situations was the thing that made me attracted to her initially. I follow them to Violet's locker, the place I should have put the letter, but I refrain from looking inside of it this time. They wrap up their conversation about whatever show they were talking about and part ways. I follow Violet as she goes to class.

I spend the first two classes with Violet just looking at

her from every angle. I notice a small scar right below her lower lip on the left side, I wonder what it's from? Maybe she had some sort of accident as a child where she fell onto broken glass. Maybe that's why she occasionally bites her lower lip, hiding the scar. I notice that her pale skin has a gleam to it when the light hits it at a certain angle. Her eyebrows are so neat and uniform that she probably takes the time to pluck them one by one. I watch her draw while she's in class, she's amazing. Each stroke of her pencil is exacting its purpose on the paper, putting slight detail into the face of a singer I don't recognize. Every time the pencil touches the paper the portrait pops to life just a little bit more. The way she makes it seem like she's paying attention to the teacher yet still totally focused on her art is masterful. I could watch her bring her creations to life for eternity.

I stop following her when it was time for lunch because I want to see how Steven is doing, or if Seth has already exacted his revenge on him. I don't put it past Seth to do something really terrible to him, someone reported him last year for bringing a switchblade to school and threatening to cut someone's dick off with it. Luckily I see his head poke above a crowd of freshman, holding a tray of food. Steven sat down at the table I used to read at in the corner, and he sat down in the chair I used to sit in.

There's no sign of Seth, but his friend Xavier is sitting with a group of kids taking the role of main torturer in his place. Tommy Squire got the back of his head slapped hard enough to propel his face into his bowl of chili, his nose dipping into it like a chicken nugget into sweet & sour sauce. Xavier than proceeded to rip Jason Streak's glasses off his face and folded them up, then dropped them on the floor. Steven looks at the event go down but doesn't do anything. He always stood up for me, why wouldn't he stand up for them? What made me so special that I was worth fighting for? Steven with his right hand, still wrapped in bandages and starts eating, pretending to ignore the bullying going on. He shoves tater tots in his mouth one after another carefully dipping each one into a puddle of ketchup on his tray. Steven takes his last tater tot and smears it in the remaining ketchup, pops it in his mouth and walks by the trash and dumps his tray's contents, and puts it in the nearby bin.

Steven casually walks past Xavier, grabbing him by the back of his long brown hair forming a matted fist and yanks down full force. Xavier is caught off balance and falls backwards head first and lands on the linoleum with a hard smack that echoed throughout the commons. Steven kept on walking as if nothing happened and sat back down at his table.

"I'm going to kill you Steven Fargo," Xavier said holding the back of his head with one hand and pointing towards him with the other steadily and aggressively walking towards him. Steven ignores him, sitting back down in the chair I used to sit in hunched over face down at the table.

"That's the same thing Seth said right before I busted his face open," Steven said not looking away from the brown circular table. Xavier takes a stutter step as he says this as he probably saw what he did to Seth, but continues forward anyways.

"Do you know what I'm going to do to you?" Xavier said looming over Steven as he remains uninterested.

"Probably try to beat me up, but unfortunately for you, I have another hand that I don't mind breaking," Steven said not budging from his blue plastic chair. "But I don't feel like fighting."

"Then you shouldn't have thrown me to the ground," Xavier said clenching both of his fists and putting them near Steven's face.

"You shouldn't have fucked with those freshman," he said.

"I was just playing around with them, you had no right to do what you did," Xavier thrusts his left fist in front of Steven's face...he doesn't flinch.

"You didn't have the right to do what you did yesterday either."

"I'm sorry your boyfriend blew his brains out," Xavier said but was unable to finish the rest before Steven landed a left elbow to gut of Xavier instantly making him double over as he tries to regain his breath. Steven stands up, the chair he was sitting in flies back. Steven loops his right arm over the back of his neck and under his chin, clasping his hands together. Steven arches his back slightly for elevation and Xavier starts flailing from the choke. He frantically tries to claw the arm that's clutching his neck but to no avail. His face turns bright red, and the rest of the lunchroom starts to notice what's going on at the table usually ignored. Steven starts to arch his back further and flex his muscles, tightening the grip even further. Xavier in an act of desperation, attempts to grabs the leg of Steven to try to trip him but before his arms touches his jeans his entire body goes limp. Xavier was unconscious, Steven choked him out. His arms dangle like ropes tied to tree limb. Steven holds the choke for a few seconds then lets go of the hold, and Xavier's body collapses as if his muscle and bones has turned to mush. It looked like Xavier was a life size marionette doll and the puppeteer had dropped all the strings.

Steven steps over Xavier's body and walks out of the commons towards the lockers. A few seconds later Xavier sits up, holding his head in his hand, obviously light headed from the lack of blood flow to his brain and stands up. It's apparent he's realizing what happened and flips the table on its side. The noise drew the attention of a nearby teacher who quickly escorts him to the office by the wrist. The only person that would rat Steven out is Seth, and he was absent. The targets of Xavier's abuse start talking amongst themselves and as a group also head to the office. I can only assume that are going to stick up for Steven, but who knows.

Violet and Dez walk inside from the main doors, missing the action entirely. It wasn't uncommon for them to take lunch outside on nice days. There are a few benches outside for kids to wait for the busses after school, but they mostly get used as graffiti targets and after school make out spots. I follow them through the hallways, they stop for a minute and talk about some report coming up that they wanted to work on together for another class, I'm not sure of the subject. They give each other a half-hearted wave and part ways. I better go to the office and check up on Steven.

I phase through the door to the office and can feel the tension in the waiting room. The secretary is mindlessly typing away as Steven and Xavier are sitting inches away from each other, presumably waiting for their turn to be interrogated. Xavier is just staring at Steven with eyes that tell him every evil thought going through his mind. The door to the vice-principal's office opens and the three Freshmen step out avoiding eye contact with Xavier while one of them gave a slight nod towards Steven as a gesture of having his back. The vice-principal steps out of his office and calls in for Steven. Xavier tries to trip him and fails, but the vice-principal notices. Xavier crosses his arm as Steven closes the door behind him. I phase through the door.

Steven was taking a seat and the vice-principal whose

name I could never remember already has his hands folded on his desk. He has a picture of two women on his desk, one of his wife, one of his child. He reminds me of George Costanza from Seinfield, except with his sense of humor sucked out of him and replaced with a hatred for children. There's a large metal plaque with the name "Richard Walker" engraved onto it. I've never been on the receiving end of his wrath but he tends to punish excessively, regardless of the rule broken.

"Mr. Fargo, will you please tell me what happened today at lunch?" Mr. Walker said.

"Yes sir," Steven said looking at his feet, not wanting to make eye contact. "I finished my lunch and went to clean off my tray. Xavier was standing over this table, I tried going around him but he stepped backwards as I was going by and he tripped over me and fell backwards. I went back to my table, he started marching towards me yellin' about how he was going to kill me. He got to me and tried to punch me so I got him in a headlock to try to calm him down and I let go once he stopped trying to punch me. That's it. I didn't mean to make him trip, and I was just trying to defend myself, I never punched him or anything."

"The three at the table where Xavier was standing over said almost the same thing...you sure you four didn't get together and talk this through?" Mr. Walker leans back trying to read Steven's body language the best that he can.

"I don't even know those kids, why would I talk to them about it?" Steven says looking up at Mr. Walker. "I walked away after it happened because I didn't want any more trouble from Xavier, or anyone else. I don't look for trouble sir."

"Well it's certainly found you the last few days hasn't it?" Mr. Walker says pointing to his hand, still wrapped tightly in a white bandage.

"Yes sir, I suppose it has," Steven says placing his bandaged hand inside the other.

"Do you have anything else you want to tell me?"

"No sir."

"Okay, you can go. If you get into anymore fights, I don't care who starts it, you'll be suspended for a week, no questions asked." Mr. Walker gives him a look as if to go away, that his presence is no longer needed.

Thank you sir. Should I close the door or leave it open?" Steven says as he bolts out of his chair, hand already on the door knob, twisting it slowly.

"Leave it open, I still need to talk to Xavier."

"Yes sir." Steven leaves the room. I'm pretty sure Steven gave Xavier a wink because he had his fist pulled back as Mr. Walker called him in. I followed Steven as he left through the office door. It's not going to take a rocket surgeon to figure out that Xavier is taking the fall for all of this. I follow Steven until I realize he's just going to his class. I go to Violet's class and watch her continue drawing her picture while pretending to taking notes. I think she might be nearing done with the picture, the details in the shading are really magnificent. She's making a character come to life like in that Ah-Ha music video.

I follow Violet through the halls to her next class until I realize she's going to the locker room. Seeing the woman I love naked for the first time may be a dream of mine, but even at this point I wouldn't feel comfortable with it. Not without her knowing, it's still not right. I sit on the lip of the stage in the commons. I see two adults escorting someone towards the main doors. It's Xavier and his parents.

"I had to leave work for this bullshit, are you serious Xavier? I have to go back to my boss and explain to him that I missed the meeting because you're a fuck up. Do you know how embarrassing that is for me? Fucking asshole," Xavier's father said slapping him on the back of the head, his hair jostling forward from the impact.

"Daniel, you're being too hard on him, he just got into a fight it's not that big of a deal. The important thing is that he isn't hurt" Xavier's Mom said putting a protective arm around him.

"He's going to be when he gets home, that's for damn sure."

"Daniel stop, you are not going to beat our child." The door closed behind them and couldn't hear any more of the conversation. Tempted as I was to follow them, I decide to sit on the lip, waiting for Violet to get out of class. You know actually, this may be a perfect way to get to know Violet better...I'll go home with her this weekend! It has to beat being around Mom getting drunk and Duncan getting high to subdue his emotional pain. Plus I can apparently think my way back there to check up on them if needed. I've never been to Violet's house so I can't teleport there I don't think.

It's Friday, so the teachers who don't hate their students let them into the commons a few minutes before the final bell rings. Some of those students begin plopping down in random chairs, slamming their backpacks or books on the table nearest them. Talk of sports games happening this weekend and some party at David Renfield's house dominated most of the conversations. The gym doors open and Violet is the last one out. She has her hair pulled back into a ponytail with a scrunchy that has a Misfits skull on it. Her face still red from whatever game they were playing in class and stands off in the corner, neglecting the chairs around her.

The bell rings. The students that were in the seats in the commons promptly stand up, grab their bags and scuttle towards the door. Violet walks out with casual strides, obviously in no rush to go wherever she is going. Her slick black ponytail floats back and forth like a pendulum. Floods of students from various classrooms breach into the commons, making their way to the main doors towards the busses. I follow Violet out the doors and the sun hits me. Since my death, the sun doesn't have a blinding effect, but I've somehow become more sensitive to brightness. Violet is standing on the corner watching the busses line up. Dez emerges out of the mass of people exiting the building and stands next to her. They talk for a minute then started walking towards the street.

I always thought that Dez and Violet lived outside of town, but I was wrong. They both walked to school, something that I never noticed. I follow them, trailing right behind them so I could hear what they were talking about.

"So, are you going to go?" Dez asks.

"I mean, I probably should right? I am partially responsible," Violet says with her head slung towards the ground with both hands in her pocket.

"You know that's not true."

"I know that you're trying to make me feel better about it, and I appreciate it. Thanks Dez." There was a long period of silence after this, I could tell neither had anything more to say about the subject. Dez finally breaks the silence.

"I still think you should go, that's all I'm saying. Matt would want you to be there."

"Oh and how do you know that?" Violet asks as they cross the road past the local gas station.

"C'mon you know how much he liked you, it would mean a lot to him," Dez says to Violet nudging her lightly in the ribs.

"I just...I just don't want anyone to blame me for it at the funeral. I don't want anyone to point at me and say 'there's the one he killed himself over' you know?"

"No one is blaming you Violet, and anyone that would is a complete asshole," Dez says reaching into her back pocket and grasping a pack of cigarettes. She removes a yellow Bic lighter that she hid in the box along with a lone single cigarette. Dez grasps it between her lips gently and lights the end with one hand. Orange embers light the end of it, smoldering while she inhales. She turns her head away from Violet and exhales the smoke into the street.

"You should really stop smoking Dez." Violet waves away stray smoke that the wind blows in her directions. "It's kind of gross, not to mention harmful to your body."

"Wow Violet, really? You sure are one to talk about hurting yourself," Dez says as she raises an eyebrow towards her.

"That's not fair Dez, you know it's not." Violet walks noticeably faster getting slightly ahead, but Dez quickly catches up.

"I know that was out of line, I'm just saying we all have our own ways of dealing with our own shit, and this happens to be mine."

"Yeah...I guess. Let's just not talk about it okay?"

"Okay. So are you going to go or not?"

"Yeah, I think I should. And if anyone says anything, fuck them, right?"

"That's right! Fuck them."

They walked in silence until they reached a small two-story pistachio colored house with brown trim. They gave each other a hug. Dez continued walking down the street and took a left at the corner as Violet fumbles in her pocket for the keys to the house. I wait for her to find the key insert it into the keyhole. She jiggles the handle at the same time as turning the key counter-clockwise. I wait for her to step inside and close the door behind her before I go through the door.

The unmistakable smell of dog hair immediately enters my nostrils. A loud clamoring coming from upstairs fumbles its way down the stairs. It's the owner of the hair I smell. A large yellow Labrador retriever rushes Violet and contemplates jumping on her hind legs. She pets the dog furiously with both hands, the dog is getting so excited that its tail is swinging so hard it's coming dangerously close to knocking a picture off the table.

"Okay Squeaky Fromme, calm down, I'll feed you in a bit, okay girl?" Violet said patting the dog on the head. Squeaky Fromme, I've heard that name before but I don't know from where. I don't think it's a band or anything, but I don't know I'll have to look it up later.

Violet makes a bowl of Fruit Loops and goes to the couch and turns on the television. She flips through the channels until she finds an episode of Seinfeld playing. She almost immediately starts laughing even though she's over half-way through the episode and doesn't know what's going on. She must have already seen the episode. Of course she has, she has good taste. She finishes the cereal, placing the bowl on a side table next to a brown porcelain lamp. She sits back on the couch with one leg folded beneath her. Once the shows ends with a classic Seinfeld standup bit about pistachios, she puts the bowl in the sink and heads upstairs. Not knowing the layout of the house I follow her instead of phasing through the ceiling into who knows what room. The entire house feels cramped; including the stairs where Violet even with her normal frame seems to almost touch the walls with her shoulders. The white sheetrock is chipped in random places and has been painted in a teal color, almost like they wanted to give it a feel of living inside of an aquarium. If this was an aquarium, I would be a shark in a ten gallon tank.

The second floor feels like I stepped into a portal into a different house. It feels like a dingy hotel from the 80's.

There are three doors to the right and one to the left. I can assume that the one on the left is the master bedroom, and I follow Violet into the first door on the right...her room.

Chapter 11

Stepping into her room was like stepping into her imagination. It was exactly the way I imagined it, or I guess the way she drew it in the painting I stole from her. Band posters slightly off kilter held up with a different color thumbtacks in each corner with noticeable holes where previous thumbtacks had been. It was messy, but intentionally so. A pair of her jeans flopping over the top of her laundry basket as if they were trying to escape. Her nightstand has a random assortment of items; a Playstation controller, loose change, a book about Buddhism, and a small sketchbook with a charcoal pencil on top of it. She has a smallish TV on top of her dresser, and I can't tell if it's there because it fit perfectly, or because it blocks out the mirror behind it.

Violet sits on her bed, shoulders hunched forward and lets out a sigh. I can tell she doesn't know what she wants to do but I can also tell she's happy to be home, and alone. She lies down on her bed on top of her white comforter with her hands folded behind her head. She closes her eyes and breathes deeply. I can see her breasts rise and fall with each inhale and exhale in her shirt. She rolls to her side and grabs the controller. She turns the console on with the controller and begins playing some distinctly

Japanese video game. I was never into the Japanese stuff, the stories always seemed too hokey and the game play was very repetitive.

I watch her delicate fingers with chipped polish manipulate the joystick and glide across the buttons with precision. I wasn't paying attention to what was going on with the screen, just her body movement. She's usually so muted and expressionless that I've never seen this side of her. I love the way way she bites the corner of her bottom lip when she gets focused, or how she runs her hand through her hair in moments of relief and gives a brief smile of accomplishment. Everything she does is beautiful, she's the woman I had hoped she would be in private in every single way. Every movement she makes plants a smile on my face as I watch the reflection of the screen on her eyes. After an especially tense moment she throws her arms in the air, dropping the controller on her knee in the process lets out a celebratory cheer. She saves her game and turns off the console, putting the controller back on her nightstand.

Violet picks up the book and starts reading cross-legged in the center of the bed. I finally work up the nerve to sit on the corner of her bed, half expecting her to reject me from doing so. I touch her comforter with my hand, it's softer than I thought it would be. The book she is reading is by someone named Sylvia Plath. I think I've heard the name before but no idea where from. Maybe they made a movie about one of her books or something.

I watch her pale blue eyes scan across the lines until she shifts to the next page. I curl around her, perching my chin on her shoulder to see what the book is about. The black fingernail polish on her thumbs grip the bottom corners of the pages. She reaches the end of a chapter, and reaches for a small slip of paper hidden near the back of the book and inserts it into the beginning of the new chapter.

As she lays her head on her pillow a slamming of a door downstairs instantly springs her back up. Violet mutters a curse word under her breath and a sigh quickly followed. The chunky clunking sound of boots coming up the steps makes Violet cringe.

"Violet I'm home," a male voice said quickly followed by the owner of the voice knocking on her door.

"Okay thanks Dad," Violet says as the door creaks open and the head of a grizzled old man peers through the crack. If Violet hadn't just called him dad I wouldn't have believed that would be her father. His grizzled face is covered with a massive white and grey unkempt beard, and a large diagonal scar from his left temple to where his facial hair begins. If I could see anymore than his head, I'm sure I would see a leather jacket with a biker patch on the back of it. I don't know what happened to Violet's mom, but I know she's not around anymore. Her dad never remarried. That just about sums up all I know about the Waits family tree.

She sighed and got up. She creeps downstairs while I

hear the shower running in the nearby bathroom. I follow her instead of playing peeping tom on an old man in the shower. Apparently Violet's dad coming home meant that she had to cook dinner. Judging from how she was haphazardly throwing pans and random ingredients on the counter in a row like a prison line-up, she didn't like this chore very much. She cuts off a chunk of butter and throws it into a pan like she was throwing a rock at a bug. While it's melting she starts cutting green vegetable, or maybe it's an herb, Mom never used herbs. She has a rhythm to it that could only come from doing it hundreds of times. She swirls the herbs in the melted butter and sprinkles salt into the mixture. Two large chicken breasts are delicately placed in the middle of the pan, and Violet swirls the butter around the poultry. She pulls out a bag of Minute Rice and puts it in the microwave. She sets the timer on the microwave for fifty-nine seconds, with a smile on her face to let me know she thought she was sticking it to the man by cooking Minute Rice one second less than recommended.

Minutes went by and she had whipped up an entire meal and put it on the plate in a way that made it look like art. I can't taste what she put on the plate but it looks spectacular, her talents as an artist seep through from the brushes and pencils to spices and utensils. I can tell even though she has a talent for it, she's only doing it because her Dad forces her. I wonder if her Dad can actually cook, but it's his way of encouraging her to do something she's good at? I don't think he's that smart. She cleans up the mess she had made and put the pan in the sink. She slips the knife she used to cut the herbs into her pocket.

Her Dad comes down almost instinctively as the plate is put on the table. He's wearing a Harley Davidson shirt and grey oil stained sweatpants, his beard still wet from the shower. He smiles when he sees the plate with yellow jagged teeth that have seen more drugs than toothbrushes. They awkwardly sit at the dinner table as if neither of them wanted to be there but were forced to.

"So, how was school?" He asked as steam escaped from his chicken as he cuts it in half.

"It was fine, nothing happened," Violet said hunched over her plate in disinterest scraping the rice off of her chicken with her fork.

"You got any plans for the weekend? I think there's a Pawn Stars marathon going on, you're welcome to join me," He says as he snaps open the aluminum tab on a Miller Lite. A creamy foam spills out of the mouth of the can, which is quickly slurped up by Mr. Masters.

"I'm going to a funeral tomorrow," Violet said looking down at her plate, stabbing her chicken with her fork.

"You mean your boyfriend's funeral?" Mr. Masters said looking at Violet, expecting her to make eye contact.

Violet clutches her fork tightly and slams it on the table. "He *is* not, and *was* not, my boyfriend Chad," Violet said giving her Dad a more hateful face than she had given me before she slapped me. Her nose scrunched up with three small wrinkles along the ridge, and she clenches her teeth so tightly I can hear her teeth grinding.

"Okay jeez Pook, didn't know you'd rip my throat out over it," Chad Waits said with his left cheek bulged out with chicken. "Anything else?"

"No, that's it," Violet said as she continues to eat as if the outburst hadn't just happened.

"Well I think I might be going to the movies tomorrow night if you want to join me, there's that new Bruce Willis movie coming out."

"I don't think I'll be in the mood after the funeral but thanks Dad."

They eat with only the sound of forks scraping against porcelain and an occasional slurping of beer. Violet eats enough of her food to say that she ate something then promptly scrapes the rest in the trash and puts her plate in the sink. I follow her upstairs and back into her room. She slams her bedroom door behind her, rattling the one window in her personal space.

Violet undoes the button on her jeans. I don't look away as if I don't know what's going to happen next, and then it does. She slides the pants past her hips, and I catch a glimpse of white lace attached to black underwear. I start to feel guilty and avert my head. I can still hear the sound of the fabric being removed from what I imagine to be perfect white milky legs. I hear her rustle in the pocket then the whooshing sound as it hit the overflowing laundry basket in the corner. I hear her tossing her blankets and the sound of a body sliding in-between sheets. I get the feeling like it's okay to look in her general direction...I'm right.

The blanket is folded, tucked under her breasts like paperweights. I know what a paperweight is, but I don't think I've ever seen one. Did people really use them? Couldn't they just, you know...write where it was less drafty? She pulls the blanket and sheet away in one swift movement revealing her legs, her horribly cut legs. Her skin on her legs is as lovely as I had imagined, but self inflicted scars plague them. Violet Waits unveils the knife she had hidden in her pants from under the covers, a serrated steak knife. I look back at her legs to notice that this type of knife may be her weapon of choice judging from the jagged inconsistency of the lines and the different depths of them. If I hadn't known any better I would have assumed she was attacked by a school of piranhas.

Violet takes the knife and slides it across her tongue, starting from the black base and working upwards, delving deeper into the muscle tissue after every divot in the blade. Halfway through the length of the blade it sliced the membrane and blood began trickling down the blade...she smiles. I don't think she's doing this to hurt herself, I think she likes seeing her blood. She pauses to watch it drip over the handle and race down to her finger. She takes her tongue off the blade long enough to lick her blood-laden knuckle where it had been concealed in her mouth moments ago inside her tongue.

Many of the scars have healed and look like small worms have been crawling just under the surface of her skin. Violet places the blade on a cut that looks like was made recently and slices it open like tape on a cardboard box. The wound opens up like a baked potato, and blood leaps out. She stares at the blood escaping her body with intrigue, as if she was studying an organism in a lab. She pulls a small black wash cloth from under her pillow, folded perfectly with the tag cleanly cut off of it. She wipes the blood clean, just to be replaced by more, which was also quickly mopped up. Two more incisions are made, this time on unscarred flesh. This seems to satisfy her more than opening prior wounds. She lets the blood form on the blade and she promptly lets it drizzle directly down her throat as she tilts her head back. The rest of her fluids end up on the washcloth until the bleeding subsides. She seems...relieved as if having blood contained inside of her was stressing her out or evacuating it gave her some sort of high.

She wipes the knife with the rag, giving it a red-smeared sheen. She opens the top drawer of her nightstand and pulls out a large brown bottle of rubbing alcohol and twists off the cap. She places the blood-stained rag over the top of the bottle and she tips it over slightly. The clear liquid exits the bottle and dampens the cloth, darkening the cloth in an almost perfect circle. The familiar smell of rubbing alcohol fills the room. It oddly reminds me of some drink my uncle used to drink with orange juice in it. I took a sip of it once when he wasn't looking and swore he had put rubbing alcohol in it. Violet folds the rag over several times and opens her legs, fully exposing the wounds she inflicted upon herself. She rubs the fabric along the wounds, putting pressure onto her skin. She doesn't like the pain judging from her clenching her fist and hammer fisting her bed.

After cleaning the cuts she throws the cloth towards the laundry basket where it lands on top of her jeans. She throws the blanket back over top of her and turns toward the wall on her side in a near fetal position. I hear a whimper coming from her, followed by something I rarely heard in my life...a woman crying.

I don't know what I should do for her, but I want to help her. If there's anything I can do...I can't talk to her...can I? I know I can move small objects, but can I use them to communicate? Even if I could talk to her, what would I say? Hey Violet sorry for killing myself and becoming a ghost, but I've decided to hang out around you without your permission...is that cool? Am I....haunting her? I mean, even if I'm friendly it's still haunting right? Maybe it's only haunting when I try to interact with the living. She looks dreadfully lonely. As cliché as it sounds, I think she needs a hug. Her whimpers continue and she lets out the most adorable sniff. As if she could hear me I cautiously lay down on the bed next to her. I was half expecting her to notice, like when you can feel someone staring at you...but she doesn't. I turn to the same side she's facing and reluctantly place my arm over hers, laying my hand over top of hers. I scoot my body closer to her, holding her, keeping her safe as she drifts off to sleep. And so do I.

Chapter 12

I enter the darkness once more, but no orb, just empty space. I walk around it aimlessly hoping to find something worth finding...but I don't. Darkness is replaced by more darkness the farther I walk...until I hear it. A slow heartbeat, my heartbeat thumping so loud I think it might burst inside of my chest. The intensity and speed of the beats increases like a dub step song building up to a drop. The sound is now so loud and violent I have to cover my ears and close my eyes to prevent it from blurring my vision. I can feel something crawling from my stomach and up to my throat. It gets stuck and my throat and I start choking, my esophagus is constricting. It feels like a baseball has lodged itself in my neck and is trying to kill me. I can feel small spikes forming around the ball, puncturing the lining as I grab the base of my neck and try to push it up.

I fall to my knees and lean my head downward to cough it up. It starts rotating upwards as if it is inside of me like a mountain climber with pick axes for limbs. I shove two fingers down my throat as fast and hard as I can to induce vomiting....it works. A rush of black bile froths out of my mouth, pushing the spiked ball out with it like a fish going downstream. I couldn't make out exactly what it is at first since it's covered in my bodily fluids. It's the goddamn prism ball. The spikes start retracting as I notice they aren't spikes, they're tiny replication of the blade Violet used to cut herself. They start retracting and I kick the fucking thing as hard as I can, and it sails into the darkness until it disappears back into eternity.

I wake up next to Violet who apparently wasn't having dreams about a psychedelic knife ball, because she's still sound asleep. I can see her shoulders move as her lungs expand and contract with each breath, so peaceful, so beautiful. I take my hand off hers and run it through her hair as it slides between my spectral fingers like a waterfall. There's a slight shift in her hips and her hand comes towards the back of her head. I wrap my hand around hers and close my eyes as my heart sinks. If I could cry while holding her hand, something I had dreamed about since I first laid eyes on her, I would. I let go as she shifts onto her back in that state between conscious and unconscious with great hesitation.

I look around the room for something to do besides look at her while she's sleeping which I'm feeling guilty about no matter how long I've thought about doing so. I need to find a way to let her know I'm here, if she knows I'm here maybe we can communicate. I have an idea...a dumb one, but it's an idea. I turn the volume down to zero on her TV, luckily they are fairly easy to push. I press the power button on her Playstation and the Sony logo appears with a short jingle. I launch the game that she was playing last. I select the "New Game" option where as expected the first things I do before beginning my adventure is name my hero. Judging from the amount of dashes present on the screen I'm only going to have six characters to send her a message with. I think about it for a moment then type the letters MATT M next to a silhouette of a man with a sword endlessly marching on screen. I go back to the TV and turn the volume back up, where a low key piano medley bellows from the speakers from the set.

Violet's head flops over to the other side, landing safely on her pillow as her hair followed a second later scattering over her face. She pushes it behind her ear with precision then sits up over the side of the bed. Her eyes squint as she tries to focus on what's on the TV. I can tell when her eyes adjust based on when her jaw drops followed up by her pupil's dilating. She just stares at the screen, looking at the door making sure it is closed. It is. She watches the character march on the screen in place for a solid minute before muttering "what the fuck?" out loud. I see an idea surge through her brain and she leaps up, making a dash towards her closet. She flings the door open and begins rummaging through who knows what. After much shuffling and shambling of boxes she pulls out what she was looking for...a Ouija board.

I've never actually seen a Ouija board in real life. Of course I've seen them on shows and movies where scared teenage girls throw slumber parties and pretend to communicate to dead people. She hastily throws the box top across the room like a ninja star where it spins through my head and lands softly on her bed. The actual contents of the box are basic, a board with the alphabet on it and a heart shaped cursor with a circle magnifying glass in the middle of it. Violet opens her nightstand drawer and pulls out a book of matches. I was always terrible with them, always snapping the match in half while striking it. Violet has apparently mastered this craft signified by her using one strike, and one match to light several candles around the room I had previously not seen. She turns the light off and sits cross-legged in front of the board on the carpet. She places all ten fingertips on the cursor and she inhales deeply. I sink half way through the floor until I'm eye level with Violet.

"Okay...I guess I should start off slow. Matthew are you here?" Violet said with more pressure on the cursor to make sure a draft didn't accidently move it. I try moving it with one hand first...no dice. I use two hands to try to budge it under her grip...nada. Okay if I'm going to get the chance to talk to her alone for the first time in my life I need to move this damn thing, but she's stronger than I expected. I raise the rest of my body out of the floor and put my entire body into moving the six inch object...it starts to move against her force. I move the cursor to the "YES" icon on the board and take my hands off of it. She sits there with her mouth agape, half in disbelief and half in amazement. I can see that she's pondering what to ask next.

"Prove it's you Matthew. If you're really a spirit or a ghost or whatever, you should be able to prove it," Violet said folding her arms still trying to remain skeptical. How can I prove that I am what I am? There's not a license I can show her that says "Official Ghost" or anything. I put my hands on the cursor once more and moved it to the letters "O" and slid it to the letter "K" taking her by surprise. I guess now I have to think of how I'm going to prove it. Turning on her Playstation and entering my name wasn't enough apparently. Slamming her door open and close seemed rude and likely to get her in trouble with her dad.

I whisper in her ear, "I'm sorry for hurting you Violet." Her eyes widen followed by a smile that can only be described as devious.

"How long have you been haunting me?"

I go back to the Ouija board which she has now given up on holding down, making my life easier. I go letter to letter, Violet saying each letter out loud as I stop on them. I sometimes have to pause to find the next letter, slightly confusing her until I spell out "I STARTED TODAY."

She already knew her follow-up question. "Why? Why are you haunting me? What do you want?"

If there was any moment in my life, or afterlife in which I could be brutally honest with zero repercussions...this was it. I respond accordingly, "I WANT

TO BE AROUND YOU."

"Why? Why would you want to be around me?" Violet asks as if she thought she misunderstood the question. I sit and ponder it, of course I want to tell her it's because I love her and want to be with her, but also don't want to scare her away.

"I WANT TO GET TO KNOW YOU." That's a good place to start right? That's what adults do on dates right, get to know each other? I died for someone I didn't even know. I can't even say I know what her favorite color is, or the last movie that made her cry...or anything.

"Why me? Why do you want to get to know me? I'm nothing special. I mean, you saw what I did to myself. Oh em gee, you saw what I did to myself didn't you?" A look of horror smears across her face.

"YES I DID" I take a long pause and follow up with the question that I know she's expecting. "WHY DO YOU DO IT" she takes a long exhale like she knew she been caught doing something wrong.

"I don't know if I can really explain it. I'm really unhappy with my life and when I'm cutting it's the one time when I feel like I have control of my life. Plus I'm ugly, so it's not like I'm going to look any worse, you know?

"NO I DONT KNOW YOU ARE BEAUTIFUL," I spelled out, noticing that the novelty for Violet to say out each letter has diminished.

"Yeah right. If I were beautiful then why don't I have a boyfriend, or friends at all besides Dez?" Violet said with sadness filling her eyes. I feel bad for her, she really doesn't understand how beautiful she is when there are so many people who are ugly on the inside that believe that they aren't.

"I WAS AFRAID TO TALK TO YOU I WAS AFRAID OF REJECTION," I said via the board game. "I ALWAYS THOUGHT YOU WERE BEAUTIFUL SINCE I FIRST MET YOU." Writing this way is a huge pain, and then I start to think about that movie Diving Bell and the Butterfly about the guy who was paralyzed except for being able to blink one eye. He wrote a book by blinking letters to a nurse...the Ouija Board was at least better than that, but not by much.

Violet sat in quiet contemplation. "I don't understand, do you think I have some reputation as a heart breaker? Is there some rumor I don't know about? I mean you are...or were a decent looking guy. Why would you be afraid?"

"IM AVERAGE UR BEAUTIFUL YOU WOULDNT WANT TO LOWER YOURSELF TO ME" I wait for a response from her, but it takes the longest minute of my life.

"And you think I'm so shallow that all I care about is looks? That's who you really think I am? If that was the case why would you be interested in someone so...putrid?" Violet says with a quasi-disgusted look on her face.

"I DONT IVE JUST NEVER HAD A GIRLFRIEND IVE NEVER HAD A DATE NEVER HAD A DANCE HOW AM I SUPPOSED TO KNOW WHAT GIRLS WANT ALL I KNOW IS THAT I WANTED TO BE WITH YOU" the cursor was flying around the board as I've gotten the hang of the order of the letters. I've been typing so long that I don't think I've ever had to select letters in alphabetic order with the exception of video games which is always a pain.

"Then why didn't you just talk to me? If you like me as much as you say then you have to know I wasn't seeing anyone, and trust me it wasn't by choice. All I've ever wanted was someone that cares about me, and I haven't found that person," Violet says as her voice trails of.

"WHAT ABOUT UR DAD" I spell out. I could tell they didn't have the best relationship, but surely she knows he cares about her.

"Hah, are you kidding me? He totally hates me. He's too much of a hard-ass to accept me as I am. You should have heard him when he caught me cutting, he treated me like a suicidal piece of shit. I had to switch to my legs because the ones on my arms were too visible. Fortunately there weren't any permanent scars. I'm not you know...suicidal that is. I don't want to die.

"ITS NOT SO BAD" I wasn't lying. Sure being dead has its downsides but overall but feel like I've gotten over a lot of the fears and anxieties from my old life.

"Hah I guess you would know right? So what's it like...you know being a ghost, or dead, or whatever?" She said with a curious look on her face as if she was greatly anticipating the answer.

"WEIRD ITS NOT WHAT THE MOVIES MAKE IT OUT TO BE"

"Oh, how so?"

"IM POWERLESS I HAVE NO CONTROL OVER MY SURROUNDINGS I CAN BARELY MOVE THIS DUMB CURSOR" I had read a book about the difference between animals and humans is that animals adapt to their environments and humans adapt their environment to them. I guess I'm an animal.

"Oh but I guess you have cool powers right? You can talk and move stuff right?"

"YES BUT SO CAN YOU"

"You know Matt, I never took you for a funny guy, but you certainly are," Violet said with a grin on her face. "Dez is entertaining but she lacks the wit that you have."

"THANK YOU AND I THINK UR ART IS AMAZING"

"Aww that's so sweet of you to say. I don't think I'm

very good. I just do it for fun, it's the only release I have that doesn't involve cutting my skin open, so I tend to indulge," She says with a smirk playfully joking about something that horrified me mere hours ago.

"YOU COULD DO IT PROFESSIONALLY," I said, and I meant it.

"Oh well I'll be sure to tell art school that my ghost friend told me I was good enough to get in, and that should be enough," Violet says cracking herself up.

"SOUNDS ABOUT RIGHT TO ME," I said and her laughter was louder and more contagious as I started laughing uncontrollably. It feels good to have a reason to be happy. I'm having a conversation with Violet and she doesn't want to slap me, in fact she's enjoying my company.

"So...do you regret what you did, you know the whole 'pwew' thing?" Violet said as she pantomimes a gun shot to the head with her hand."

"NO REGRETS IF I WAS ALIVE I WOULDNT BE SPENDING TIME WITH YOU RIGHT NOW AND YOU WOULD STILL BE MAD AT ME SO THIS IS WORTH IT," I say and look up at Violet. Tears are streaming down her face like a character in an anime, a single line from the corner of her eye all the way down her cheeks. Great now I think she's mad at me. "DONT BE MAD."

"Why would I be mad? It may be morbid but it's the

sweetest thing anyone has ever said to me. Thank you Matthew it means a lot to me. If I could hug you right now I would," Violet said extending her arms out as if expecting an embrace from a loved one. I lean in towards her and wrap my arms around her, placing my hands on the back of each shoulder blade. The expression on her face changes, "I can feel you. Your hands feel warm Matthew, it's nice." Violet attempts to wrap her hands around me but fails to miss the mark. Her right hand and part of her arm end up where my heart should be, and her left ends up somewhere in my ribcage. It's the thought that counts. It's a thought that I wish would never end...but it does.

I go back to the Ouija Board and quickly spell out "THAT WAS REALLY NICE" and she nods in agreement.

"I've really enjoyed our chat, but I think I should go back, we both have a big day tomorrow."

"OK CAN I SEE YOU TOMORROW"

"I can't really stop you now can I?" Violet says as she winks in my general direction. "But I think I'd like that, so yes I'll see you tomorrow. Do you want me to go to the funeral?" I move the cursor to the word "YES" and leave it there. "Okay well see you tomorrow then. Where are you going to go?"

"HOME TO CHECK ON MOM AND DUNCAN"

"How do you get there? Is there some sort of ghost transportation system?"

"I CAN TELEPORT"

"See I told you there were cool special powers! You're practically a part of the X-Men. Good night Matthew and hope you enjoy your teleportation."

"WILL DO GOOD NIGHT."

Violet stands up and makes her way back to bed, realizing that the music from the video game was still going. She turns the system off using the controller and rolls over to the corner. I watch her fall asleep before going back to check on Duncan and Mom.

Chapter 13

The house is quiet. There are no lights on in the living room and the television is off. The sound of a single fly in the kitchen buzzing about permeates the building. I float through the ceiling into Duncan's room. He's laying in bed in almost the exact same position that Violet was before I left, curled up and facing the wall. He wasn't crying, it was worse...he was sobbing. I've seen Duncan upset but he wasn't nearly this upset even when Dad left. A mixture of snot and tears swirls on his face like a cauldron. The composition drips off his face and onto the bed sheets. He looks up briefly for me to see his bloodshot eyes, I can't tell if it's from crying or if he's high, or a combination of the two. He keeps mumbling the same thing over and over again, which was completely unintelligible until he roared it.

"Why did you do this to me Matthew? Why did you hate me Matthew? Fuck you Matthew!" He said this slurred together and repeatedly as if it were his mantra. My heart drops. I want to tell him that it's not his fault, that I don't hate him...but he wouldn't believe me. He wouldn't believe that a ghost is talking to him, and even if he did he's too stubborn to admit I was right. I wish I could just smack him in the head and tell him, but I can't.

He's also not one for physical contact unless I'm a punching bag so hugging it out isn't going to help matters much. I say the only thing that I can say in hopes that it means something. I tell him I'm sorry but as expected he doesn't hear it, or pretends not to.

The sound finally stops and Duncan rolls over to the other side. His hand emerges from his body and reaches to the floor, reaching into his jeans pocket. He pulls out something small and dark that I can't make out in my hand. His other arm slithers into view and grabs the other end of the object, pulling into view a blade. It's obvious that he took care of it based on the oily gleam coming off of it. Duncan places the handle in the palm and closes his fingers around it. A beam of light from the moon enters through the window and hits the knife, illuminating his face in a dark blue glow. He outstretches his arm and rolls the sleeve of the plain white shirt. He takes the knife and brushes it against his arm like he was a chef sharpening a knife, just grazing the skin.

Duncan I swear I will slap the shit out of you if you even think about cutting yourself. Duncan tightens his grip on the handle and his hand shakes, making the blade tremble right over the skin. A single translucent arm hair becomes the first victim to Duncan's self-torture. The sniffling and crying begins again as Duncan squints his eyes and resumes his mantra cursing me. Duncan turns the edge of the blade towards his skin and starts to seesaw it into his flesh. Duncan grits his teeth and clenches his eyes in discomfort. I reach over him and grab his hand with both wrists...too late. Blood oozes out of him like magma leaking out of a fissure, dripping down his biceps and around his elbows where it dropped to the sheets. Duncan had not foreseen, or just didn't care that the blood would have to end up somewhere once it exited his body. He stared at the flow of blood like some sort of Rube Goldberg machine.

Duncan tosses the knife towards his nightstand; it spins in the air like dancer doing a pirouette. He sits down at his desk and pulls out the ceramic ash tray that he made as his pottery class last year, and a small pile of loose lined paper. He places his elbow over the ceramic bowl and lets the dark red plasma collect inside of the tan colored dish. Duncan never smoked so Mom got suspicious when he brought it home, if only she knew what he was actually going to use it for. It appears Duncan's cut was more precise than I had first thought, it looks like he hit something major intentionally. The bowl fills quickly, and thin layer of the liquid builds at the bottom. After several minutes nothing is dripping off him, and what was remaining was sticky and drying to the skin. Duncan shakes his arm as if he was shaking the last bit of milk out of the carton. There was already a bottle of rubbing alcohol sitting on his desk, and it's quickly splashed over his wound, cleaning it out and washing some of the blood off his skin and onto the desk.

Duncan Masters separates the top piece of paper

from the pile and places it in front of him, dipping his right index finger in the blood and scraping the excess onto the side of the ash tray. His fluid soaked hands begin writing on the paper in a handwriting that's almost identical to his regular penmanship. While I can't make out what he's jotting down, I notice that the blood looks like beet juice on his fingers but dries to a weird brown on paper. He finishes writing his macabre message and takes a second sheet of paper and lays it down next to the first. I read over his left shoulder to see the message that he wrote.

"Why didn't you talk to me about this before taking your life?" He sits for a moment for something to happen, but what? Is he expecting a response from me? Even if I didn't feel weird about using my brother's blood as ink, what would I say that would make him feel better? He's grieving for the loss of his brother in which he feels slightly responsible...there are no words. I'd regret it if I didn't try though, if for nothing else than for Duncan. I dip my finger in my brother's blood and hover it over the page, hoping the magical right words will pop in my head...they don't. The reason I didn't tell him was because I knew he would talk me out of it...and I didn't want that. I start writing the only letters thing that I can...the truth.

I respond on the blank page, being careful not to waste any of the blood, knowing that if it ran out before I finished the message that he would gladly supply more. I write small but precise, ensuring it's as legible as possible. Even though it's a short sentence, it's the only real answer

that I have for him. "Because I was a bad brother."
Duncan stares at the paper in disbelief. He didn't seem to
notice the letters popping up one by one but instead
noticed the entire message became visible as if it was
delayed ink and not his own fluids. He shakes his head
while still staring at it.

"I wish that were true Matty, I wish that were true,"
Duncan said as if disappointed by my answer. I try to write
a response to his doubt but he grabs the ashtray before I
get the chance. Duncan empties it out into the bathroom
sink, and runs water to wash the rest of it down.

Duncan goes back into bed, and I check on Mom,
who's fast asleep with empty bottles sprawled around her
bed like they were worshipping her. I float to my bed and
lay there hoping to get sleep that never comes. Light
beams through my window and the glare from my
computer monitor reflects into my face. Duncan starts
stirring moments later; even on the weekend he can't
resist the urge to get up early. Mom is fast asleep and
given how much she probably drank the night before,
she'll be pissy when she does eventually wake from her
slumber.

I follow Duncan on his jog. I'm finding it easier to
keep up with his frantic speed in death more than I did in
life. Duncan makes another stop back in the secret spots
in the woods, sitting on the stump toking on his pipe. The
longer he smokes the more trouble he has igniting the Bic
lighter, it takes ten minutes before he's determined he's

the proper amount of high. He resumes his jog but at less vigorous pace, as if he was just racing to get high. He runs until he reaches the rail road tracks, about three miles from home before turning around, as if he hit his checkpoint. He seems distressed but also very calm, maybe it's from the pot, but maybe it's from the numbness. When he finally makes it home he stops at his secret entrance, albeit for only a moment to contemplate smoking again, but ultimately decides against it and carries on back home. By the time he reaches the door the back of his white shirt was soaked with his own sweat. He takes a deep breath and goes through the door. Mom is in the kitchen pretending to be a mom, even greeting him, but Duncan ignores her. Duncan goes into the bathroom, I don't follow him.

I hear the shower start and float downstairs, Mom is cooking eggs in a basket, the only fond memory I have involving her and cooking. It's a simple enough dish: use a small glass to cut a small circular hole into a piece of bread, we use a special cup with an own on it for this purpose. Place a skillet on medium heat and throw in a tablespoon of butter...never margarine. Let the butter melt and place the bread in the pan, then here's the great part...crack an egg into the hole of the bread! After the bottom cooks a little you flip the bread and the egg at the same time, and if you do it right...the yolk won't break. After the egg cooks on the other side it's ready to serve! Here's the surprise twist ending, the piece of bread you cut out of the middle, put it back on top to conceal the egg like a hat. Duncan always liked to break the yolk with his fork, spilling the contents over the bread letting it soak in. I never liked my yolk to touch my bread so I always had Mom cook my yolks all the way through, which usually meant she burns it. When Dad was still around she used to make it for all of us Sunday mornings before church.

Duncan comes down the stairs dressed in a suit. I haven't seen Duncan in a suit since Aunt Tabitha died of a stroke on Christmas Eve a few years ago. She was supposed to show up our house that evening and never came. We all made jokes about how she ditched us to watch a Matlock marathon, or a six pack of Corona was calling her. We didn't find out until two days after Christmas, and since then we always got really nervous if someone showed up to family functions late.

"I made you breakfast Duncan," Mom said sitting the plate down on the kitchen table as she takes off her apron and drapes it over an empty chair. Duncan sits down without saying anything. He takes the circular piece of bread off the top and places the whole thing in his mouth. Duncan pokes the egg with his fork like a Roman attacking an enemy with a spear. Disappointment fills his face.

"You overcooked the eggs," Duncan said dropping his fork on the plate, refusing to eat.

"Damn it Duncan that's how you always liked them. You always liked the yolk cooked all the way through," Mom said picking up the plate, and raising her voice as she's obviously aggravated.

"That's how Matthew liked them. You do remember Matthew don't you? Or did you always just ignore him so much when he was alive that you forgot everything about him now that he's dead?" Duncan said with his still turned to her.

"How dare you? You little shit." Mom said slamming the plate towards the linoleum floor. The plate shattered like a brick going through a window, the egg stayed intact in the middle of the bread, but pieces of porcelain scattered throughout the room. "I have to bury my son today and you're worried about the goddamn eggs? Fuck, Duncan." Mom did a little hop over the large sharp chunks and went upstairs without saying anything. Duncan shakes his head and gets the broom and starts cleaning up the mess.

By the time Mom comes down the stairs dressed in a black dress, Duncan was finished cleaning up the mess. They spoke at nearly the same time. "I'm sorry Duncan, I shouldn't have lashed out at you like I did. We're both going through a really hard time and I shouldn't let it affect how I treat others...I'm sorry."

"I'm sorry too Mom. I took something out on you that I shouldn't have," Duncan finished his thought by extended his arms outward. They hugged. "You ready to get this over with?" Mom nodded. They left the house, Mom locking the door behind her and double checked the handle to ensure it was locked. It was. They got into

Mom's car and she drove, even though he offered.

"Hey Mom. Remember back when I was about eight and Matt stole some money from Dad's pants that were in the dryer?"

"Yeah, I was so pissed about that, but not nearly as pissed as your Dad was. You know how he was with money."

"I did it Mom, Matthew had nothing to do with it."

"What? Why would you let him take the blame? He even admitted that he was the one that did it," Mom said in total shock. I remember when that happened. Duncan never explained why it was important to him. I just knew he was my older brother and when he tells me to do something, it's usually in my best interest to do so. Even if that means lying to get into trouble.

"Dad always held me to such a high standard that I knew he would take it really hard."

"But why did you take it Duncan? It's not like you to do something like that."

"There was a concert I wanted to go to with Jason, you remember Jason right?"

"Oh I remember Jason Statler all right," Mom said with an obvious disapproving tone.

"And that's the exact reason I didn't want you guys to

know. Otherwise I would have to tell you who the band was, what kind of music they played and who I was going with. Answering any of the three would have led to me not going."

"Well now that I already know who you went with, what band was it?" Mom's curiosity was peaked. It may be she wanted to take her mind off of the fact she was driving to her own son's funeral, or it may be genuine interest.

"Ozzy Ozbourne, well I guess saying Ozzfest would have been more accurate, but he was back playing with Black Sabbath." Duncan is getting more excited the more he talks about it. Mom smiles.

"Oh honey," Mom says almost in a condescending tone, but now with a dopey grin. "Sabbath was the first concert I went to with your dad. I enjoyed the show, but every ten seconds Tom would lean over to me and say 'Did you see how Iommi shredded that solo?' or 'after all these years Ozzy still has it right?' I still have the ticket stub in my jewelry box, but I honestly don't know why." Mom stared blankly towards the windshield as rain drops started bombarding it.

"What, really?" Duncan says in complete disbelief, mouth agape.

"Yup. Your dad loved all that music. I was never that into it, but I always pretended to be just so I could be around him more. I still have his vinyl collection in the garage; feel free to scavenge through it."

"Dad won't mind?"

"If he cared he would have asked for them by now. I'm sure he's bought them again on the computer by now, you know how he is with his music." Mom was right. Dad never went anywhere without his music. He used to have his brown miniature briefcase full of cassettes for the car, and bought a new car just because it had a CD player already installed a few years later. "Remember the Christmas that I bought him an IPod when they first came out? I've never seen him so happy in his life. He spent that whole day putting his music on it and making different playlists."

"Yeah I remember. It was like opening that box made him a different person. What was that playlist he made for that summer that he always played in the car?" Duncan asked.

"Hot Summer Jams. I wish I could have made him as happy as that damn iPod did," Mom says as she purses her lips, holding her emotions back.

"Have you talked to him lately? It's been awhile since I've gotten an e-mail from him."

"I called after Matthew." Her sentence was cut short by a flood of tears. She lets out a soft whimper and slams a fist against the steering wheel. "The fucker never even called back. He never even let me know that he knew his son was dead. He never called me to ask me if I was okay. That whore of a girlfriend probably deleted the message." She recklessly throws her hand against the wheel again, this time with three open handed strikes. More tears follow. Duncan reaches in his pocket, pulling out a small plastic package of tissues. He holds one in front of her face while still looking forward. Duncan was always so prepared.

Mom says "Thank you," drying her eyes before wiping her nose. The rest of the car ride was silent, occasionally being interrupted by a bump in the road, or the stereo from a car with its windows down next to us at a stoplight.

Mom parks the car at the cemetery, closes her eyes and sighs, her trademark for preparing herself for doing something she doesn't want to do. We never believed in funerals inside of churches where everyone cries over the corpse. We do the burial but even then, we make it a brief event. There's no reason to drag out a depressing situation longer than you need to. Duncan gets out of the car and stretches, prompting Mom to follow suit. A preacher greets her and shakes her hand after he gives his condolences He stood well over six feet tall. His milky white complexion contrasted with his dark black hair. His frame is tall and lanky to the point where I almost think he's on stilts. He smiles and his smile seems almost sinister with missing teeth. His Adam's apple is protruding to the point where I almost think his neck may be pregnant, or an alien is about to burst out of it. He gives Duncan a nod, and he returns it.

They walk past row after row of tombstones each in a different state of decay. Some have chipped corners that lay nearby, while others are so old that the names are no longer legible, making it impossible to know whose body lies underneath the stone slab. I see something out of the corner of my eye, but when I turn my head it disappears, or I think it does. I focus intently at a grave nearby, of a 14 year old girl who died weeks ago. I stop and focus my eyes almost like I'm looking at one of those 3-D pictures, and something comes into focus. A translucent figure, skinny and frail dressed in tight and frayed jean shorts and an Aeropostel shirt. She was on her knees pounding the ground with her fist wailing like a siren. The noise pierces me like a spear through my skull. The more I listen the more I'm drawn into it. I can make out words incorporating into her shrieking. She kept saying "No" and "I'm not dead." She doesn't notice me. The name on her tombstone reads "Abby Marcus".

I look at the grass and move on, hoping not to see anything, or anyone else that disturbs me as much as that. I catch up with Duncan, Mom, and the preacher where they are standing by a large rectangular hole in the ground. It's my grave. A huge mound of dirt is next to the open grave with three shovels stuck into it like flagpoles. The headstone is already in place, I read it.

IN MEMORY OF

MATTHEW J MASTERS

1995-2010

SO IT GOES

Vonnegut. My epitaph is a quote from Vonnegut. I always loved his way with words and with life. If there was one person I would have liked to meet, it would have been Kurt Vonnegut. Who knows, we're both dead now, maybe I'll get the chance. No one knew I was a big Vonnegut fan except maybe Steven, but even then it's not like I walked around quoting him all day...strange. I peer down into the hole that will be the resting place for my body until the world blows up and my bones float endlessly into space. The sun is shining directly overhead and I can see down to the bottom of the pit. I wonder if they have some machine that makes the holes for them or if they still use a shovel. It seems like it would be hard to make such a perfect shape so far underground by hand.

Duncan offers another tissue to Mom as she touches the tombstone. She weeps onto the stone forgetting the tissue is in her hand, or not caring. She apologizes to me profusely now hugging the stone as if it were me. Duncan clenches his eyes and takes a deep breath trying to gather his composure.

People start showing up. Distant relatives I haven't seen since I was six, friends of Mom's, and teachers from school. All greet Mom and Duncan and all say they are sorry for her loss as if it's the only thing you can say to someone grieving. Dennis Greggs, a friend of Dad's shows up and talks to Duncan for a few minutes, not bringing up anything that's happened. Dennis always liked Duncan, even though he stopped coming around after Dad left. Duncan didn't bother asking him if he knew how Dad was doing.

I see three heads bobbing towards us in the distance, and I instantly recognize all three: Steven, with a black guitar case, Dez with her hair freshly dyed black with purple highlights and Violet, who was already crying judging from the makeup smears under her eyes. Violet was squeezing Dez's hand so hard that it was turning red. She was wearing make-up which is rare, but it was already running down her pale face. They walked up to Mom at the same time, who was now staring at the headstone but more composed than before.

Steven spoke first. "Miss Masters, I know we didn't always see eye to eye on things, but I'm really sorry for what happened. No one wanted to see that happen to Matthew, no one. If it's okay with you, I wrote a song for Matthew that I'd like to play during the funeral if that's okay with you."

"That would be nice Steven. I'm sorry I treated you so badly. You're not a bad kid, I was just worried my son was going to get caught up with the wrong crowd. Thank you for everything you've done for him."

"You're welcome Miss Masters. If there's anything I can do, please let me know."

"Hey Steven."

"Yes Miss Masters?"

"Did Matthew...you know, tell anyone he was going to do this?"

"No way. No one knew a thing. We all knew he was upset and embarrassed over the note thing, but we thought it would blow over and be fine. No one saw this coming. I would have called you, or hell even the cops if I knew something like that was going to happen. I don't think there's anything anyone could have done."

"Thanks Steven," Mom says as he walks away with his hand around his guitar strap.

Dez and Violet go up together as if they were Siamese twins locked at the hands. Violet speaks first.

"Miss Masters. We don't know each other but, I'm Violet. I'm so sorry for all of this. I feel like this is all my fault." Violet eyes release more tears with every word. "I know I don't deserve it, but I need you to forgive me. I need you to forgive me for not helping him. I just feel like I could have done something, you know?" Violet breaks down completely. She drops to her knees and sobs into her hands. Dez takes a step back as Mom kneels down in front of her and wraps her arms around her, placing one arm around her shoulders and the other in such a way that her hand is on top of her head.

"Shh. It's okay Violet. This isn't your fault. It isn't anyone's fault. Matthew did what he did and we all have to suffer through it, but it's no one's fault." A brief wind gushes by and Mom's hair meshes with Violets, hiding both of their faces and their tears. Mom struggles to whimper out "I forgive you Violet." Mom leans her head back and looks her in her beautiful eyes, "I forgive you Violet." Violet immediately reacts by embracing her again with their heads side-by-side.

Violet in a half squeak, half whisper says, "Thank you." Mom kisses Violet on the forehead, Violet stands up, and Mom nods to Duncan to give her a tissue which she gladly accepts, wiping away both her tears and those of Moms. I notice some of Violet's make-up smeared onto Mom's cheek. Dez gives Mom a nod and she returns it, Violet quickly finding Dez's hand again, keeping her other hand free to clear away any tears. The preacher taps Duncan on the shoulder and Duncan walks away.

The preacher tries to gather everyone's attention so that the funeral could begin. We stand in silence for several minutes until six men came into view, each holding a handle of a light brown colored box, my coffin. I only recognize two of the men, my brother Duncan, and my best friend Steven; with his guitar still slung behind his back. A second group of men who I assume work here are setting up small metal tubes around the grave and attaching flat green ropes between the tubes, creating a checkerboard pattern. The casket is lowered between the metal pipes and onto the green ropes, suspending it in air. A small motorized crank is attached and my body is lowered into the ground. The green straps are retracted and the pipes are taken away.

The preacher starts talking like it's a speech he's performed thousands of times. There's no emotion in his speech yet most of the people have tears in their eyes. One of Mom's guests brought a baby, which its cries are the only sound other than the preacher's eulogy, and besides the occasional sniff of the nose. The preacher finishes his speech which gets a small solemn applause. Mom shakes his hand and thanks him. He then opens up for anyone to share a story or something they would like to say. Mom steps up next to the preacher.

"No mother should ever have to bury their child, especially like this. Matthew was a good kid. Even during pregnancy he never kicked when I was sleeping. When he was a baby he would never cry just to cry, only when he needed something that he knew I could give him. He loved to explore, make people happy, and always wanted to learn more about the world. It's a shame that he didn't get the opportunity to learn more, and see all the things he wanted to see. We will never get to see what he will become as an adult. We will never know who he could have helped, who he would marry, or what his kids would look like. All that we know is that he's gone, and he's not coming back, and I'd give anything to be near him right now." A tremble in Mom's voice grows with each word she says until she barely makes out the last sentence. She couldn't have said more even if she wanted to.

Steven begins to unzip his guitar case, taking out his guitar. I don't know much about guitars but I can tell it's new and it's a really nice acoustic. Steven steps next to the preacher and starts to talk.

"I'm not very good with talking about my emotions, and this whole ordeal has put me through a lot of emotions that I haven't been through before. I've never lost anyone this close to me before, and it hurts. I knew Matty was hurting, but he should have told someone, he should have just talked to me about it. Damn it Matt, why couldn't you have told someone what you were going to do so we could have stopped you? I didn't know how else to properly convey my emotions, I've never been a speechwriter, or even nearly as good of a writer as Matt was. Instead of that, I wrote a song that I hope will mean something to someone, and I hope Matt can hear it wherever he is."

Steven started the song using a familiar chord progression that he's been working on. When he belts out the first lyric about me, everyone starts to tear up. As the song hits the chorus I find out the name of the song is "Miss You Matty" as it's repeated several times. As the song progresses his voice fills with sorrow and he struggles to make it through without crying. As the last chord of the song rings through the air, Steven hangs his head and says, "I'll miss you Matty" and places his guitar back into his case. He steps back into the crowd, a few people around him giving him a pat on the shoulder, telling him he did a good job.

A few distant relatives say a few words about me, none of which I really take to heart. If they hadn't bothered to talk to me, or even see me in the last five years I doubt they really care that much. The preacher makes a last call for anyone to say their last words. There's a shuffling in the crowd, someone from the back who's making their way forward. It takes me a moment to recognize the person who's standing in front of me. At first I don't believe it, but the scowl that Mom puts on her face lets me know that it's real. It's my Dad.

Chapter 14

Dad looks mostly unchanged but he cut his hair shorter than usual and has gained a little weight. Five years ago, the last time I saw him, he was in pretty good shape and had shoulder length hair. I guess his new girlfriend didn't like him that way. He can feel every eye on him, even the wind stops to acknowledge his presence.

"I don't really know what to say. I just heard yesterday that I lost my son. It's a phone call no one wants to get. It's something that I haven't even had time to process, but here I am, looking at my son's coffin. There's nothing that can be said that will bring him back, or I would have already said it. Son, I miss you, and I love you, and I wish there would have been something I could have done. Thank you," Dad said as he walks away from the pit and stands next to Mom who gives him a look of death. He looks at her and quickly sees her displeasure that he even exists.

The preacher says some parting words and gives the signal for those who brought flowers to throw them on the casket already sunken in the hole. Single flowers get tossed into the air to fall deep into the ground landing on different parts of the wooden box. Men begin grabbing the shovels and tossing dirt in the hole with a distinctive thud when it lands. Some of them were crying as they were doing so, tears mixing with the soil before it was flung onto me. The grave filled quickly.

I sink beneath the dirt and enter my casket. I need to see my body one last time. It's pitch dark, almost as dark as the afterlife/dream world is. I use my hands to feel around, I touch my face. My nose is cold and stiff, and my ears rigid and damp. I feel the skull where the bullet entered my skull; they covered the entry point well but I can still tell there's a soft spot. This used to be my body. My soul used to belong in that body. That's the body that Mom gave birth to. That's the body that played Transformers with Duncan. That's the body that loved Violet. That's the body that killed itself. Even though I know that's still me, it feels like we're separate entities now. It's almost as if I'm a parasite looking for a new host after discarding the old used up one.

I float above ground, and for a second I feel like everyone is staring at me. Once I realize this is absurd it hits me that they are having a moment of silence and all looking downward. I see several people whose eyes are wide open, and others whose eyes are closed as if they fell asleep while standing. After the silence is over they all tilt their heads back up as if they were a squadron of robots being turned on at once. The crowd starts to disperse and spreads out. The ones that felt more obligated to come than anything left without saying anything to Mom or

Duncan.

Dad treated this as more of a social event than anything, shaking hands and laughing with old friends. I could feel Mom's anger rising as she witnessed this take place. They rarely talked, and when they did it always turned into an argument. I have a strange feeling this won't be any different. Mom stomps towards him with tears and vengeance in her eyes.

"Can I talk to you?" Mom said less in a asking way, and more of a telling one.

"Yeah give me a minute babe," he responds, still with his back facing her.

Mom spoke in that harsh yet low voice that let you know that she was losing her shit, but didn't want the whole world to know. "I am NOT your babe. Your babe is some cum guzzling slut with a meth addiction that I wouldn't let my children around for a goddamn second." This caught his attention. People started backing up far enough to act like they weren't paying attention, but not so far that they couldn't hear every word.

"You have no right to say things those things to me or my girlfriend, not today, not at my son's funeral."

"He stopped being your son when you walked out on us."

"I wouldn't have left if I didn't have to share a bed

with such an intolerable bitch." She slapped him, and I don't blame her. She turned away and for a moment he followed her, and then just let her walk away. Dad softly shakes his head while it hangs downward, followed by a deep sigh. His friends step closer to console him, but he bats off their attempts with his hand. I want to hug him, but I also want to slap the shit out of him harder than Mom did.

"I think it's better if you leave Dad," Duncan says giving him the look a parent gives their child when they mean business. "Nothing personal and it's great to see you, but not like this." Dad hesitantly agrees kicking every bouquet of flowers that crosses his path.

I trail behind Mom who is already sitting in the car, both hands gripping the top of the steering wheel and head planted firmly where the airbag would deploy. Her head drops back and lets out a long primal scream as she begins to beat the steering wheel with both hands. Her hands begin to turn red and skin begins to tear, but she continues the onslaught. If Duncan hadn't opened the passenger door she may have turned her hands into bloody stumps before quitting. She looks surprised to see him, but also surprised that she forgot to lock the doors.

"He's such a fucking asshole!" Mom said resuming her position she was prior to the beating.

"I know he is Mom. He just doesn't understand, and he never will. I know it's not the same as bringing

Matthew back, but you'll always have me." Duncan puts his arms around her and she gladly accepts them. She sobs on to his shoulder until every last emotion pours out of her. Dried tears cover her face and she looks drained. She places a hand on each of his shoulders and thanks him, and follows it up with another hug.

"You ready to go?" Mom said, half crying.

"I don't think I'll ever be ready to leave Matt behind forever, but I guess we better." Mom starts the car and drives off. The further they drive away, the longer between words spoken between them. If only they knew I was still sitting in the back seat, where I always sat when Duncan called shotgun. They don't speak until Mom parks the car down the old rocky driveway.

"We're going to be okay Duncan, right?" Mom always asked questions just for reassurance.

"Of course we are, this is just another beginning for our family. First we lost Dad, now we lost Matthew, but we always have each other Mom."

"I guess you're right Duncan." Mom steps out of the car and walks into the house without looking back to see if Duncan was behind her. She rummages through a cabinet and pulls out a bottle of liquor. The wake would be later on that afternoon and she didn't want to be sober for it.

I better go see what everyone else is doing. I think about the graveyard and it appears in front of me. Most of the people have dispersed, but I see a black guitar case sticking out of a group of people. I head over to see Steven who was shaking people's hands and telling him what a wonderful job he did. He took the praise graciously but he was grinning more than I had ever seen him. No one other than me had ever really commented on his guitar playing. Steven doesn't get a lot of compliments. Steven looks at his watch and tells the group that he has to go.

Steven starts walking down the road in solemn silence. Cars pass by him but his head never deters from being pointed to the ground. The cemetery wasn't that far from town, his mom must be picking him up somewhere. He starts whistling the tune from Kill Bill that Daryl Hannah used. I heard that she was really weird and lived in a teepee for a year one time. I didn't even know they still made teepees, but I guess if you're Daryl Hannah you could get one.

Steven crosses the street to go into the gas station which is commonly referred to as "The Shit N Go" based on their C health food rating and burritos that have you doubled over in stomach pain in no time. I never really went there after they took out the arcade machines. I remember Mom honking the horn after getting gas because Duncan and I went extra rounds in a heated Mortal Kombat 2 battle which ended with him hurling an ice ball at me, and exploding my character's body into a scattering of ice shards and internal organs. Duncan never played video games after a certain point, and he was never that great at them, but for whatever reason in Mortal Kombat 2 he was king.

Steven goes to the cooler in the back, passing isles of overpriced cereal, emergency car supplies, and baby food. Steven opens the door to the refrigerated drinks and a cloud of icy air blasts him in the face. He stands there an extra second or two, as if the chilly draft had paralyzed his body. I knew before he reaches for it, that he was going to grab a Vanilla Coke, the only thing I ever see him drink besides water. He stands in front of the glass case at the counter looking at corn dogs, burritos, and pizza pockets that may have been sitting under the lamp for days. He makes the right decision by paying for the drink and not requesting anything out of the glass box of doom. Steven puts the change in his pocket and tells the cashier to keep the receipt.

Steven pushes the door open with one hand as he holds his soda with the other. As soon as he steps outside he opens it and takes a long swig. Mid-drink two figures that were hiding to the sides of the door come into view and shove Steven to the ground face first, catching him off-balance. His soda spirals out of his hand sprays on a hood of a blue Corvette parked in the handicapped parking spot. His guitar swings around and clips his own head before falling aimlessly on the sidewalk. The instrument lands string side down making a dramatic clung as if it knew what had just happened. I recognize the figures as being Seth and Xavier. Seth puts his enormous sneaker between Steven's shoulder blades and presses down hard as he tries to get up. Steven's nose grinds against the pavement. Layers of skin lay engraved on the ground as his arms flail outward.

"Hey you little fuck, not so tough now are ya?" Xavier said bringing his head to Stevens's level. Steven tried to spit on his face, but he narrowly missed, and the saliva hit a nearby wad of dried gum instead. He gets up to his knees just to be shoved back down by Seth's sneaker. Seth removes his foot and leaps onto his back, putting his entire body weight on top of him. He sinks a gigantic hairy arm around his neck like a furry anaconda. Steven tries to slide his fingers between his own chin and Seth's arm, but to no avail. Steven has to know that Seth was trying to choke him out, but luckily his form is awful. "I'm gonna choke you out and smash your fucking skull in." The way Xavier was cackling leads me to believe he wasn't joking.

Steven springs his arms back like an action figure and grabs Seth by the ears and starts pulling them forward. Seth lets out a yelp with enough pain in it to let Steven know he caught Seth off guard. Steven slips his head under Seth's arm and quickly rolls from under his weight before he realizes the escape has taken place. Now standing Steven delivers a kick to the stomach of Seth so hard that I hear two bones of his ribcage slide against each other like tectonic plates. Xavier blindsides Steven with a right hand to the back of his head. Seth, still whimpering in pain, holds his chest in agony from Steven's kick. Steven stumbles forward, tripping over Seth's body but regains his balance after a few stutter steps. Xavier and Steven square off, waiting for the other to make a first move. Steven fakes a left jab to see his reaction, and then follows it up right hook to his chin, Xavier's legs buckle like they were momentarily made of taffy.

Steven takes advantage of Xavier's weakened state and dives for his legs, lifting both of them into the air, and driving Xavier's torso into the ground. His nose is quickly met with Steven's elbow. He quickly swipes another one across his face; blood begins pouring out of Xavier's nose. Xavier scoots back so the white cement wall of the gas station allows him to sit up. Steven cups Xavier's neck, holding his head steady for the incoming strike which ends with a cringe-worthy thud of Xavier's head against the brick wall. His eyes show the pain that he's going through. He opens his mouth in agony and blood drips down his throat.

Seth who has now regained his composure, grabs Steven's shirt collar from behind and pulls it back, choking him with it. Steven stands up to alleviate the pressure, and in one move slips out of his shirt revealing his tan body. Seth looks stunned as if a magic trick was just performed in front of his eyes, still holding the shirt in his hands. Steven doesn't hesitate to punch Seth in the face in his state of amazement. Seth responds by pushing his

foot into Steven's stomach, sending him back into the
glass door, making it rattle and ringing the entrance bell.
Steven rebounds quickly and lunges at Seth with another
fist, but he is ready for it as he dodges the blow. Xavier
grabs the guitar case and rams the fat end into the side of
Steven's head, buckling his knees. Seth follows up with an
overhand right to the dead center of his forehead.
Steven's eyes roll in the back of his head and falls
backwards. His head bounces off the pavement with the
unmistakable sound of bone breaking. A pool of blood
begins to form from under Steven's skull. He doesn't
move.

The gas station door opens and the cashier comes out
screaming. He feels the need to wig out on Xavier and
Seth before checking to see if Steven is okay. I'm not so
sure that he is. He's still unconscious with his eyes closed,
the blood is spreading out like spilt water on a coffee
table. He tries to wake him as Xavier and Seth scatter off
in different directions. I follow Seth, I can't let him get
away with this. Not today, not on the day they bury my
body. Steven will either be okay, or he won't be, there's
nothing I can do about that. I catch his shadow turning
onto Brook Street. I find him two blocks later with his
hands on his hips trying to catch his breath. Fat piece of
shit can't run five blocks without stopping. He resumes at
a slower pace.

He takes a left on Elm, then a right on Dense where he
fidgets in his pocket for his keys. The house if you want to

call it that has seen better days with three different colors of panels, one window slathered in duct tape, and the other with a blanket covering it. If houses were alive this one would be on life support. I float through the door before Seth opens the door. Unfortunately for Seth this place looks worse on the inside than it does on the inside. Empty pizza boxes and plates with unrecognizable food clung to them litter the living room. As Seth enters he sees a mouse scurry off a plate and into the kitchen, taking a corner of a pizza crust with him. His dad is sleeping on an old orange couch that has pieces of fabric missing and dark dried stains from decades ago. The TV must have been a freebie of someone who bought a HDTV, it was old, worn out and probably weighs a thousand pounds.

His dad shifts around on the couch upon Seth entering, still half asleep. He flips over and he has a black unkempt beard with hairs sprouting out randomly, as if trying to escape the rest of his face from impending doom. His plain white shirt has blotches of faded yellow from absorbed sweat, and is rolled up above his stomach which pours over the couch. His bloodshot eyes open as he grabs a beer that's sitting on the floor and takes a drink.

"Where the fuck have you been?" Seth's father asked after belching from his drink.

"Out with Xavier, just foolin' around," Seth said avoiding eye contact and trying to creep towards the hallway.

"I told you to stop hanging around that faggot. He's just waiting for the chance to turn you gay. Some cum guzzler trying to turn my own son gay." Seth's father takes a swig of his warm beer. "Guys like that should be shot."

"Dad, Xavier is not gay," Seth said giving his dad a disappointed look. "And even if he was, so what? What does it matter if he was?"

"What does it matter? Son, has he already turned you into a fairy? If he made you suck his cock you tell me right fucking now and I'll put you both out of your misery," Seth's dad said, now furious. His large hands crush the beer can, spilling amber liquid onto the already stained carpet. He hurls the can towards Seth's head, he dodges and it lands in the kitchen with a clang, followed by the squealing of a mouse nearly hit. "What does it fucking matter? I can't believe you. If you weren't my son I'd assume that you were the fag trying to convert him from being normal."

"You're right dad, he's prolly a fag," Seth said as he walks down the hallway away from his dad's abuse.

I follow Seth into his room, I would have known it was his without seeing him close the door behind him by the Jay-Z poster and the hole that was presumably kicked into it. Slightly crooked posters of movies like Scarface, Boys in the Hood, and Goodfellas are slathered around the room. Magazine clippings of rappers fills the gaps between movie posters with small black pinholes where previous rappers once stood. XXL magazines are stacked next to his bed, along with various empty soda bottles. A small TV sits in the corner with a DVD player built into it. Seth takes off his shoes, throwing them at the door and turns on the TV. Seth watches some movie about gang members that I don't recognize, and has this kid killing a guy with a potato at the end of his gun acting as a silencer.

It doesn't take long before Seth's dad knocks on the wall followed by yelling for him to turn it down. Seth responded by turning up the volume during a shootout between rival gangs. The clinking of shells off the ground inspires more yelling from his dad, but Seth ignores it. Seth eventually gives up, turns off the TV and just lays down listening to music. I don't know what song it was, but I know I heard Ludacris on it. His door swung open, his dad stood in the frame.

"I've told you a million times to shut off that coon music," Seth's dad said, breathing heavy.

"Dad, stop it, you know that's racist, and you know I hate it," Seth said looking at his dad in shame.

"I'm sorry but that's what it is, nothing but mud people trying to think it's okay to get normal kids to be acting like them."

"How can you just forget that Mom is black? How can you forget that I'm half black? Do you even understand that?"

"You're right, your mom is black," Seth's dad says downing half of his beer that he got before storming in the room. "But look what she did to you. That tar bitch left us both Seth. That's what they do best, they run."

"She left because you fucking hit her," Seth said, standing close enough to him to smell the cheap beer on his breath.

"Don't you get in my face boy, or I'll hit you so hard it'll knock the nigger right out of you," Seth dad said smiling the way only bad guys do in movies. Seth's lips start pouting and tears start welling up in his eyes. Seth half shoves him out of his room and slams the door hard enough to make a pile of CD's stacked on his table to fall over. He turned the music off, lays flat on his bed, and tears come down the sides of his face. He slams his hand down against the bed, and pulls his pillow up near his face and screams into it. I actually feel sorry for him, I still hate him for everything he did to me, but I feel sorry for him. Maybe it's not his fault he's such an asshole. I don't think he had much of a chance not to be, given his dad is the one raising him.

I better go check on Steven and make sure he's okay. I close my eyes hearing only the whimpers of Seth and the occasional snorting of snot. I wish myself to Steven's house and open my eyes.

Chapter 15

Steven rarely invited me over to his place. He lives in an apartment less than a mile from the school. It's a really nice place, but he still feels embarrassed about living in an apartment, and I guess I can see where he's coming from. I remember vaguely living in an apartment before we moved into our house when I was little. I love Steven's place, but I've also really liked the idea of living in a little block of people who all friendly with each other. I'm sure that never really happens, and there may be one of the people you even know, let alone talk to. Steven said the people down the hall were Indian and every Sunday would cook, making the whole building smell like curry powder. I'm in his living room on the first floor of his complex. The living room was quiet but I can hear light screaming coming from the back hallway.

"Ow quit it, that burns!" It was Steven's voice for sure. I follow the voices into the bathroom in the hallway. Steven was sitting on the toilet lid with his shirt off, and his mom had a cotton ball in one hand, and a bottle of rubbing alcohol in the other. I don't envy Steven right now for a few reasons. His jeans are tattered, his shirt laying on the floor has a three inch slice across the shoulder, and another one in the back. Cuts like red worms laid across his face in random patterns. I can assume that whatever was under the cotton ball was the worst of the damage. I was right. A deep gash above his eyebrow came into view; the cotton ball was a weird mix of blood and dirt. She threw it in a small trash can where it was greeted by a dozen or more bloody orbs. She tilts the bottle against a fresh ball from the bag lying on the sink like miniature clouds.

Steven winces as a fresh dose of alcohol is pressed onto his face. Steven clenches his fist and bangs it against his leg three times to cover the pain.

"You need to stop getting in these fights Steven," Mom said, pressing hard against his head.

"I'm not looking for them Mom, Seth just has something against me."

"You know how hard his family life is. It's hard to blame him."

"Uh, no it's not. I wasn't feeling sorry for him when he was trying to stomp my freaking head in."

"He used to be your friend Steven."

"Yeah, he used to be, until he the incident, and he started trying to beat everyone up. I didn't stick up for Matthew because I like Matthew, I stuck up for him because it wasn't right what he was doing. I couldn't take it anymore, you know?"

"Yeah, I know what you mean, Wobbly Bear," Steven's Mom said scuffing up his hair. Wobbly Bear? Is that seriously his nick name? I crack a smile only because I think if I laughed they may be able to hear me. That explains why his mom always called him "WB" around me and never knew what it meant. Every time she said it around me he gave her the "Mom, knock it off" look, and I wasn't going to push it. His mom throws the cotton ball away and takes a step back, admiring her handiwork.

"I think it's as good as it's going to get, just avoid Dad until it heals more up. You know he would freak if he finds out." This was true. Steven's Mom was the "cool mom" that everyone loved, but his dad was the overprotective parent that asks a million questions, and blows things out of proportions. If Steven's Dad found out about the fight, he'd want the FBI involved. "If the gash on your head heals up, I can just tell him it was a skateboarding accident. But he may try to sue the skateboard for making cement so hard." She laughed at her own joke. They were good parents and they worked well together. She's a funny but eccentric redhead who loves her son more than anything, and his dad is overly serious but cares about Steven more than his watch collection, which is saying something. Steven's dad has over 30 watches, one for every possibly occasion that he cherishes more than almost anything. He's bald and wears coke bottle glasses; if he was short he'd look like a moleman.

Steven goes to his room, turns off the light and turns

on his Xbox. I can hear him grinding his teeth as he boots up the game and muttering something to himself. He grips the controller as if he's trying to snap it in two as he waits for his first match to start. He places his headset on almost like a mission control operator at NASA and I can tell by the look in his eyes that he's not in the mood to mess around. He's in a free-for-all match where it's every man for himself. He starts in an urban type environment with his back against a brick wall and carrying a shotgun. He sees someone barreling towards him. He meets him with a shotgun blast to the head at near point blank range, first kill for Steven. He runs into a building across the street with boarded up windows; he checks the corners making sure no one is hiding out. He sets a landmine at the entrance to cover his tracks. He heads upstairs and breaks one of the windows open to have a look around, he doesn't see anything. He hears gunshots not too far off, and he heads back downstairs behind a counter, a safe distance from the land mine. He hears footsteps coming near him, he sees an enemy soldier come onto his screen. Steven snickers right as he steps on the explosive device, "boom" Steven says out loud. The explosion not only kills the assailant but blows away the boards and glass from the windows.

Another player nearby notices the explosion and goes cautiously goes in to investigate. The player tosses a grenade into the building, but it ricochets off the counter he's still hiding behind. It explodes, kicking up dust on his TV as he enters the building. He crouches in and checks his corners just as Steven had done. Steven has his gun pointed between the counter and the stairs, waiting for the character to come into view to press the trigger. Steven's grin gets wider as the enemy walks past him without noticing him. He creeps behind the character as he's ascending the stairs, pulls out a knife and slams it into his back. It's an instant kill. Steven flees the abandoned house and runs into the streets. He gets seven more kills before anyone even gets a shot off. He racks up five more after that before someone actually gets a kill on him.

I teleport my way to Violet's house and make my way to her room. Before I enter I can already hear the giggling that's unmistakable as teenage girls. I phase through the door and smile, Violet and Dez are on the floor with the Ouija board between them. Both of them had their hand on the cursor.

"I swear I was talking to him," Violet said with her hand across her heart. "I swear Dez."

"Uh-huh, then why have we spent the last fifteen minutes staring at a piece of wood touching hands?" Dez said giving Violet a suspicious eye. She told Dez. I'm not sure if I should be happy about this, or really hurt.

"I told you I didn't know exactly how it works, I just know that it worked last time. I've used the dumb thing dozens of times, but last night was the first time it actually worked."

"Well if the devil doesn't get in contact with us soon, I'm watching Criminal Minds."

"You and that damn show, I never understood it, it's the same damn thing every episode."

"Yeah, but if it's amazing every episode, why would you change anything?"

Violet sighs, and rolls her eyes and throws the pillow she was sitting on at her, she dodges. "As much as I'd hate to miss the opening scene of the dumb show, we should try again."

"Okay, okay, let's do it. But I'm serious; the TV is going on in five minutes unless something happens pronto."

"Okay, I guess I'll ask again. Matthew are you here?"

I don't know if I want to respond. I feel betrayed that she told someone else something so special to me, but also it means she didn't think she was crazy and that maybe I mean something to her. A long pause happens as I hover over the game. I put my hands on the cursor and try to move it, but it's harder with two hands than it was with just Violet's delicate touch.

"This is bullshit, come on Violet, this is dumb," Dez says, taking her hand off. Violet takes her hand off as well and places it on Dez's shoulder. I start moving the cursor as no one is touching it just for dramatic effects. I spell out the words "IM HERE".

Dez looks at the board in shock and terror as if she was waiting for a monster to suddenly pop out and decapitate her. She gives Violet a suspicious glare as if it's a prank. She smiled in a way that said, "I told you it was true." Dez is still speechless, Violet asks the next question, "How are you Matt?"

How am I? Oh jeez Violet lemme see, I just went to my own funeral today and that was really uplifting until my Dad crashed it, then my best friend got beat up by the school bully who I later felt bad for. In other words, I'm great. I respond with a factual statement since I don't think sarcasm will translate very well through Ouija board. IM STILL DEAD. She laughs, I guess sarcasm does translate from beyond the grave.

"Were you there today, at the funeral? At least I don't have to think about the answer to this one. YES.

"What's it like seeing your own funeral?"

ITS SAD THAT MY FAMILY CAN ONLY COME TOGETHER ONCE IM DEAD.

"Yeah I guess that would be really disturbing, but all families are fucked up in their own little way. Even hers," Violet says, pointing, to Dez. I already knew something about her home life wasn't great, but I didn't know what.

"Hey, that's none of his business," Dez said, crossing

her arms and giving Violet a stern look. "So what do you want Matthew?"

TO KILL YOU

"What? Oh my God Violet what the fuck did you just do?"

JUST KIDDING I DONT KNOW WHAT IM DOING

"So there's not some great plan you have to follow to make it into heaven?"

NOT UNLESS I MISSED ORIENTATION

"What's it like...you know to be dead?"

IT ITCHES. I'm having a hard time giving Dez straight answers, but regardless it's cracking Violet up.

"So seriously, why are you back on earth and not in heaven?"

I THINK I HAVE A JOB TO DO

"What do you think the job is."

I WISH I KNEW

"Must be hard to do a job when you don't know what it is."

YES IT IS

"So why are you here, following us?"

TO SEE IF SHE LIKES ME. I move the cursor so that the pointy end is directed towards Violet.

"So, does she?" Dez says with a sly grin.

I DONT KNOW ASK HER

I know that is really putting her on the spot, but I don't care. There's something about being dead that makes you not care about consequences, since I've already paid the biggest one. Dez and I both look at her, waiting for an answer.

"To tell you the truth, I've always liked you Matthew, as a friend," This wasn't exactly what I wanted to hear. The woman I love never thought anymore of me than just a nice guy to be friends with. "But last night changed everything. I never really got to know you, and I wish that I had Matthew, you are really someone special. I'm glad I'm getting to know you now, but I'm sad that it's too late you know?"

YES I KNOW WHAT YOU MEAN

"The funeral was really nice Matthew, it was touching," Violet said putting her hand over her heart in sincerity.

IT WAS GREAT UNTIL DAD SHOWED UP

"I figured by the way everyone acted around him that he wasn't well liked."

HE WASNT AROUND TO BE HATED

"I'm sorry, but I also know how you feel. I'm sure you've noticed it's just me and my dad here."

I NOTICED

"Is there anything you want to ask me? I hate being the one to ask all the questions."

WHY DO YOU CUT YOURSELF

Dez cuts a look to Violet, and Violet looks hurt. "Violet, you told me you quit, you told me you fucking quit! How long have you been doing it?"

"I don't want to talk about it," Violet said, avoiding eye contact with Dez.

"I don't give a shit if you want to talk about it or not, you promised me, remember?"

"I remember."

"Do you? The ghost in the room seems to think you're still doing it."

"Because I am Dez, I've been going through a lot recently. I've only done it a few times."

"Are you going to stop?" Dez asks as she gets in her face. There's a long period of silence. "Are you?"

"Yes."

"When?"

"When I have a reason to."

"Well I'm sorry I'm not a good enough reason to do so. You and Casper here can go fuck yourselves." Dez stomps out of the room, and a moment later the sound of the front door slamming follows.

"I wish I could hold you right now, at least for a moment you know? It seems like you're the only one that really gets me you know? It's weird to say, but the person who's already left this world is the one person I'm not worried about leaving me."

I wrap my arms around her and phase in. I can tell by the look in her eyes that she can feel the warmth of my limbs around her. "Is that you?" Violet asks. I whisper in her ear to tell her it is. Her eyes widen even more as if this was the moment that it actually hit her. "I thought being touched by a ghost would be cold, like they always say, but I'm glad it's not." She lowers her head on my shoulder, and she starts to cry. Her tears drip through me and soak into her shirt. I can feel the vibrations of her body trembling, and I honestly don't know what to do. I feel like there should be something I can say to her to make it all okay. There's not.

She breaks the embrace and gives me a nod to follow her...to her bed. She lies down under the covers and rolls onto her side, facing the wall. She reassures me and tells me its okay as if she knew I was apprehensive. I lie down next to her, and wrap my arm around her shoulder, dangling it over her neck. "I know it's not the same, and that I can just barely feel you, but it's just nice knowing you're here." I squeeze her a little tighter so that she can feel it, and after a moment or two, I can hear the unmistakable sound of a woman snoring. I would love to lie here forever, but I feel I'd fall asleep as well and I am in no hurry to meet the weird psychedelic orb thing again. I'll go check on Mom and Duncan.

Chapter 16

I teleport back home, and the atmosphere was drastically different from the last time I was there. For one there were people, tons of them, but also it was festive. Balloons scattered around the room bumping into each other haphazardly like bumper cars. Bottles of water and cans of soda laid over every available inch of counter space that didn't already have a paper plate with snacks on top of it. A few of the adults had bottles of beer; Mom of course was included in these people. There were two main groups of people that immediately formed cliques in two separate areas. The people who were friends of Mom's were over by the couches where she had been drunk, yelling at Duncan a few nights prior. The other group was gathered around the kitchen/dining room table, these were mostly people that I knew personally or family; Duncan was with this group. A few family friends, school mates, and even teachers were sitting around talking. The longer I sit in with them I realize they're swapping stories...about me.

"Did I ever tell you the story about the time I tricked Matthew into the dryer?" Duncan said with a Western Family Lime soda in his hand and eyes glazed over from the pot. "I told him there was money in the dryer, he must have only been five at the time. He crawled in and I shut the door behind him. I didn't know how to work the thing so I just put it on the spin cycle and pressed the start button. With every loud thud came a muffled voice begging to be let out. I tried to pull the door open but I was laughing so hard that I couldn't compose myself to do so. When I finally got it open he looked as dazed like a boxer after being knocked out. I asked him if he found the money, when he shook his head I closed the door again and told him to look harder and then pulled the dryer door back open." That last part got big laughs.

Duncan was always really good to me, but when we were younger he got a certain glee out of tricking me. Usually this didn't involve me tumbling inside a major appliance, but sometimes it did. It was almost like I was became an adult when he decided I was too old to pick on, or maybe it was that Duncan was the one who was growing up, either way I'm glad it stopped. Duncan has grown up a lot since Dad left, maybe he felt like he had to be the man of the house once he vanished. He takes better care of Mom than Dad ever did that's for sure.

Mr. Spalding, my former Creative Writing teacher migrated over from the couches to the dining room table. He was dressed in blue jeans, a black shirt, and a beer in his hand, and by the way he was walking I assumed it wasn't his first. He flops down into an empty chair next to Kevin Tape, one of Duncan's friends. Mr. Spalding takes over the conversation saying what a good kid I was and what kind of future I had as a writer, but slowly drifted into stories about his college days. It doesn't surprise me that he a lot of crazy stories to tell, he was fairly young and even though he was well composed in class, could tell when he cut loose, he cut hard. As soon as his stories wandered into telling people about the book he was writing there was a knock on the door. I wonder who the late arrival is? Everyone else seems to be curious as well, judging from the amount of eyes fixated on the door. Even though I could go through the door and see who's on the other side, I liked joining in the suspense with everyone else. Mr. Spalding hobbled over to the door and twisted the knob.

It was Steven. The gash on his head was covered with a comically large band-aid, and a circle surrounded his left eye the color of a blue moon. The parts of his body that weren't covered in an AC/DC shirt, were covered with scrapes and cuts. He held a hand in the air as a general greeting to everyone around, and his arm reached right into an ice chest, pulling out a lime soda. Duncan approaches Steven before anyone else feels obligated to.

"What happened to you?" Duncan asked, giving an inquisitive look.

"Another day another fight my friend," Steven said, drinking most of the can with one drink.

"I'd hate to see what he looked like!"

Steven chugs the rest of the soda, throws it into the trash from ten feet away and responds, "They. You would hate to see what *they* looked like." Duncan remained silent. "It is what it is I guess, some people just can't let shit go."

"Hey do you want to take a walk and take the edge off?" Duncan makes the universal sign language of smoke a joint by pressing his finger against his thumb and putting it against his lips, inhaling slightly. Steven thinks about it, almost as if morally indecisive.

"Fuck it, why not?"

They left, and I followed them. As expected they went up the road and into the break in the woods. Duncan was slightly nervous, I bet it's the only time he has taken anyone else up there. He reaches into the stump, pulling out his stash and a lighter. He puts a joint between his lips and lights it, smoke flowing out of his mouth. Duncan passes it to Steven and he examines it for a moment before taking a drag off it. Steven hands the joint back to Duncan, then quickly bends over coughing, smoke pours out of his mouth like opening the oven after Mom was cooking. Duncan takes another hit and Steven finishes his coughing fit by spitting in the bushes.

"You alright?"

"Yeah, I think so. Sorry for being such a noob at this."

"No problem, everyone has to start somewhere right?

Just don't take such big hits, that'll get you every time."

"Thanks for the tip. I never would have took you for a druggie."

"I'm not, not really I guess. I just need to take the edge of every once in a while you know? Unfortunately the stress has been stacking up recently," Duncan says taking another hit, passing it back.

"Yeah, I know what you mean. Hey I'm not judging, I'm here with you. I just always viewed you as being so straight laced and everything you know?"

"Yeah I know. Sometimes you got to put on the image of the person you want to be, instead of the one that you actually are. I guess it's one part fake it until you make it, and one part being someone you would envy."

"I'm sorry you lost your brother."

"I'm sorry you lost your friend. It's been rough on everyone. I want to thank you for being there for him. You really meant a lot to him. I just don't know if I'll ever get over it. I don't know if I'll ever not feel responsible for Mathew's death."

"You know it wasn't your fault. Matthew did what he did," Duncan cut him off.

"He used my gun. He broke into my safe, got my gun and shot himself with it. If I didn't have the stupid thing it never would have happened. Matty would still be alive, he'd be here with me right now and none of this shit would have happened."

"Duncan, I get that, but I mean I'm not beating myself up. I was his best friend and I didn't have the slightest clue. I don't blame him, I blame the fucker who put up the letter all over school. And I blame Violet."

"Why do you blame her?"

"She fucking posted it on face book and tagged him in the picture, saying how pathetic he was." He was right, and I totally forgot about that. Something about that doesn't seem right. She doesn't seem like the type that would do that knowing her now. Maybe someone else did it, or maybe she meant it, but only felt bad once I killed myself. Maybe her liking me now is just because she feels guilty about what happened. I don't want to believe that, but there's an odd feeling inside me that can't shake the possibility.

"I dunno man, that seems really fishy, something doesn't add up with all of that. Why would she do that? I'm not that close to her or anything, but I never pegged her for the malicious type. She strikes me as the type to go home and cry about it and maybe write some bad poetry about it." Duncan chuckled at this, hell so did I, because he wasn't that far off.

Steven takes another hit, gives it back and tells him he's done. "I've never done this before. I'm going to be alright right? I'm not really feeling anything yet."

"Oh you'll feel it on the walk back, it always hits you on the way back. C'mon, lets go."

Duncan puts the stash back into the stump and they start walking back. After three steps I can see that the pot has officially hit Steven. He looks at his hand for a few seconds, and then runs it through his hair several times before catching up. "This is pretty damn amazing Duncan. This feels like I'm in a dream, like everything is real, but it's not."

"Not sure if you knew this or not Steven, but this world isn't real," Duncan says looking him in the eyes. It took several seconds for Duncan to crack a smile. He was never much of a joker, which made it all that much funnier when he decided it was time to pull a gag. A wave of relief went over Steven's face once he was sure that it was a joke. His head keeps moving from left to right like he's been blind his entire life and he's experiencing sight for the first time. Pot apparently heightens your senses or it dulls them so much that any sensory input is amazing. I'll have to add smoking pot to whatever you would call a bucket list for things you wish you would have done while you were alive.

A few of the guests had left during the smoke break, most of them were Mom's friends; however Mr. Spalding was also nowhere to be seen. A man in his 40's was exiting and sniffed the air around Duncan to let him know he that he knew what he had been doing. Duncan didn't seem to care. He grabs a handful of peanut M&M's from the candy bowl on the counter, shoving most of them in his face at once. They sat back down at the now vacant kitchen table and shared more stories about me. Mom was still drinking and was getting to the point of belligerent. I have a feeling Mom is going to have a breakdown in front of everyone, and I don't want to see that. I'd rather spend the rest of my night with Violet.

Chapter 17

"Get the fuck out!" Violet said, throwing a pillow at her dad. "Just leave me alone okay?"

"Violet, no daughter of mine is going to cut herself. Don't you understand that it's crazy?" He was pissed, this was apparent but he seemed frantic and unsure what to do to solve the problem.

"Dad, I didn't do it, why won't you believe me?" Violet starts tearing up. "I didn't do it. I've quit cutting dad, I've quit, why won't you believe me?"

"Because I can see the fucking scars on your legs Violet. Why do you think I'm that fucking stupid? My knives have been disappearing and I can hear you crying in your room all damn night. How do you expect me to believe that you're okay and not hurting yourself again? C'mon Violet, at least try to keep your promises to me."

"I know I promised you that I'd stop when I came to you for help the first time, and I did, it was just this whole Matthew thing...it got me starting again, but I'm over it now, I don't want to do it anymore." Violets cheeks are gleaming with tears. Her chest is expanding and retracting with heavy breaths rapidly, I can tell she means it.

"I want to believe you Pooky, but damn it you lied to me about it. You can't just keep cutting yourself every time something bad happens. This time it was the Matthew kid, last time it was your Mother. What is it going to be next?"

Violet cut him off, "I don't have a mother. If I had a mother she would be around now wouldn't she? I don't want to hurt myself anymore daddy, I don't. Please just believe me. I know I haven't been a perfect kid, and I know you worry about me, but I mean it, I think my life is a book, and I'm finally getting to the good part," Violet said giving him the sad eyes with a slight smile. "Just believe me."

He lets out a big sigh as if he was holding his breath for several minutes. "Okay, I'll tell you what. Promise me you'll never do it again, and if I ask you to prove it, you show me. If you can do that, I'll let this slide. But damn it, I mean it this time. If I catch you again, we're gettin' you an evaluation and you're taking whatever pills they prescribe, and I don't care how they make you feel. You're the only lady left in my life, I need to keep you safe." His voice started softening, and they hugged. She apologized again, and he left.

I whisper in her ear, "You better keep your promise."

"So you saw that huh? I wasn't lying, I don't plan on cutting again...thanks to you."

"What did I do?"

"I do it at times when I feel like no one cares about me. First it was Mom, she left so I thought 'hey no one cares if I start cutting so why the fuck not' you know? Then Dez came into my life, and I thought she cared about me, so I stopped for a long time, but things with her have been messed up the last few months, so I started again. Then the day I saw the note, it made me mad. Not because I didn't like it, I just didn't want to believe it was true. I didn't want to believe someone would like me that much you know? I always dreamed about having someone I knew I could depend on, but I never thought it would happen for me. I kinda resigned myself to being the single girl forever. Maybe get some pets so I'd have someone to complain to occasionally."

I whispered in her ear, "I think you would have made an awesome crazy cat lady." She smiled then laughed.

"You're a fucker, but I like you anyways," she said with her smile persisting. She sat on her bed with her legs crossed, and I sat next to her. We talk for hours. We talk about our childhoods, who are favorite ninja turtle are, why Freakzoid! was so awesome, our favorite episodes of The Simpsons, and of course our favorite bands. We got on YouTube and I showed her Tom Waits, and she showed me Reverend Horton Heat. She lost her shit when she found out I never listened to Weezer's album Pinkerton. She still buys all of their albums hoping it sounds like it only to be constantly disappointed. We listened to it from beginning to end...twice, then we discussed my thoughts of it. I loved it. Not just because the music was good, which it was, but because it meant so much to her. Besides her drawing, I rarely see raw passion out of her.

As the distance between her yawns gets closer, her eyelids droop lower. "You should go back to sleep," I whisper in her ear.

"Only if you'll join me and keep me company." She gives me this look that I've seen in movies, but I've never had directed towards me. It's attraction, she's attracted to me. I feel my stomach drop and I suddenly become so nervous I can't move. I'm standing in her room looking her in the eyes. She likes me. This is really going to happen. I can feel my eyes widening. My heart would be pounding if I had one. I don't know what to do. I know I should make the first move, but what is the first move? I've never done this before, not even close. Her back was turned against me; I press my lips on the back of her neck. I hear her inhale deeply. I kiss her neck again, this time slower, having my lips linger on her skin. She turns over and faces me, she's biting her lower lip in the left corner and whispers to me "Kiss me."

I lean in and close my eyes, focusing on making sure my body stays physical. I feel the pressure of her lips against mine. She grabs the back of my head and pulls me closer. I feel her mouth crack open, and I follow suit. It takes a moment for me to work up the nerve to move my tongue inside hers, but when I do hers meets me half way.

Our bodies fuse together, sending what feels like an electric shock down my body. Her tongue twists and turns around mine like an octopus's tentacle wrapped around its prey. I feel her pulling away from me, her tongue pulling out of my mouth, and I hesitate as I don't want the moment to end. "Will you lay down with me again?" she asks. I tell her I would, and I do. I wrap my arms around her tight, thinking about how much I want to tell her I love her, as I drift off to sleep.

Chapter 18

The darkness returns, and so does the orb of light. The way its pulsating is different now, it's not longer at a regular beat. It's...hectic now, I can't make out a pattern to it, almost like its sending out Morse code. Like a bullet it jettisons into my mouth and lodges into my throat. It works its way down into my chest, and I can feel it beating inside me, where my heart should be. I can feel its energy surging throughout my body as if it was pumping cosmic energy through me. I can not only feel the heat emitting out of me, but: also see it like a sort of radiation in a comic book. The aura around me starts changing colors in rhythm with the beating inside my chest. It's trying to communicate with me, but I just wish I knew what the national language of the afterlife was.

I focus on my breathing and I shift the energy inside me through my lungs. After several minutes I could shift the all the energy to any part my body, making it feel like a cement block. I put everything into the tip of one finger and my entire body starts leaning forward. I'd be lying if I said I didn't put all the energy in my dick, some things we may not be proud of, but I'm at least willing to admit it to myself. A crippling pain hits my stomach, and I drop to one knee, using a hand on the ground to brace myself. Multi-color liquid flows out of my mouth in a puddle floating in space in front of me. Once I've purged all of the afterlife ooze out of my system, I wake up lying next to the woman who I want to spend the rest of my afterlife with.

Violet's House:

It's still dark and Violet is still asleep. I hug her, I hug her like I've always wanted to hug her, I hug her like I've always dreamt of hugging her. Her hair waves against my face like a thousand threads of silk, I smile. It almost makes me cry, I have what I've always wanted, the woman that I love. I brush my hand through her and she starts to shift and turns over to face me. Even with morning hair, she's the most beautiful person I've ever seen. She smiles, which in turns makes me smile more. It hits me that I don't have to try to stay in the physical world around her, my body knows it needs to be shown around her. She sees me appear, tells me good morning and gives me a kiss.

I run my hand through her hair and ask her what she's going to do today, she shrugs. A long moment of looking into each other's eyes is broken up by a knock on the door. She gives me the look like I need to hide, so I disappear myself. I guess she thinks her dad wouldn't approve of her sleeping in the same bed with a ghost.

"Hey, you decent?" her dad didn't bother waiting for a response before cracking the door open.

"I am as long as I have the blankets over me I am," Violet says sitting up and holding the blanket up to her collar bone. I think the collar bone is actually called the clavicle, but I wouldn't swear to it. He averts his eyes, looking at the floor even though he's pretty sure he doesn't need to.

"I'm going to the store, and wanted to see if you wanted to tag along. Thought we could have a little bonding time like we used to you know? Maybe go to breakfast at Terry's Diner like we always used to do, remember that?" I could tell by the smile on her face that she had.

"Yeah I remember, let's do it! Do you think they still have the peanut butter milkshakes?"

"I dunno Pookie, it's been a long time since we've been, but they might. Go on and get dressed and we can leave," Violet's dad said as he exited the room, closing the door behind him.

"Do you want to come with us?" Violet asked while getting dressed hiding most of her body with the blanket.

"I better not, you should enjoy the time alone with your dad. I'm going to check in on Mom and Duncan."

"Suit yourself, you're missing out on some fantastic

milkshakes." This was true. If I'm thinking of the right place they have a chalkboard with 30 or so flavors and you can combine them in any way you want. It's one of those grimy diners that plagues every small town, but a banana, chocolate, and peanut butter shake dubbed "The Elvis" does sound really good right about now.

"I'll probably be waiting for you when I get back, bye," I say as she waves at me, and I return it. After the best day of my afterlife, and one of the weirdest dreams ever, I go to check up on my family.

Home:

Everyone is asleep and the house is trashed. Mom passed out on the same couch she was on before I left with a bottle of wine still in her hand. Trays of rummaged food scatter the house with loads of crumbs trickling along the floor like a schizophrenic breadcrumb trail. The snoring of Duncan is the only noise filling up the space. His clothes smell like weed and his breath smells like whiskey, no wonder he's sleeping so hard. I only know its whiskey because it's what Dad used to drink and I remember him slapping me with one hand and his bottle of Jack Daniels spilling onto me with the other. I'll never forget that smell, and I don't like smelling it on Duncan.

I gently slap him in the face to wake him up but to no avail. I sit on the edge of his bed until he starts to groan, covering his face with his hands which until now I never noticed how lanky and slim his fingers are. After several minutes of reluctantly getting up, he makes his way into the bathroom to take a shower. Once he gets out I avert my eyes while he gets dressed. I make myself appear physically while his back is facing me. I whisper to him, "Duncan it's Matthew." He stops looking for a shirt and turns around, our noses are almost touching. I smile, he screams.

"W-w-w-what?" This was rare, Duncan losing his shit isn't an everyday occurrence. I wave at him, and he rubs his eyes hoping I'll vanish when his vision refocuses, but I don't. "Oh God, the letters, is that what summoned you? I knew that was a bad idea, I shouldn't have taken his advice, I knew it was dumb," Duncan continues to ramble until I interrupt him.

"That's not why I'm here."

"Is it to haunt me? You're here to haunt me because your death was my fault aren't you? I'm sorry Matthew, I'm sorry I did this to you. I wish I could take it back, I wish I could change it. Forgive me Matthew, please forgive me." Duncan drops to his knees with his head slung between his shoulders sobbing.

"There's nothing to forgive and I'm not here to haunt you, I'm here to tell you it's okay." That sounded a whole lot better than telling him I was here to spy on him some more while my girlfriend was drinking milkshakes. He still thinks he's hallucinating and I can't say I blame him. "I love you Duncan, and I never got the chance to tell you that when I was alive."

"I love you too Matty, you are...I mean were my baby brother. No matter what, you'll be in my heart." The heartfelt moment was interrupted by a knock on the door.

"Duncan, ten minutes until we leave for church, you need to be ready."

"Yes Mom, I'm getting dressed right now."

"I'll leave you to go with Mom to church. I would come along but I don't know what happens when ghosts go to church. I'll be back tonight and we can talk. You better hurry up, Mom won't wait." Duncan knew this was true and got dressed quickly. We never went to church on a regular basis but every once in a while she'd decided it was important to go that week. I can understand why she chose this week.

"Okay...I'll see you tonight I guess. I really do miss you Matthew," Duncan said while putting on his dress socks. I vanish from his sight but still remain in the room for a few minutes. Part of me wants to go with them to see what happens when I do go to church, but I figure it's probably not the best idea, and Violet may be back by now.

Violet's house:

She wasn't home yet, so I spend a good amount of

time going through music she has stored on her laptop. You can learn a lot through the music they listen to. There was a lot of the music I expected, an entire discography of Nirvana, Sublime, and Smashing Pumpkins, but also songs I didn't expect her to be into. I can assume it's the stuff she's embarrassed to admit she likes, or maybe stuff Dez burned for her. Songs from Pink were right next to Pink Floyd and Ke$ha was next to The Kennedys. I'm not sure how she would feel about me going through her stuff, but she also didn't password protect any of it, so I'm not sure I'm to blame in this situation. She probably figured her dad wasn't tech savvy enough figure out how to turn it on, let alone dive into it.

I see a folder called "Writing" and double click it, bringing sub-folders named by year and month. I open one up and quickly realize it's all journal entries. Is it right to read this? Of course not, but how can I not? How can I not get to know the deepest darkest secrets of the person I love? I hesitantly look at the screen and read a random entry.

"If you're reading this, then you will die in ten seconds unless you bang your head against the nearest wall while singing the words to Smells Like Teen Spirit backwards! Okay now that you're dead, or if I just saved your life here's what happened to me today. Soooo I have something really big to tell you, something top super secret. There's a boy I think I like. He's really sweet, and funny and I haven't talked to him yet but I think he might like me by the way he looks at me sometimes. We have one class together, and I always catch him staring at me, but as soon as I catch him doing it, he turns away. I'm hoping that's a good sign. I'm sorry that I can't tell you much about him, because I don't know that much about him. He's the type the generally keeps to himself. I mean he's not a loner or anything, he has one friend that he's around all the time. It's one of those Odd Couple situations where it's two friends that couldn't be more different than each other, kind of like Dez and I. I bet he's a really good kisser, I don't know why, but I think I might have a secret power that I can tell who's a good kisser and who's not. The exception to that rule is that I can never use this power on myself. I guess that I don't have to be too self conscious since I've never kissed anyone before, but who knows maybe Xavier Michaels will be my first. Here's for hoping!

Violet Waits"

My fingers are trembling, and I can't tell if it's coming from a place of pain or anger. I think it's both. How the fuck can she have a crush on Xavier? Why don't I mean anything to her? Why did she notice when he looked at her but didn't notice when the same god damn thing happened to me? Why doesn't she care about me? Why is she pretending to like me now? Is it pity? Does she think I'll hurt her if she doesn't? Fuck her, how dare she do this to me?

The front door opens then closes shut, great perfect

fucking timing. I close the laptop and put it back on her desk. Every step I hear her take up the stairs makes me grind my teeth harder and harder. By the time I hear her on the other side of the door I feel like I might explode. I want her to hurry up and get in here and on the other hand, i don't think I can stand to look at her face.

She comes in the room smiling, with a smudge of peanut butter on the edge of her lip. "Matthew you here?"

"How dare you?" I say to her standing right behind her, not making myself visible to her in as loud of a voice as I could muster.

"What's wrong Matthew? How dare I what?" Violet asks, acting like she doesn't know what she's done, pretended to be startled.

"I thought you liked me, I honestly thought you cared about me." My voice hissed through the room like a serpent.

"I do care about you Matthew, I don't understand what's going on." She starts to cry, but I can tell she's faking it. I open the laptop and the screen lights up with the truth of how she feels about me. She looks surprised like she didn't think I'd catch onto her, like I was too dumb to catch onto her game.

"Matthew, you read my diary? You went through my shit? How dare you? You have no right to go through my stuff and you know that!"

I snap words off in her ear. "I would have no right, except when I find something like I did. You lied to me Violet. I did nothing but love you, I blew my fucking brains out because I couldn't stand to live in a world without you, just to be drug back to it like this." She's in full blown tears now, but I still don't believe they are real.

"That was last year Matthew, that was before I even knew you liked me. I don't have a thing for him anymore, it was a fleeting thing. Yeah I had a crush on him, but no nothing ever became of it and you know why? Because I saw how Xavier and Seth treated people like you and Steven. I don't have feelings for him anymore. Are you trying to tell me you never had feelings about anyone else but me?"

"That's exactly what I'm saying."

"I don't know what to tell you Matthew, I'm sorry. I really am, I didn't mean to hurt you or upset you."

"So when you slapped me, you didn't mean to hurt me? Do you expect me to believe that?"

"That was a mistake and I told you that. Matthew, I'm sorry I'm so fucked up, but I promise you I don't have feelings for Xavier anymore, please believe me, please."

"How can I believe you when you've been lying to me this whole time? You had a crush on my bully, how the fuck do you think this makes me feel? The person I love the most wanted to kiss the person I hate the most." I can't control my feelings anymore. I clench my fist and shift my weight into it and hurl it against the laptop screen. It shatters into a thousand fragments of glass all around her desk.

"What the fuck are you doing?" Violet flails her arms in disbelief. I finally get a real reaction out of her.

"What about the Facebook post?"

"What are you talking about?" Violet flails her arms in frustration, or the fact she just got caught.

"The Facebook post where you posted the fucking letter, saying how pathetic I am."

"I don't even have a Facebook account, I don't even know what you're talking about."

"I can't be around you right now, I'm afraid of what I'll do." She keeps talking but I don't listen, my heart can't listen to anymore of her lies. I need to let my anger out and there's only one viable place to do so.

Seth's house:

Seth's dad was still passed out from his previous nights beer binge, and judging from the collecting of beer cans around him he drank an entire case by himself. Good, fuck him, I hope he dies and Seth finds his body and decides to follow the same path as his damn dad. I can hear his music blasting through the hallway even before I walk through his door. He's tying his battered Converse shoes as I walk through then attaches his chain wallet to his pants. His face is still cut, but he seems to be healing, maybe I can help open a few of those back up. I phase my leg in to trip him, he stumbled over thin air, cracking his forehead against the wall. He looks around bewildered, looking for what he stumbled over but finds nothing. That felt good.

He leaves the house and cuts through several yards. He dashes down a small alley between Dagan and Turla street, this is my chance. Sporadic patches of grass in the yards of abandoned houses with dilapidated metal fences are the only witnesses for what's about to happen. I wrap my arm around Seth's neck, looping it around his neck and grabbing my bicep for leverage. I can hear the sounds of a person choking that wasn't expecting it. I use my other hand to press the back of his head forward to put further strain on his neck. "You're going to pay for everything you've ever done," I whisper in his ear in as raspy of a voice as I could muster. He wriggles his body around trying to escape the clutches of my choke with no success. He grabs at his throat meeting my invisible arm and tries to pry it away. In a single action he tilts his chin up and makes his body goes limp. My grip slips and he tumbles onto the gravel.

His dreadlocks' scatter across the ground like spider legs shifting as he gets up. I kick him in the stomach, and I see him tightening his abs in response to the pain. As he stands up he looks around for the assailant, but instead found a fist in his face. His neck recoils and looks behind him, finding nothing but another punch, this time landing in the back of his neck. Seth blindly swings his left hand around like a hammer whiffing through my head.

Bewildered that he didn't connect with the attacker Seth turns around in circles, looking for a person he won't find. I grab a handful of his hair like bundle of long cigars and yank them as hard as I can. His knees buckle, feet wobble, and the back of his head hits first, grazing a rock along the left side of his head.

Blood spiraled around the rock as if nature was intentionally making art as it seeps into the gravel road. He dabs two fingers over the wound then shifts the blood between his thumb as if he was expecting some results. I place my hands around his neck and squeeze, and he winces with pain as he tries to get a stream of air in his lungs.

"I'm going to kill you Seth! I'm going to choke you until your lungs collapse, and your heart stops beating. I'm going to choke you until your body turns cold Seth. Seth, I'm going to rip your fucking throat out of your neck. I want whoever finds you to think you're some unfortunate animal that got mauled by a bear."

He attempts to open one of his eyes, I use my other hand to slip my fingers in his eyes, putting pressure on both of them, he starts flailing his legs. He pushes my hand away from his face, then covers his eyes with both hands. My grip loosens as he turns over on his side and onto his stomach, still covering his eyes. He tucks his head and shifts his body up like a giant turtle. I wail on the back of his head. Blow after blow crash into his head like raindrops in a storm, I start to hear him crying. "Keep crying you little bitch, I hope your dad beats the shit out of you for being such a faggot." Seth lifts his head up, only to meet a haymaker to the side of his temple. His body slumps over and goes limp, the punch has knocked him unconscious. I always watched boxing matches and wondered what it's like to throw that punch that knocks someone out...it feels good. It feels like you're a machine that was designed specifically for dominating other people.

"Seth? Seth is that you? What the hell are you doing down there?" A voice said in the distance. The crunching of gravel beneath his feet became more erratic as he drew closer. It was Xavier. He leans over him and turns him over like a boulder. Xavier grimaces as he sees his face. "Who the fuck did this to you?" With no response he shakes him by his shoulders. He places his hand over the left side of his face, covering several cuts and scrapes. "Wake the fuck up Seth." Seth did wake up, but he tried to open his eyes only to find both his eyes were swollen and could only partially open one of them. The other was totally donezo until the swelling went down.

"Hey Xavier," Seth said with a smile planted on his

broken face.

"You scared the shit out of me Seth, I thought you were...dead. Who did this to you?"

"Dunno, never saw'em. I thought it was Steven but it didn't sound like him." Seth turns his head to the side and spits out a mixture of mucus and blood. "Can you do something to make me feel better?"

Xavier leans in and presses his lips against Seth's. "How's that?" It takes me several moments to realize what was happening as he kisses him a few more times. "You should be feeling great by now."

"C'mon and help me up. Let's go to your place and watch the game."

"That sounds great Seth," Xavier said carrying all of Seth's body weight to help him up. I feel the anger drain out of my body like a car with a gas leak, I feel better. I feel satisfied. Violet has a crush on a homosexual.

Steven's House:

Steven was on the couch watching My Strange Addiction and laughing hysterically at a woman who dresses up like a baby. His mom was sitting on the opposite side of the couch nearly in tears. Seeing them two of them with completely different reactions to the same piece of entertainment is a little bit jarring.

"How can you find that funny?" Steven's mom asked with a tissue being softly applied to the corner of her eye. "It's so sad."

"Did you miss the part where she's shopping for new clothes that don't make her diaper show? That's hilarious." Under normal circumstances I might agree with Steven, but right now it makes me sad. It makes me sad this miserable fuck is dressing like a baby can be happy, but I can't be. She can be alive, but I can't be. The show ended with a black screen with white text telling us if she had changed her ways since the filming of the show, she hadn't. Good, fuck her. The show ended and Steven got up, taking a nearly empty glass of water which was on the floor by his feet to the kitchen. He went into his room and I followed him.

"Steven, it's me, Matthew," I whispered in his ear and watched his hair stand up on his arms. He turns around and jumps a few feet back.

"Oh shit! fuck, fuck, fuck, fuck! Don't hurt me Matthew, I'm sorry, I'm so sorry, I'm so sorry Matthew." With his back against the wall he slid down until his ass is planted on the carpet and slung his head down. A slight wheezing sound emits from him, then he starts sobbing. "Don't kill me Matthew, I'm sorry I fucked up and I know I'm responsible, but I can't fix it." He keeps rambling on and apologizing.

"I'm not here to hurt you, I'm here to tell you

something. I saw what Seth and Xavier did to you yesterday. I tried to help but I couldn't. But I got'em back Steven, I beat the shit out of Seth."

"W-what? I'm fucking losing my mind. Get out of my fucking head!" Steven hit himself with his palm several times against his head. I grab his wrist; this gets his attention.

"Look at me, you're not crazy, you're not losing your mind. This is me, it's really me. I know it's fucked up and crazy but it's me." He looked up at me with wet dilated eyes.

"Okay. I still think I'm crazy but I'll play along. What do you want? Why are you haunting my house?" He was still holding his wrist in the air where I had kept it, even though I was no longer restraining him.

"It's not like that, I'm not tied to a house. Movies are bullshit, who would have guessed? I'm here because I beat the shit out of Seth for you. Did you know he is..." I didn't know exactly how to put it, so I waited for him to fill in the blank.

"Gay? Yeah I know, Matthew. Why the fuck do you think it hurt so fucking bad when my girlfriend left me to be with him? He wasn't even attracted to her, he only got with her to get back at me. Do you understand how fucked that is?" He was right, I hadn't connected the dots yet between Seth being gay and Taylor. I guess that explains why the relationship didn't last, he did it out of pure spite. "How did you beat him up? Can you do that?"

"I'm not exactly sure how any of it works to be honest, but I've learned how to affect things in the physical world."

"Well I gotta tell you, you're voice sounds wicked awesome. It's like your voice, but really raspy, almost like one of the black riders from Lord of the Rings."

"Thanks, I think? Steven, I don't want you to blame yourself. None of this is your fault, this is all my fault."

"I told you to write the damn letter, then I gave you the wrong locker to put the letter I told you to write in. I fail to see how it's not my fault."

"I pulled the trigger. No one did that for me, it was a decision that I made by myself. If you would have even suspected it, you would have done anything to stop me, right?"

"You know I would have done anything Matty to stop you, ya sneaky bastard. I would have murked ya myself if I knew you would do something that dumb." This made me laugh, but I didn't let him hear it.

"Steven"

"Yeah buddy."

"I heard the song you played for me. I was there you

know, at the funeral. I really liked it, it meant a lot to me. Thank you,"

"You're welcome. I thought it was corny when I wrote it, and felt like a total doofus when I was standing there playing it for everyone."

"It was really touching, everyone loved it," I said over a loud knock to the apartment's front door. I can hear the muffled voices of Steven's mom and a strong male voice that was sort of familiar, but I can't place why. Steven's mom calls out for him, but her voice is shaky...something's wrong. Steven takes a deep, nervous breath and stands up, and exits the room. I hear a jingling sound, almost like the janitor at the school with the key ring with a hundred keys. I hear a loud metal snapping noise, I phase out of his room and into the living room where Steven's face was pressed up against the wall, with a wall clock just inches above him. There's a police officer standing behind Steven, clicking together the handcuffs on his right hand, the left were already restrained. The police officer was the same one that Mom had talked to after my suicide. I don't remember his name, just his voice. He was reading Steven his rights and his mom starts sobbing.

"He was with me all day officer! He didn't leave the house today, there's no way he could have hurt that boy, there's no way!" She was now grabbing the sleeve of his shirt, pleading with him. "He didn't do it, you have to believe me."

"Mrs. Fargo, since Steven is legally an adult, I have to take him in for questioning. If he didn't do anything wrong, we won't have an issue, but I still have to take him in for questioning." This didn't stop her death grip on his shirt. I wanted to choke him out so Steven could escape, but that would just get Steven's mom arrested. No one is going to believe that a ghost did it. Steven starts crying.

"I really didn't do it officer, I swear I didn't." Steven gets tugged away from the wall and is led in front of the officer towards the door. "I didn't do it, I didn't do it, why won't you believe me? I didn't beat up Seth" The officer said nothing. Steven's mom grabs her purse, pulling out a cigarette and lights it, sitting on the couch, tears dripping onto her smoke. The confession of a man addicted to sniffing gas emits from the TV, drowning out her sorrow.

My House:

Mom is once again passed out on the couch with a pool of vomit drying on the ground next to her feet, a nearly empty bottle nearby. I need to be with Duncan, I need something in my life that's stable, someone that understands, and someone that I can rely on. I need to talk to Duncan. I can hear the music playing in Duncan's room, it's Metallica, but I don't know which album. It's unusual for Duncan to be playing music loud outside of the time he's in the garage working out. I phase through the door, and I don't know the emotion I'm feeling. It's pure anger, the type of anger I felt when I saw Xavier's older brother Brian smash the skull of a kitten with his foot; but I also feel severe disappointment by what I see.

Duncan is sitting in the corner, one hand against his head, the other is rubbing a knife against the skin of his arm. The cut skin flops over the side like sliced lunch meat. He lifts the knife and begins carving a chunk of flesh near his shoulder. Blood begins trickling down his bicep and onto the sheets. The only thing audible besides the knife tearing into skin which sounds like tearing off a band aid slowly, is Duncan sobbing incoherently. I take a step into the room and realize his other hand isn't on his head, it's holding a gun, and the gun is against his head. Another step and I see printer paper scattered around the room all with large reddish brown words written on them in blocky letters like a kindergartner would write. The papers were all around the room, and even though none of them were identical in the style or size of the letters, they all said the same thing, "I'm sorry."

A small bowl with a thin layer of blood lay at his feet. He had been cutting and using the bowl to collect his "ink" he used to write the notes to me. Tears drop into the bowl making a *plop* sound as it hits the collected liquid. I see something shiny in the bowl, but I can't tell what it is. He bangs the stock of the gun into his leg either to distract him from the pain in his arm, or the pain in his heart. Duncan puts the gun next to his head and before I can stop him, pulls the trigger.

-click-

I slap the gun out of his hand, it twirls in the air like a baton and lands by his bed. I grab the collar of his shirt with both fists and breathe in his face like an enraged bull. "What the fuck are you doing Duncan? You're my fucking brother and there's no way I'm going to let you waste your fucking life after I wasted mine. I don't care if I have to haunt you for eternity; I'm not letting you hurt yourself for as long as you live. I will be ripping the throats out of doctors trying to pull the plug on you before letting you die."

His eyes went white and I thought he was going to feint. Panic sets in his face and he scrambles to his feet, kicking over the bowl, revealing a small pile of bullets hidden in the murky depths of the blood. My grip tightens, and Duncan scrambles, trying to get away, but I force him down on the ground. "No, you sit and fucking listen Duncan. I always looked up to you, and I still do. You need to get your shit together and be the person that Mom needs you to be. Do you think it's a coincidence that Mom's life is falling apart the same time you decide to smoke pot and act like a piece of shit? Look at her, she's in pieces and you can't even try to help her like you always helped me. Do you know why I didn't talk to you about what was going on with me, Duncan? Because I knew you would talk me out of it, and I didn't want to be talked out of it, I wanted to be irrational."

Duncan finally got the courage to speak. "I-I'm sorry

Matthew. I guess you can tell that from the notes I left you, I was just trying to summon you, you know like before." Duncan began to regain his composure. "But I never wanted this for me, I never wanted to fail you, or Mom. When Dad left, he made me promise him that I would take care of you, and watch over you, and I thought I was. I didn't, I've failed everyone in my life Matthew, everyone! I was supposed to be the man of this family, but I can't do it anymore Matthew, I can't do it, I'm just not strong enough." Duncan slams the pistol against his leg again, this time more lackluster as if more out of frustration than anger.

"You have less to worry about now, I don't need you to take care of me Duncan, I took care of myself. Mom is still alive right now, but who knows how long until she drinks herself into her grave; help her like you wanted to help me. How would she feel if she had to bury *both* of her children in the same month? If you kill yourself you'd be killing her too. Do you *want* her to die Duncan? Duncan, do you?" I was screaming at his face now, I'm sure if I were alive spit would be flying out of my mouth as I spoke. I grab his chin and shove his head backwards, it thumps against the wall.

"I don't want Mom to die, I don't." He begins crying again, his eyes bloodshot, either from the crying or the drugs...or both. "But I don't know if I can do this Matthew, I don't. I'm tired of being the strong one, I'm tired of the pressure, I'm tired of being the person everyone wants me to be. I don't want to join the military Matthew, I just wanted to make them happy, I thought it would bring them back together; it's all I ever wanted. I hate working out, I hate running, but the thought of our family being together made me smile as I was doing it. I didn't want to be from a broken home, but now I don't have a choice, it's already broken no matter what I do."

"He left *us* Duncan, don't get that twisted. He left us because he didn't care about us, he didn't want to be in our lives anymore. He chose another woman over me, over you, and over Mom. Fuck him. How dare he show up at my funeral like that, like nothing happened, like he actually cared?"

"He does care Duncan, that's why he showed up. He showed up because he loves you."

"Then why did he not show it until after I was dead? Why couldn't he show it when I needed him? He showed up to see his friends, not us. I should kill him myself that worthless piece of shit." I realized that my hands were tight around Duncan's neck, when I release them a red indentation of my fingers lingered. Duncan forces oxygen into his lungs. For the first time in his life...*he* looks scared of *me*.

"Please Matthew, just leave me alone, let me be."

"Promise me you won't hurt yourself."

"I promise."

"I'll be back in the morning to make sure you're okay. If I find you dead, I'm going to kill Mom. I don't want her to go through another death in her lifetime but her own."

"I believe you."

"Good. Duncan, I love you." I don't wait for his response before I leave. I have someone to talk to, someone I have unfinished business with. I go downstairs and kiss Mom on the forehead, still passed out, then I teleport to my destination.

Violet's House:

The sound of her heart breaking immediately fills my ears. I thought movies were exaggerating when a break-up happens...they aren't. For the first time with her I feel like I'm seeing something that I shouldn't be seeing. I know she can't hurt me but I feel endangered as I near closer to her, as if she's an unpredictable wild animal. I try to find the right words to say, to even introduce myself to her, to let her know I was in the room with her; but the words never come. She's in her bed in the same position that we were in last night when I was holding her, with her back to me. I grab her shoulder and pull it back lightly, careful not to startle her.

She didn't even turn around before she spoke, "What do you want? Did you come back just to make me feel like a whore again? If so I'll save you the trouble, because I'm still feeling like a whore from the last round."

"I came to apologize, and because I need you." She remains silent, which I guess it means she'll at least hear my apology. "Violet, I love you, I've loved you for a long time. I loved you before I even spoke to you. You mean more to me than anyone else in my life."

"If you love me so much then why did you say that shit to me? Why would you be so fucking mean to me?"

"I lost control. I went through your diary, which I know I shouldn't have done. I apologize for that, it was totally a wrong thing for me to do. I did it to try to get to know you better. I want to know everything about you Violet. I want to know your every want, thought, and desire. Then I saw what you wrote about Xavier, and I just lost it. The thought of you liking anyone other than me drove me nuts, and it made me feel like you didn't like me at all. I committed suicide because I thought I couldn't be with you, it's kind of ironic that it's what caused us to become close. It doesn't excuse it, what I did was terrible, but a lot of good has come out of it you know?" She remains silent as if thinking about whether to accept my apology or not.

"Can you explain what you mean by that? What good came out of it?"

"I got to meet you, I got to actually talk to you? Do you know how many nights I laid in bed thinking about how the next day I was going to work up the courage to talk to you, only to never do it? I wanted to so bad but anytime I saw you in the hallway I would just stare at you and freeze, unable to do anything. Only in death was I able to overcome this fear and do what I feel like I was meant to do. I'm sorry I hurt you Violet, I just felt threatened and I reacted poorly, there's no excuse for it. And I invaded your privacy which I had no business doing. I crossed a major line and I knew it was wrong even as I was doing it. Violet do you forgive me?"

"I'm still pissed at you Matthew, but yes I forgive you. If you do it again though I'm calling an exorcist!" She smiled and made a cross with two of her fingers and while giggling says "The power of Christ compels you. The power of Christ compels you!" I had never seen the movie The Exorcist but it was one of those references that everyone gets. It made me smile, so I kiss her even though it slightly catches her by surprise. Her tears brush against my face. I think she thought the finger cross *would* actually stop me. "So where did you go after you left?

"Thank you for forgiving me, it really means a lot to me, and I understand you being mad still. Honestly, today was the worst day of my life," I look down and let out a deep sigh. "Steven got arrested because of something I did, and I'm worried about Duncan."

"What did you do to Steven, and why are you worried about Duncan?" She raises her eyebrows and shakes her head in confusion.

"Duncan has fallen apart since my death, I caught him trying to kill himself. He's broken. He's broken because of me. And Steven, I beat up Seth...like bad. I think he may have been admitted to the hospital and they must have thought Steven did it. He was crying as they hauled him off. I wish there was something I could do to make it better."

"I'm really sorry Matthew, I don't think there's much you can do except learn from it."

"There's something I want to ask you and I don't know how to bring it up. I think I found the perfect solution to resolve all of this. From you being lonely, to us not being able to really be together. It's going to sound crazy at first but I really think this is what's best for us both." I take a dry gulp as I prepare to ask the woman I love the most important favor I've ever asked anyone in my life. "I think you should kill yourself so that we can be together."

Chapter 19

"What are you trying to say? A-are you going to try to kill me?" Violet scoots away from me several inches while not taking her eyes off me.

"No of course not but think about it. This is the solution, this is the way that we can make it work. If you kill yourself, you'll be a ghost just like me and we can finally be free. We could be together the way we want to, the way it should be. Don't you want that?

"Matthew, you know that I want to be with you, but is this really the right way?"

"Is there any other way to do it? I feel like you're being hesitant and I don't understand why."

"You really don't understand why I'm a little standoffish about killing myself? You went through it yourself, you can't tell me there wasn't a moment when you hesitated, when you thought you might be making a mistake. You almost didn't go through with it, didn't you?"

"There was a moment when I didn't want to pull the trigger, but that was only because I was uncertain of what would happen after I died. You don't have to worry about what's going to happen after you die, you don't have to fear death."

"You said yourself that you didn't get a handbook to the afterlife, you can say all day long that if I do it everything will be great and we can be together but how do you know Matthew? I know you hope we can together if this works, but what if it doesn't? What if I go to heaven and you're stuck here wandering aimlessly wishing I was still alive, living my own life?"

"But that won't happen."

"You don't know that Matthew! You know what happened to you, but you don't know what's going to happen to me. You're putting me in a position where I want to trust you, and I want to believe you, but I don't know if that's what I'm supposed to do."

"It is Violet, this is what's supposed to happen. I wish I could tell you how I know it's going to work out, but I just know that it is. I know it's scary, but you're just going to have to trust me, it's going to be for the better."

"How can you say that? Matthew, you've seen the lives of everyone around you crumble because of what you did. You saw your mom go back to drinking, you saw Steven getting hauled away in handcuffs, and you had to stop Duncan from ending his own life. All of those things were caused because you took your own life Matthew. What makes you think that the people who care and love me would be in any better of shape? I don't want my dad to have to go through what your family did, I don't want my dad to have to bury me. He will blame himself, he will think he failed as a parent, and I don't want that; my father is a good guy. How can you be so selfish and only think about yourself? You thought it was okay to ruin the lives of everyone you care about, so it must be a great idea for me to do the same? You would really be okay with me hurting everyone I know and love just so that we could be together?"

"Violet, I know that it be really hard, but you know they would get over it, it will take time to heal but they can move on, and we can be together. This is the only way to make it work. We can't keep doing this while one of is dead and one of us is alive, and I don't see myself becoming alive again anytime soon. This is the only shot we have, and you're right I don't know for sure what's going to happen when you die, but I think this is what's supposed to happen. I think when we can finally be together in the afterlife that we will both get to go to heaven...together and live for eternity together. I know it sounds crazy, I don't want you to make that decision right now, but I want you to think about it."

"Okay, I'll think about Matthew. I've never felt so close to someone but at the same time felt so far away from them you know what I mean?" Violet said hunkering her head down.

"I do know what you mean, I felt that way since the

moment I knew you existed Violet. It wasn't life holding me back, I was holding myself back from life. I do regret what I did Violet, because if I would have just walked up to you and asked you out, this whole thing would have been prevented. I'm just glad we found a way to make it work even through all of it."

Violet lets out a big yawn, followed by an outward stretch of her arms. "Hate to break the news to ya, but I need to go to sleep, I have to go to school tomorrow."

"Okay, I guess I'll go back home so-"

"Stay with me." I nod and she crawls into bed. I curl up next to her like I had done the night before and everything felt right.

Chapter 20

Darkness consumes me once more, with no source of light making itself known. I feel it in my stomach again, and I know what's coming. I stick two fingers down my throat to induce vomiting. Black sludge drizzles out like thick tar out of a barrel. The tar is so dark that I can only see it because it's darker than the rest of the emptiness. What seems like gallons of the sludge trickles out before I feel normal again. It starts pulsating in front of me to an unknown, seemingly random rhythm. Every time is pulsates it grows a little larger, somehow growing mass from out of nowhere. It makes some sort of slushing and slurping sound as it grows, and it splits near the bottom forming two blobby legs. The rest of a human body is formed but without any distinct features. It resembles myself in some sort of odd fashion, same height, same build, but void of any definition. It reminds me of Shadow Link from the old Legend of Zelda game.

The dark me stares at me as if angry, as if had expectations of me that went unfulfilled. I disappointed it. A ball of light comes down from the void, appearing out of nowhere. It drops into the hand of the shadow me, where it starts to take form. It turns into a gun, but not any gun...Duncan's gun. I stare at the alternate dimension version of the gun I used to end my life as light emits and glistens from it at the same time. Shadow Me puts the gun to his temple and pulls the trigger of the gun, a blast of light explodes out of it like firework explosion in the sky. The radiant white lights launches beams through the head of Shadow Me, causing shards of him to fall to the floor. Something beneath the black exterior of Shadow Me is peaking through like a hollow chocolate ball with a prize inside. Shadow Me falls to his knees and slumps over, almost mechanically as if it's some domino in a Rube Goldberg machine. The prize inside the shell begins to make itself known...the ever-changing psychedelic juice begins pouring out of what *was* Shadow Me's head.

Once all of the swirls of colored gel leaves the body, the Shadow Me disappears into nothingness, leaving only the gun behind. The psychedelic blob starts taking form into a person, it's me...but not me; It's the same height but seems taller due to proper posture. His facial features were nearly identical to mine, except more defined and enough muscle tone to make Duncan jealous. Is this who I'm supposed to be, or maybe the optimal me living up to my fullest potential? Optimal Me kneels down and picks up the spectral gun off the ground without lowering his head, as if he knew where it was *supposed* to be. Several dark figures begin walking in unison at an equal distance from Optimal Me, and Optimal Me begins firing the gun with the precision of a sniper. Dark figure after dark figure begins dropping, headshot after headshot until the three survivors are within feet of him. It's like watching a Jason

Statham action movie watching the black entities being dispatched. He fires two shots back to back, and two shadows fall forward, almost bowling him over like a domino. A sinister grin overtakes his face as the last bullet lodges itself into the left eye socket of the last assailant. The body crashes into the ground and Optimal Me drops the pistol, it hits the invisible ground without a noise. His body turns blinding white, and as if abducted by an alien light, ascents upwards. He's raised so high and so far away from me that he becomes the size of a pen light towards the sky. I wake up.

I jolt upwards as I regain consciousness. If I had sweat glands my face would have been soaked with perspiration of a fever dream. Violet is gone but I hear the rabid swishing noises of someone brushing their teeth in the bathroom across the hall. I hear her singing a song to herself half-heartedly as she brushes, I think it's What I Got by Sublime but I could be wrong. I hear her spit, and rinse, then spit again before hearing the light switch click off. I hear her footsteps creek towards her room, I need to talk to someone about my dream. I need to make sense of it, I need to understand what it is, what it was telling me. Violet steps in and looks around for me, I make myself visible and tell her I need to talk. She tells me to make it quick because Dez is going to meet her in a few minutes.

I explain the dream to her, and she gets the same bewildered look that I've probably had on my face this entire time.

"So, if you murder shadow people you get to go to Heaven?" Violet said squinting with one eye and wriggling her nose at the thought.

"I don't know. It's like they want to teach me, but they don't want to tell me what they want to teach me."

"You know for someplace that you want me to go, the afterlife sounds like a huge cock tease," Violet says rubbing her tongue against her gums trying to get minty taste of toothpaste out of her mouth...or spread it around.

"Why would killing people be the answer? Do you think it matters what kind of people it is?" I know Violet doesn't have the answers to the questions I'm asking but I hope verbalizing it helps. It didn't.

"Maybe this is how you become a grim reaper! Maybe you have to kill a bunch of people whose time has come and you work your way into heaven by doing it as sort of a part time job!" She was jumping up and down with excitement at the prospect. Can't say her idea is any less crazy than any of mine. Maybe she's onto something, but how would I even know who to kill?

"Possibly, but I don't want to go offing people in hopes that I'm trying to be a grim reaper, I might go to ghost prison for that."

"T-there's a ghost prison?" She said with bugged out wide eyes as if I had just crushed her dreams of being an afterlife criminal.

"I don't know but there has to be some sort of punishment system right? If I can do good things and go to heaven I'm sure if I do bad things I get sucked into hell."

"So you think that killing people is good? Because you know, you kinda just said that." It was true, I did just say that killing people would get me to heaven like some sort of religious nut. Maybe I'm trusting these dreams too much? I should probably rely more on my instincts and less on listening to things I barf up.

"No I don't, but these dreams, they feel like they are guiding me, like I should be doing what they tell me." I feel like an idiot once I start hearing what I just said. I never believed in psychics or people who interpret dreams, so why am I so willing to believe it now? Just because I'm dead doesn't mean everything I experience isn't real, does it? This could all just be a dream and any moment I'm going to wake up in front of my computer writing my love note to Violet, and tell Steven about this elaborate dream I had about killing myself. I don't think that's going to happen though, I think there's a reason that I'm a ghost in limbo, and I think there's something I can do to make it to heaven. I don't want to be stuck in this body alone for eternity. I just want to be with Violet, no matter how I have to do it. "Are you about to leave for school?"

"I'll be leaving for school but I won't be arriving. I have something I need to do today, and I don't want you following me while I do it...it's personal." I don't know what she plans to do, but my gut reaction is to follow her and find out despite her wishes. I can't betray her though, not again, not after what happened with the journal. If I break her trust again, I'll probably lose her forever.

"Okay, I'll go check on Duncan and Mom, I guess I'll meet you back here later on in the afternoon?" She nods, and then she gives me a hug, followed promptly by a kiss on the lips which almost went through me. She smiles as she pulls away from the kiss and gleefully skips out the door.

Not being alive frees up a lot of my time. There's no eating, no taking shits, no showering, no driving. I can just do whatever I want to do without having to think of anything else. It has its downside though, it takes away my routine. When I wake up, I don't know what to do, there's no maintenance I need to maintain, no teeth or hair to brush, no clothes to put on, no shoes to tie. The only thing I feel the need to do is take care of the people around me.

My House:

Mom had started to stir in the couch, knocking over nearby bottles with flailing limbs. A bottle of nearly full Jameson begins spilling onto the carpet making a glugging sound. Duncan's body is lying in his bed, legs contorted in awkward positions as if was practicing for Circ du Soleil. No blood, the safe is locked and after several seconds of looking at his shoulders...he's breathing. He kept his promise, and I hope my empty threat to kill Mom if he had killed himself had something to do with it. It shows he still cares, and if I want Duncan to live, he needs something to care about. I better let him sleep. I don't think him missing one day of school will hurt anything, especially given the situation with just burying his brother. I feel like for once in my life, I helped Duncan.

I go to my room and I turn my computer on and open a word pad. I start writing out my dream, hoping to make some sense out of it. First I write just the facts of it, from throwing up the black blob to the murder of the other shadow people. Then I start jotting down some of my thoughts of what it could mean. It boils down to three main theories.

Theory 1. I need to kill nine people

Theory 2. I need to kill nine shadow people in the afterlife.

Theory 3. I need the gun to kill 9 more people and I'll get to go to heaven.

Theory 4. The dream didn't mean anything

I wish the theories were in order in which I believed the most, but it was just as I thought of them up. All four completely plausible but I knew only one of these would be correct. I don't think it's Theory 2, I haven't even seen any shadow people, so how would I kill them? Where would I even go looking for them besides the one I barf up in my dream? I made sure to note the number, it has to be important, I don't believe it to be nine for no reason. I don't think it's Theory 3 either, it seems improbable that the weapon matters more than the actions. That leaves Theory 1 and Theory 4, and so far I don't believe it to be nothing, why would it be? I may not know what the dreams mean, but I can just *feel* that they are trying to tell me something. That just leaves Theory 1, the one about me having to kill nine people. Even if it's not nine, the fact remains that I need to murder someone, with the potential of it being multiple people.

Who would I kill, who *could* I kill? Maybe I could just sneak into a random prison, go to death row and off nine people in a row, just going cell to cell. Sure the guards would wake up and think something crazy had happened with nine bodies in nine locked cells, but to be honest, something crazy *had* happened, just not a something they would figure out. I guess I could choke out people in their sleep, especially if they can't hurt me. Even if I could work up the courage to kill them and it works, I'd be leaving Violet. I don't want to leave Violet, I want to be with Violet, but if it comes to a situation where I can't be with her...it's nice to have a plan. This will be my plan for my path of salvation if my afterlife with the woman I love fails.

I save the text file to my desktop and shut down the PC. I check on Duncan and he's still asleep, now snoring. I write him a note telling him that I was proud of him and I head back downstairs where I hear Mom stirring. I don't believe my eyes, she's cooking. It's not that she's cooking that surprises me, it's that she looks half-way competent in the kitchen. The fire-alarm isn't even going off, and she has two burners going on the stove. I know what she's cooking by the sound of the popping of bacon in its own rendered fat, and the steady sizzle of eggs. Eggs-in-a-basket. She flips the bacon in the pan with the same spatula she would flip the eggs with, Mom never worried about cross-contamination of food. She grabs the bottle of Jameson sitting in front of the blender and takes a deep swig from the bottle, a single gold drip rolls down her face like a Midas tear. She wipes it from her face and flicks her wrist, splashing the droplet onto the floor. She continues cooking. Watching her do something like cook breakfast should be comforting and nostalgic to me...but it's sad. It's sad that she can't make it through breakfast without a bottle next to her. It's hard to see her fall so hard, and even harder to know it's because of me. I'd give anything to just have my family back the way they were.

Mom sets up two plates on the table and slides the eggs surrounded by bread on the plate with a thud. I could tell by the sound that the toast was burnt on the bottom, but the eggs look perfect. She pours the bacon grease over the crispy-on-the-bottom bread, it soaks up leaving a glistening layer on top of it. Mom snaps the blackened bacon in half like brittle pretzel sticks and lays them next to the eggs-in-a-basket. I can hear Duncan shambling down the stairs one at a time with no rhythm to his movements. He sits down without acknowledging Mom, hunched over his plate. He pokes the fork into the yolk, letting it spill over the bread, soaking into the pores of the bread the way he likes it. He eats and Mom joins him without speaking a word. The sounds of chewing and clanking of silverware and the occasional sipping of water which Mom had brought over is adding to the awkwardness in the air. They finish eating without a word to each other, not even a glance. Duncan puts his dishes in the sink.

"We're going to need to talk soon," Mom said to Duncan's back.

"What do we have to talk about?" Duncan said walking past her nearly bumping her with his shoulder.

"Us Dunc, we need to talk about us. We need to work past this and get back to being a family."

"We don't have a family Mom. Our family was broke up when you let Dad leave. Matt's gone now, and next year I'll leave, then you'll be alone. You'll be alone to drink every goddamn day without having to worry about cooking me breakfast in the morning. You'll be free to drink so much your liver will just burst with excitement." Duncan doesn't turn around to look at the tears forming in her timid eyes, he simply stammers back upstairs.

Mom stands there crying with her arms folded like she

doesn't know what to do with herself. She looks around the living room, seeing nothing but the empty bottles and trash that have made a home in the carpet and furniture. Her face starts to twist and turn in agony and pain, occasionally dabbing a tissue at her eyes that she' clenching in her fist so tight that it's matted together. Mom empties the bottle of Jameson into the sink and drops the empty bottle into the trash with two fingers with her arm extended as if she was discarding something rancid. She picks up two bottles of wine on the kitchen table and grabs them in one hand, they clank together with every step as if it's some alcoholic musical instrument. She continues the process of pouring out the partially full bottles and throwing away the empties until they are all gone. She even goes through the refrigerator and pours out the peach wine coolers that Mom got sick off of and refused to touch ever again. She takes the trash out and closes the door behind her.

I want to believe her, I want to believe she wants better for herself...but I don't. I don't think she has it in her to do the right thing, but she never has. I want her to change so bad, but she's never shown me that she can, so why do I feel so shitty for doubting her? It's because she needed me isn't it? I thought it was the tragedy breaking us apart, but maybe I was the glue of the family, and not Duncan. Now the glue is gone and my family is peeling apart like a withering sticker.

Duncan is sitting on his bed, hunched over. I whisper

in his ear "Guess who?"

"Oh gee what other ghosts do I know? What do you want Matthew?" I don't think Duncan has ever been this short with me before.

"I just wanted to see how you were doing."

"You know how I'm doing, you left a note while I was sleeping, remember?" I forgot about the note until he mentioned it. I can't tell if he's upset with Mom or with me about threatening him last night. I don't think asking him is the right move.

"Yeah, I remember. I just wanted to see how you were holding up."

"I'm fine. I go back to school tomorrow, so I guess my life can start getting back to normal tomorrow."

"Yeah I guess so. If you need to talk, or need anything really, let me know Duncan."

"Yeah I'll do that. I'm going to go for a run."

"Okay, I guess I'll see you later on."

He doesn't say anything else and I guess he assumes I left, or just doesn't care if I'm still around. I wait until he leaves and watch him run up the road out of his bedroom window. I think things are finally starting to get back to normal.

Violet's House:

She didn't get back for a few hours. I wasted an hour sitting on her bed and thinking of all the things she could be doing, but nothing comes to mind. What could she possibly be doing besides going to school on a Monday morning? A doctor's appointment, sure but she was happy about going wherever she was going. Her dad also didn't quite seem like that type that would seek medical attention unless it was dire. Every noise I heard outside made my stomach sink as I expected to hear the door open soon after. When I did hear the door open it surprised me, I didn't hear anyone coming down the street at all. She came in the room bewildered with a smile, she called out for me when it hit me that I didn't make myself visible. I make myself appear lying on her bed and it made her giggle.

"What are you doing there silly?" Violet asked with her hands on her hips. She sits down on my feet without even the slightest bit of hesitation.

"Just trying to think of what you could have been doing this morning, that's all."

"Well you don't have to wonder, you can just ask, you know." I wasn't used to this form of blunt honesty from anyone but Duncan.

"So spill it. What were you doing this morning that was so important and that's made you this happy?" I sit up in anxious anticipation of her answer.

"I've been thinking about what you said, and what you asked me. I think you're right, I don't have that much going on in my life. To be honest you're probably the best thing going on in my life right now. Giving you up would mean giving up on the only person that I know loves me no matter what. It doesn't matter if I fail a class, get an "A" or just cry and cut myself, you're going to be there for me. That means more to me than anything else."

"I do love you no matter what and you're right, I'll be there for you no matter what. So what were you doing this morning?" She's hesitating on telling me what's going on, I think this is how she acts when she's nervous. I've never seen her nervous before, it's kind of cute.

"Well," she said and a deep breath, let out a sigh, then a smirk followed. "I was talking to Dez. I needed to see her one last time." She waited for my reaction to what she said by biting the corner of her bottom lip.

"You mean...you're going through with it?"

"Yuppers! She's my best friend and I thought if there was one person I would want to say good-bye to it was her."

"That's very sweet of you, in a morbid sort of way." Her smirk got bigger.

"Well...she also was the only person I knew that had

access to enough sleeping pills to do the job," she winks at me.

"You're a jerk." I laugh and throw a pillow at her, it hits her square in the face. She pulls out the bottle of pills and shakes them in front of me. "This is what we call a matin' call in Boone County." I didn't catch the reference she was making but laughed anyways.

"So yeah...I think tonight's the night. I think we should treat it like our last night together, you know in case it doesn't turn out the way we want it." I nod as a slightly sad look crosses her entire body.

"A-are you okay if it doesn't?" I ask, almost not wanting the answer.

"It can't be much worse than this, can it?"

"I think it will be a million times better when we're together. I mean together together you know what I mean? So what do you want to do with your body the last day you have it?"

"Use it." She grabs the back of my head and pushes it towards her. Our lips meet with an explosion of passion. My tongue slips into her mouth and our entire bodies twist into each other. She nibbles on my ear lobe as I kiss down her neck to the collar bone. She moans in my ear as I lick up the other side of her neck. She takes her shirt off revealing a white bra holding two perfect breasts inside them. She catches me staring at them and smiles. Violet takes my hand and places it on her chest then kisses me.

We make love. I don't know how different it is than when two normal people do it since I never did when I was alive, but it's better than I had hoped.

We lay in her bed just staring at each other, holding each other for hours. This is the life that I want, this is what I've always hoped I could have. Dumb thoughts cross my mind, like "Can I get her pregnant?" and "Did I do it right?" I don't think I'll ever know. She just smiles likes the expression is permanently stuck on her face. "What are you so happy about?" I ask.

"Because I like you Matthew." She kisses me.

"I like you too." I brush her hair out of her eyes.

"Can we watch a movie together?"

"Of course, what do you want to watch?"

"The Shining, the Kubrick version obviously."

"Okay, it's one of my favorites. Did you know Stephen King was inspired by a real hotel to write the book? I would kill to stay in that hotel."

"Maybe we should go together and haunt it, though I don't think we would be alone in that venture." She wiggled all her fingers at me to invoke the amount of spookiness that it would entail.

"Already making vacation plans for us eh? Go ahead

and put the movie on." She puts the movie in her Playstation and we cuddle and watch the Torrance family slowly delve into madness. That was actually the only thing about that version of the movie I didn't like, Jack Nicholson's character seems crazy from scene one in the office talking to the manager to being frozen in a hedge maze. The made-for-TV version sucks, but at least they nailed that slow transition into madness better than Nicholson did, who just naturally comes that way.

I also never understood the mind behind writers who could sink to such dark levels. There's no way you can spend hours writing about really horrible things, close your laptop and feel happy the rest of the day. It has to linger around them like a stench that they can't wash off until they finish it. Maybe the stench never goes away and it just builds on top of them novel after novel and eventually they stop and can't take it anymore. I guess it's possible they have a switch in their brain that they can just turn on for "writing mode" and flip it off when they're done. I could never do much horror writing, I just wrote dumb science fiction stuff with a semi-fresh angle, I never had to dwell on the content.

Wendy and Danny escape in the snow mobile and Jack is wandering the maze with axe in hand yelling incoherently. He sits down, gets frozen and credit start. We let the credits roll as we hold onto each other, talking about the movie as the chilling music continues.

She gives me a look, followed by a nod, and pulls out

the pills. I ask her if she wants to leave a letter, she said
she didn't. The only thing she wanted to say was whatever
she told Dez earlier. I ask her if there was anything she
wanted to eat or drink, and that if it works she wouldn't be
able to taste food or drink again, but you could still smell
it. No wonder most ghosts are pissy. She plants the palm
of her hand in her forehead and tells me she'll be right
back. She returns with a Barq's Root Beer and a smile on
her face. I ask her why out of all the things in the universe
she wants a Barq's. She rolls her eyes and lets out a
dramatic sigh and responds.

"And here I thought you were a fan. The almighty
Barq's Root Beer was the last thing Kurt Cobain, my Lord
and savior drank. The can was found near his body half
empty."

"That stuff would make me want to blow my brains
out too," I said.

"You're such a jerk, you know it's great, and we both
know he was murdered." She carries on about the
"evidence" of how she "knows" it wasn't a suicide. I knew
most of the details, but she got into the gritty details of it
all. I wasn't sure what to believe about it, there's really
compelling arguments to be made on both sides. "You
know the weird thing about Barq's is that the regular
version has caffeine, but the diet version doesn't. I was on
a caffeine-free kick for a while and was drinking regular
Barq's religiously because I thought it was "safe" like the
diet version was. My 30 day accomplishment was less of

an accomplishment once I made that little discovery." She takes a quick drink, and I can smell the aroma coming out of the can. I never liked root beer, the burn always bothered me.

My heart drops with each drink she takes, because I know at the bottom of that can is the start to the end of her life. It's as if it's a liquid hour glass, counting down her life with every sip. I hesitate, then speak up, "So, if this doesn't work, I want to say that I'm sorry for hurting you, and I never meant to ruin your life."

"Babe, you didn't ruin anything and you have nothing to be sorry for. You know how miserable I was in my life, but you've made me happy. So even if this doesn't work, isn't it worth it to know that I'm dying that way? I won't have to worry about being old and miserable. I can die young, beautiful, and in love. What else could I want?"

"I guess you're right. Are you ready?" She nods. She pops open the orange container and dumps 20 or so pills into her hand, a few spilling over, falling onto her bed. She shovels them in her mouth like popcorn, using the remaining soda to wash them down with. I hear her swallow hard several times, a slight pain and discomfort in her eyes.

"I don't know how this works, I guess I'll just lay down. Will you hold me?"

"Of course I'll hold you. Nothing would make me

happier." We lay there waiting for the large dose of medicine to overtake her body. With each passing minute I can see her eyelids getting heavier, and her smile getting dopier. I tell her I love her and squeeze her hand, her smile widens, and her hair falls over her nose. I brush it back and give her a kiss on her forehead. Her breathing gets heavier, deeper, and more of a rhythm. She keeps talking, but the space between words lengthens, and become less coherent.

Her eyes close for a moment, then she forces them open, albeit slightly. "If you're wrong about this, I'm gonna call the Ghost Busters and have'em zap yer ass." I laugh, then smile, then let out a spectral tear. Her eyes close again, then her entire body relaxes, she's asleep.

"Goodbye Violet, I hope to see you again soon. I love you."

"I love you too Matthew, I love you too." She smiles and squeezes my hand.

I place one hand on her wrist to feel her pulse, and the other on her chest for her breathing. I was never good at checking pulses, but I got the hang of it. As soon as I felt pulses from the heart slow down, the breathing would follow suit. It's seconds between beats now, I can feel the life slip out of her. Her chest is now barely raising, the breaths she's taking are no longer deep, they're shallower. Her lungs are already shutting down. I can't tell if I lost the perfect spot on her wrist, of if her heart stopped beating. I put my finger under her nose for ten seconds and feel no exhaled breath coming out of her. I put my ear to her chest and feel no movement inside, just a warm beautiful husk. I kiss her on her cheek and give her one last hug. I whisper in her ear, "I hope I know what I'm doing too Violet." Violet Waits is dead.

Chapter 21

Her body lays motionless. I don't know how long this is supposed to take, or if it's not going to work at all. The room starts getting dark, as if someone was dimming the lights. All the objects in the room disappear in the darkness, as if they are fading out of existence. A bright light emits from below me, below everything. Unlike the blinding white light from my dreams it was a swirl of tense red and orange. Something comes out of the hole...or someone, all I can see is flowing white material like silk or satin drifting up towards me. As it gets closer I can tell there's definitely something under the white cloth by the way it's flowing, it seems to be flowing around it. It's almost like whatever is inside of it is what's causing the ripples in the material. The rest of the room has completely faded out and it's just Violet's body, me, and whatever is about to approach us.

As it gets closer I realize it's not just big, but tall. Whatever it is stands about twice as tall as me and broad as a heavyweight MMA fighter. It could be some sort of otherworldly demon escaping from the portals from hell or a cosmic refrigerator...I just can't tell. I can feel the stillness of it, it scares me and I don't know why. I shouldn't be afraid of anything, I'm already dead. It solemnly stands in front of me, towering above me. The white silk is a robe almost like you see druids wear in fantasy movies, but pure white and light as a feather. A grey hand emits out from the cloth like granite stone, cracked and weathered. He moves through me and next to Violet.

A voice from under the hood mutters some words in a language I've never heard before and stretched out his fingers over her chest. He lowers his hand slowly like a pendulum lowering upon a victim. Once his hand is fully inside her, I can tell from his wrist that he's clenching the rest of her. He slowly pulls his hand out, almost like one of those claw machines with the stuffed animals in grocery stores. Something white is caught in the grip of the massive grey/green hands. It's Violet, or at least her ghost. I see her translucent fingers wiggle, then her head jolts back to life. Her entire afterlife-body is now out of her physical-body though she's still not fully aware, like she's drugged. The creature that's holding her lets out a satisfactory grunt in a tone that it cannot have been human.

She places both of her hands on the thing's massive wrist and tries to push off of it. He doesn't budge. He drags her downward, back towards the red and orange orb where it came from. I look into the reddish orb and see what it is...hell. Flames like solar flares burst out of it and screams of terror could be heard emitting out of it. The creature is a demon trying to take her back to hell.

I see the look on her face, her face that is actually paler than it was before. She's scared. The creature dragging away Violet isn't moving very fast. I grab the back of the cloak and tug on it; it's a lot rougher than I thought it would be. The entity turns its body towards me, I can feel a rush of warm breath come from under the hood. I can feel the grin from its face even though I can't see it. His other hand relinquishes me from his grip on his cloak and carries on.

"Let go of her!" I yell as I barrel towards them at full force. I grab its wrist and try pulling back one of his Twinkie size fingers. Violet reaches out and grabs onto my shoulder tightly. The creature places its other hand on my chest. From its pinky to thumb stretches from the base of my neck to my navel. He pushes me away with a quick shove, my grip loosens and I fly backwards into the vast emptiness. I keep spinning head over heel several times before I regain my balance. I look around for them before I spot them above me, and they are getting closer to the red orb where it came from. I rush towards them, feel like a salmon swimming downstream to the inevitable bear waiting at the basin.

As I get closer, I start building speed, I wind back my fist like Superman in a comic book and plant it in the back of its head. It stumbles forward, bending over slightly from the waist and turns around. I catch a slight glimpse of its face...it's not human. It has murky red eyes that almost seem to come to a point like a dagger. Its lips protrude out of its lifeless face, and has nothing but a gaping hole where its nose should be. It grunts and a puff of steam comes out of its nostril holes and faces me directly. It reaches for my chest but I dodge out of the way and tag it again in the head once more. Before I have time to react his gigantic fist hits me in the chest like a wrecking ball. He can't hurt me but he can make me feel pain and disorient me. He stares at me for a moment, presumably to determine if I'm giving up. I haven't. I follow up with an overhand left which lands at its right temple. I follow up with an uppercut to his chin and its head snaps back like a Batman Pez dispenser. I pry its fingers off one-by-one using both hands while it's dazed. The first three fingers loosen and Violet slips out from his grasp.

"You need to follow me right now!" I yell to Violet as I move towards her body. She hesitates.

"What's going on?" She asks slowly moving with me but uncertain if she should be or not.

"Bad things, very bad things, you need to trust me right now." She hesitates a moment longer then matches my speed. I reach out my hand without even looking back at her and she grabs it and gives it a light squeeze. I smile. We get within feet of her body. "I need you to go back inside your body."

"But…"

"It's the only way we can get back right now."

"My body is dead, why would I go back?

"Just do it! We don't have a choice, I'll protect you Violet, I promised you that."

She doesn't say anything but she moves towards her body, still floating in space. Violet looks at her body with morbid fascination and dips into it like a girl testing the pool water, toes first. She starts submerging herself in her body, unsure what she's supposed to be doing, or how she's supposed to be doing it, but I'm hoping she'll figure it out because I don't have a damn clue. The last of her body, her left hand, the hand that just squeezed mine melts away into her physical body.

A cold hand grabs my ankle, and tugs hard. I get flung downwards back into the darkness as I see the creature approaching Violet's body once more. I rush back towards them with his body looming over hers. I grab his ankle and yank it as hard as I can. He moved, but not nearly as far as when he had done it to me. I go towards Violet's body, I make it to her knees before I feel the Granite Monster's hands on me again. I use my other foot to smash his face several times, but his hand remains on me. It crawls up me like a bear climbing up a tree and latches itself onto my back. It reaches around with both hands and plants all of its fingers into my chest and begins pulling my chest apart. I can feel the very fabric that I'm made out of tearing apart as if I'm a knitted sweater that's being unraveled. I extend my arm toward Violet's shoulder to inch closer to her, but my strength starts giving out the more the monster rips me apart. The monster starts laughing and I can feel its muggy breath on the back of my neck.

I manage to scoot and inch closer to Violet, but the monster tears away at my body the harder I resist. I reach for Violet's mouth, grab her chin and pull her mouth open like a hatch. As I feel my shoulders start to separate from my body I can feel my chest no longer exists. I've been torn into two with thin neck tissue stretching between my pieces. I reach forward inching my fingers into Violet's mouth, traveling over her tongue like maggots and down her throat as far as I can reach.

My body gives out, I can hear the skin of my neck stretching off the rest of my body and a solar wind breezing through my chest cavity. The monster laughs and removes its cloak, reveling what it is...a true monster. The closest thing I know to describe it is a golem. A giant rock monster twice my size carved from one granite block. It grabs my head in its fist and squeezes. Everything goes black, and I feel nothing.

Chapter 22

Vomit. Barf. Upchuck. Spew. Puke. These are all the words I know to describe what was coming out of Violet Wait's mouth in copious amounts. Her eyes are still closed but her body is expelling everything inside of her without her consciousness. She's on her side but it spills over her chin, down her neck, and splatters randomly around her, congealing in piles. Goops get caught and interwoven in her hair while the rest covers the blanket like warm chunky pudding...and root beer. The unmistakable stinging smell of root beer mixed with the noxious smell of bile permeates the room, filling every square inch. I put my hand on her chest to see if she's breathing. She is. The expulsion of vomit slows down considerably and I ensure she stays on her side, I always heard you can choke to death flat on your back and we've had enough experience with death tonight.

She cracks her eyes open, and gives a light smile like in an action movie where you're not sure if the main character is dead or not. The smile quickly fades when she notices the sticky vomit on her cheek. I hug her. I hug her so tight that the puke makes a squishing sound. I kiss her temple, the only place on her face that's dry and tell her I love her. She touches her face, unintentionally smearing liquid across her face. "You're gonna need to take a long hot shower." I tell her as her face quickly switches to a smile and hugs me.

"I'm so happy Matthew, I'm so happy to be alive!" It hadn't occurred to me until just then that I was back to normal. My body is in one piece. That feeling of being ripped apart, I don't want to feel that ever again. I don't want to meet whatever the rock creature was again either.

"I'm sorry to put you through that Violet, if I would have known that was even a possibility that could have happened I wouldn't have even tried it."

"It's okay Matthew, I know you were just trying to do what you thought was right." Was I? Was I trying to do what was right, or just trying to get what I wanted? "I'm gonna go wash this shit off me. Would you mind taking the sheets off? Just put'em in the hamper and I'll take care of'em."

"Of course. Make sure to get it all out, some got in your hair," I said and she cringes. She leaves the room and I take care of the sheets oh so carefully not to spill anything on the carpet. Throwing them in the clothes basket helped the stench a little, but it's still present. I have a feeling she's about to take the longest shower of her life.

Steven's apartment:

I teleport to Steven's house and hope for the best. I hear voices coming from his room, but they sound angry and tired. Steven is arguing with his dad about what he was thinking when I phased through the door.

"How many times do you I have to tell you I didn't do anything?" Steven said throws his arms in the air in frustration. "Why would I even be here if I did Dad? If I did it I would still be in jail wouldn't I?"

"You can't just go around being the hero defending everyone Steven, you have to pick your fights. You can't just pick them all." Steven's dad said screaming inches away from his face.

"And you can't be the hero when you want to be either. You can't just fucking swoop down when I'm in trouble to lay the law down like you're an actual fucking father to me. I never see you, all I have is Mom and my friends."

"You're crossing the fucking line Steven. You know goddamn well I'm trying to be home more, it just hasn't worked out yet. It's getting there Steven, I just have to work through this last project and it'll slow down for me," Steven's dad said.

"Okay great I'll make sure to tell Seth he can stop harassing me soon because my dad is wrapping up his project.

"Damn it Steven, try to reason with me. I try to do what I can. I just need you to keep a low profile for a bit okay? I just want the best for you and this shit isn't helping."

"I do know what you mean, but like I told you a thousand times. I didn't do anything. I don't know who did, Seth terrorizes everyone! He has a ton of enemies who would love to jump him like that. You know what I'd like Dad? Do you want to know what would make me respect you a little bit? Respect me when I tell you something is the truth...believe me"

"I-you're right, I'm sorry. I need to start treating you like the adult that you are. I just want the best for you. I don't want you to make the mistakes that I made as a kid. You have to understand that all a father wants for his son is to live a better life than he did. I haven't done that very well lately." Steven's dad grab's him and embraces him; Steven is shocked at first like being attacked by a bear, but wraps his arms around him reluctantly.

I feel like once again I'm intruding on a private moment, albeit an awkward one. I step out into the living room and sit down next to Steven's mom and watch My Strange Addiction as she cries over a woman who eats the stuffing from couch cushions. I laugh.

My house:

Mom is sitting at the kitchen cable under the chandelier light sipping coffee out of a cup that has Garfield on it. Mom loves Garfield, but I never saw the appeal. I go to Duncan's room to find it empty, including the locked gun safe. I go to the garage to find Duncan doing chin-ups on a bar mounted over the door frame. After he does ten in a row he drops down to the floor.

"Boo," I said. He jumped slightly, then smiled.

"Hey Matthew, what's up?" Duncan was breathing hard and sweat soaked through his grey AC/DC shirt. I can't tell what it is but Duncan seems normal, or at least like his old self.

"I've had a lot free time since dying, so I'm just checking up." I thought I said that last time I saw him but couldn't remember, I hate reusing jokes.

"I quit smoking. I smashed the pipe and threw the rest of my stuff in the woods. I figured maybe I could still go out there and do something more constructive, maybe I'll start drawing again." Duncan used to draw comic books when he was younger but dropped it a few years ago when he decided that you couldn't be an artist and in the military.

"Maybe we could finally finish that project we started a few years ago? Remember it, the one about the superheroes that were professional wrestlers? We had all of those characters written up and everything."

"Yeah, maybe we should. I probably won't get much time after I graduate."

"I think Mom is doing better too," I said and Duncan gives a nod of approval. "I don't know if she's kicked the booze totally out of her system but she seems to *want* better for herself again." Duncan nods again. "Even if I can't be here creeping around forever, you still need to take care of Mom. You know she's not strong enough to handle all this on her own."

"I made you that promise and I have no intention of breaking it."

"Thanks Duncan, and even though she may not say it often, you know she loves you...and so do I."

"Right back atcha," Duncan said smiling and giving me a wink and giving me the gun hand.

"So, what happened to the gun?"

"Cops took it as evidence when they did their investigation, but they returned it to me. I didn't like having it in my room, even in the safe. I made sure it's safe and out of the hands of anyone that could potentially get at it. But there's something I need to tell you, and I'm not happy about it, and definitely not proud of it." Duncan let out a long sigh. He's not the type to hide anything from me, I have no idea what he would do that he wouldn't be proud of. "I looked at your computer. I don't even know why I did it, but I felt like there was something important that I was supposed to find. I saw the list of explanations for the dream you had."

"Oh. I mean I wish you wouldn't have because you know I didn't mean for anyone to see that I was just writing out my thoughts." I wanted to be mad, but I knew it would make me a huge hypocrite after everything that had happened with Violet.

"Listen I know it was wrong and I apologize, but I want to help. I was thinking about it, and I don't want you to murder anyone, prisoners or not. I don't think it's you that has to do it, I think it's the gun. I don't want you to murder them, and I'm sure as hell not going to do it either. I don't exactly have a plan but I think something will present itself, some opportunity for that gun to take other people's lives by someone else's hands is going to present itself. I can feel it."

"Okay, I mean I guess I'll have to take your word for it. I'm not really worried about it right now to be honest. I'm happy right now to just to be there for the people I love. Moving on to my afterlife is a little scary to be honest, because it's the only unknown left that I have."

"I feel like I owe it to you to eventually let you move onto Heaven. It may take a while, but I'll pay my debt to you," Duncan said.

"Thanks Duncan for always having my back. I need to check back with Violet. I'll be back later on tonight."

"All right. Take care."

Violet's house:

I teleport back to Violet's house to find her already on her bed with her sketchbook in her lap. I don't want to bother her so I sit next to her, invisible, watching her draw. It's a sketch of her from a bird's eye perspective on a hill in the middle of the night. She's staring up at the stars with her hands bracing herself behind her. A transparent figure that's presumably me has his arms wrapped around her. Most of the major detail is done, she's adding the stars and the moon, and a tree with a bunch of different birds in it.

"Hey," I whisper in her ear. She jumped.

"I'm never going to get used to that. Scares the shit out of me every time. How long were you watching me?"

"I lost track of time. I could watch you draw all day, it's pretty entrancing."

"You're silly," Violet said, leaning in for a kiss.

"Violet, I love you."

"I love you too Matthew."

Epilogue

Dear Steven,

Violet and I are still together. She's in college now at an art school living the dorm life with a roommate. While she's in class I do the things in life I've always wanted to do; backpack through Europe, watch the sunset over mountains in Japan, and explore the pyramids in Egypt. Her roommate Jill doesn't know about me. She's pretty oblivious in general actually. But the moments when we're alone in her room are priceless. We snuggle up in her bed and I just watch her draw for hours. She does a web comic in her spare time that is actually getting quite popular. It's about a super-cool chick who works at a coffee shop that has a best friend who's a ghost who always gets her into trouble. Oh I guess I should also mention that Violet did have a part time job at a local coffee shop, but I rarely made trouble for her.

Mom is doing great! Okay, maybe great is an exaggeration, she's still Mom, but she's kicked the booze completely. She got married, yup Mom re-married. One moment she was single and getting her life together and the next she married my creative writing teacher Mr. Spalding. Violet asks me if I'm technically a Spalding or not now. Duncan never changed his name, out of respect to Dad, even though he never attempted to contact him. Mom says he it was because he didn't have to pay child support anyone, I think it was because he felt guilty. Mom sold the house because it reminded her too much of all the bad things that had happened there and Mr. Spalding and her got a small place together next to the park. She spent most of her free time in the garden, tending to her beds of iris and tulip flowers. She quit her job after Duncan graduated and spends most of her time volunteering at a suicide hotline for teens.

Mr. Spalding decided to quit his job to peruse his writing career full-time. A short story collection he wrote called *Earth Landing* which is the title bearing story he borrowed from me got a really good reception. On the dedication page it listed only two names, Mom's and mine. It got published by a semi-major publisher and made enough to fund his first full length novel about a struggling writer who slowly poisons himself to write about the pain. From what I heard Mom say on the phone to her friends, she really liked the first draft.

Duncan didn't sign up for the military. He told me that going through what he did with me was too much, and he couldn't bare the thought of Mom losing him after losing me. Instead he joined the police academy, and after a year or deciding it wasn't for him he became a prison guard. A year later he was transferred to Texas for a big promotion at a maximum security facility. He seems to really enjoy it. When he wasn't stopping inmates from stabbing each other with shivs we worked on finishing our graphic novel series. We self-published it and got it on several store shelves in the Dallas area and it's sold fairly well. He hopes to one day to be able to live off doing it, and I don't blame him. I enjoy doing the writing, even though I can't take credit for it.

I heard Xavier decided to be a prison guard as well, but from what I hear it didn't straighten him out. He's pretty good at scaring the shit out of people so maybe he'll find a good career at it. He had to do something after his dad was killed in a drunk driving accident. I attended the funeral out of respect but not even Seth showed up. I don't think there was a lot of love lost. Seth and Xavier broke up shortly after high school. I don't know what happened but I think Seth is repressing his tendencies.

Steven. Out of everyone that we expected to do well in life, no one expected you to really succeed. I was telling Violet you got tied up with a gym and ended up getting into Mixed Martial Arts training. I showed Violet the tape of your first fight, the one you won in 46 seconds by submission. Then I showed her the fight in the UFC, fighting the top fighters in the world. Okay so I had to admit to her you have a *little* help in those fights from some unexplainable force that may or may not have swayed the outcome a few fights. But to your defense, I didn't sink those anaconda chokes for you, you did that yourself. If you win a couple more fights convincingly you might get a title shot and be on top of the world. Sorry we don't talk that much anymore, but I know you're living the rock star life now. I guess I just wanted to tell you that I really miss hearing you play guitar, don't give that up.

And me? Well besides spying on my family, writing graphic novels, watching my girlfriend draw, and fighting in MMA brawls, I've been hanging out in hospitals trying to help those cross to the other side. I'll be honest, I'm kinda hoping to meet someone like me, but it hasn't happened yet. Maybe I'm a special case and I'll be a ghost forever, or maybe something will happen to boost me into the next stage of reality. Until then I'm going to enjoy what I never got to in my life. The weird dreams have stopped for whatever reason which has really freed up my time to get everything done. If I were to give any advice to anyone that's living it would be to do the things you want to do. Don't hesitate to tell the person you love how you feel about them, and if there's something getting in the way of getting what you want...find a way. Don't let fear control you, control your fear and you will bend the world to its knees.

Be with you always,

-Matthew Masters -

In Love and Dead